CATHEDRAL
OF BONES

CATHEDRAL OF BONES

A. J. STEIGER

HARPER

An Imprint of HarperCollinsPublishers

Library of Congress Cataloging-in-Publication Data

Names: Steiger, A. J., author.

Title: Cathedral of bones / A.J. Steiger.

Description: First edition. | New York : HarperCollins, [2021] | Audience: Ages 8-12. | Audience: Grades 4-6. | Summary: Fourteen-year-old Simon, with mediocre magical powers, and Alice, a young girl transformed into a monster, work together to discover a cure to her enchantment and uncover secrets of their pasts.

Identifiers: LCCN 2020011103 | ISBN 9780062934796 (hardcover)

Subjects: CYAC: Magic—Fiction. | Monsters—Fiction. | Shapeshifting—Fiction. | Secrets—Fiction. | Fantasy.

Classification: LCC PZ7.S8178 Cat 2021 | DDC [Fic]—dc23

LC record available at https://lccn.loc.gov/2020011103

Typography by Alison Klapthor

Interior art by Brandon Dorman

21 22 23 24 25 PC/LSCH 10 9 8 7 6 5 4 3 2 1

❖

First Edition

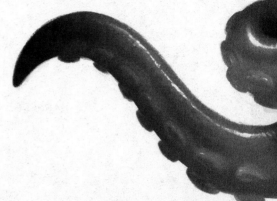

To Mom and Dad

That is not dead which can eternal lie,
And with strange aeons even death may die.
—*H. P. Lovecraft*

In the beginning, there was Chaos.
And out of Chaos came both darkness and light.
—*The Book of Azathoth*

Part I

A Curious Affliction

Simon Frost was very young, perhaps six, when his mother left on a pilgrimage to visit a Gaokerena tree in the mountains. Her destination was far away, on the western fringe of the Continent, near a tiny town called Splithead Creek. She planned to spend a week meditating at the foot of the tree, her consciousness entwined with its roots and branches.

His father was opposed to the journey, unsurprisingly. There was a long argument.

"What do you need to travel all that way for?" Simon's father asked. "We have one of those trees here in Eidendel, right in the middle of the bloody city."

"But each tree has a different voice," his mother replied.

"Trees don't *speak*."

"They do if you listen closely, dear."

"Don't 'dear' me. You're always doing this."

"What? Leaving you alone with the children? What a *dreadful* fate. Come now—Olivia is practically raising herself, and Simon is the most docile and sweet-natured boy you could ever hope for. They won't give you any trouble. Will you, Simon?"

She packed up her bags, humming while his father scowled at the back of her head. Her imp, a furry, orange, newt-like creature with tiny iridescent wings, buzzed around her room, gathering random objects for her—a hairbrush, a flask, a tiny silver jar. Simon watched from the doorway, biting his lower lip.

His mother dropped a kiss onto the top of his curly-haired head and said, "Now, be good for your father. He has a very important job at the Foundation Headquarters, working for dull little men and women who aren't nearly as smart as him, and it makes him grumpy at times. But he loves you very, very much, and he won't bury himself in his research while I'm away. Will you, Aberdeen? He'll tuck you in and kiss you good night—yes, *every* night—and you won't even know I'm gone."

Simon didn't want to be left behind. He tugged on her sleeve and pleaded for her to take him with her. But she just chuckled and told him the journey would be very dull for a child.

"Perhaps when you're older," she said, "we can go together. Animists like us must cultivate a bond with nature. It's the source of our power, after all."

"You don't need a bond with nature in order to tap its energy," his father grumbled, "no more than you need a bond with kerosene oil in order to light a lamp. You just have to know how to use it."

His mother rolled her eyes. "We're not having this debate *now*, Ab."

"The children miss you when you're gone, you know."

His mother didn't reply.

She left the next morning. Simon's father spent the entire time muttering about her habit of talking to plants and flitting off to Spirit-knew-where. "She can't stay put," he said. "One of these days, mark my words, she'll just float away on the breeze like a dandelion seed and disappear. Oh, stop sniffling. I'm not being literal. She'll come back. She always does."

And she did . . . that time. She returned smiling, with a dusting of new freckles on her arms and nose, and swept Simon and his sister up in an embrace.

"Did you bring us any presents?" Olivia asked, grinning breathlessly.

"Of course. Don't I always?"

To Olivia, she gave a hand-carved bone bottle filled with a flaky gray substance.

"Summoning ash!" Olivia squealed, clutching the bottle against her heart. "What will it bring me? Can I call a wraith?"

"The surprise is half the fun, darling. Don't use it on your own, though. Your father and I will supervise."

To Simon she gave a book. "This isn't from my trip," she said. "It's a special book of my own, one I loved as a child. And now it's yours."

The book was enormous and heavy and bound in a dark, creaky leather that resembled withered reptilian skin. When he ran his fingers over it, he felt tiny, hard bumps here and there. There was no title on the cover, but on the first page was a symbol drawn in ink: a disembodied, octopus-like tentacle coiled around a sphere. Beneath that, in jagged, thorny script, was the title: *Elder Gods: An Introduction.*

He turned another page, to an illustration of a monstrous serpent with an eerily human face. A thread of ice ran through his blood. The creature prowled through a jungle, pulling itself along on stubby arms, its jaws clamped around the waist of a man it was in the process of swallowing. The man's legs kicked helplessly in the air.

The next page began, "*Yig is the serpent god, also known as the Father of Serpents, and is primarily known through the legends of the Sunari folk in the pre-Foundation era. Some sects worshipped him and offered him sacrifices, while others—*"

Large hands snatched the book away from Simon. His father clutched the book, glowering at his mother, who stared back with wide, innocent eyes. "What?" she said.

"Do you really think this is an appropriate gift for a six-year-old boy?"

"*I* was six when I first read it," she said. "I adored it. It's a bit ghoulish, I suppose, but who doesn't love a shiver on a moonlit night?"

Scowling, his father leafed through the book. "Look at

this. Human sacrifice? People turning to stone?" He snapped the book shut. "He already has bad dreams. But that's not even the issue." His voice lowered. "We've talked about this before."

She gave a delicate sigh and averted her eyes. "All right. I suppose I'll wait until he's a bit older." She ruffled Simon's hair. "I'll find you another present."

When Simon was ten years old—shortly after what Simon's father would come to refer to as "the Incident"—his mother left again. This time, she didn't tell anyone where she was going. There was only a brief note: *Forgive me for this, but there is something I must do. Wait for me. I will return.*

Simon waited. A year crept by, then another . . . and another. He stopped checking the mail. He tried to hold on to those words—*I will return*—but with each passing month, his hope dwindled a little more. She was a dandelion seed, and the wind had carried her away.

Chapter One

A smoggy, feeble sunrise glowed in the skies of Eidendel, illuminating the city's steeples and clock towers. Gas lamps stood on street corners, pools of yellow light in the gloom. Pigeons scattered as a line of street-sweeper imps trundled past on stubby, purple-scaled legs, gulping down bits of litter and muttering their monotone chorus, *"Gubble, gubble, gub-gub-gub."* The previous night's rain had mostly stopped, but the streets were still deserted, aside from the occasional carriage clattering past. A few damp pedestrians hurried by in overcoats and umbrellas, heads bent.

Simon sat alone on a bench, eating a mincemeat pie. He glanced across the street and tensed. The old woman was still there.

She had been watching him for several minutes now. Every time he looked, she was standing in the same spot, like a statue. Bedraggled, graying blond hair framed her gaunt face, and a leather satchel hung from one shoulder. She wore mismatched shoes and clothes even more patched and worn than Simon's robes. The tufted brown feathers decorating her numerous filthy braids almost blended with her hair, as though an owl had exploded on her head.

She looked familiar. Now that he thought of it, he was pretty sure he'd seen her wandering the streets around here before.

"Er . . . hello," he called. "Do you need something?"

She approached. "Do you seek the truth?" she asked in a thin, scratchy voice.

"Uh. What?"

Her sharp, glittering gaze remained fixed on him. The irises were a dirty yellow. "Are you looking for answers to questions you dare not ask?"

He shifted. "I don't know what you're talking about."

"Yes. You do." She smiled. "I'll ask again. Do you seek the truth?"

His mouth had gone dry. She was looking at him so intently, as though she *knew* something about him. "Yes?" His voice came out a little squeaky.

She pulled a rolled-up newspaper from her satchel and offered it to him. "Then per'aps you'd care for a copy of the *Eidendel Underground*! Only one gilly."

He blinked, deflated.

Oh.

"I promise you, it's worth it." She leaned forward and added in a conspiratorial whisper, "It tells the *real* stories. The ones the Foundation don't be wantin' you to read about."

Simon almost told her that he worked for the Foundation. He was even wearing his brown apprentice robes—hadn't she noticed? Granted, they were a bit shabby, but even so. "No thank you."

She went on, unfazed: "They say there ent been any Abominations created since the War of Ashes, but that ent true, you know. Abominations walk among us. The gubmint never stopped experimentin' on humans."

Gubmint? Oh—government. "I'm really rather busy . . ."

"How about some dried frog pills?" She held out a tin with a crude painting of a smiling frog's head on the lid. Its half-closed eyes expressed a state of transcendent bliss. "These little beauties help you remember your past lives. *And* they boost male portency." She gave him a snaggletoothed grin and a wink.

"I think you mean potency," he muttered. "And I'm only fourteen. I don't—look, I'll just give you the money, if you really need it."

Her eyes widened, and her nostrils twitched. "*Well.* If you ent interested in the truth, then there's no helpin' you." She walked away, grumbling to herself.

Simon watched her disappear around a corner then took

another bite of his pie, which was rapidly crumbling to bits in its grease-stained paper wrapper. There were certainly some colorful figures in Eidendel. Part of the city's charm, he supposed.

A sweeper imp waddled toward him on all fours, nostrils flaring in its wide, fishlike face. Amethyst scales glistened in the morning light. "*Gubble*," it croaked.

Once Simon had finished eating, he dropped the wrapper to the cobbles. The imp's tongue shot out, snapping it up like a fly. Its throat bulged as it gulped down the wrapper. "*Gub-gub.*"

"You're welcome." Simon stood and walked back toward Foundation Headquarters, a towering building of gray stone. It dwarfed everything around it; a flock of gulls flying past, high above, looked like white specks against its walls. Atop the roof, a wagon-sized, carved phoenix reared, engulfed in marble flames, its beak wide open in what was probably meant to evoke a triumphant battle cry. To Simon, it looked as though the poor creature were screaming in pain.

The first time he'd set foot in this place—the same building his father had once worked in—he'd felt a rush of awe and excitement. This was the epicenter of the Foundation, the wellspring of power, the beating heart of the entire Continent. The strongest, most influential Animists in the world came here to develop their talents, share research, and discuss matters of policy.

It hadn't taken long for that sparkle of wonder to fade. Being physically close to power, he'd learned, did not mean sharing in it.

Simon walked up the wide stone steps to the main entrance, shouldered open the massive, solid oak doors, and stepped into the spacious marble lobby of Foundation Headquarters. A wave of cool tingles swept over him, from his head down to his toes, as a security ward registered his energy signature. The sensation was always a little creepy, like invisible fingers poking around inside him. And for some reason it made his nose itch. He sneezed.

Robed figures bustled through the lobby, back and forth, taking no notice of him. Imps crouched on their Masters' shoulders or flitted along behind them on iridescent dragonfly wings, carrying scrolls or letters in their mouths. A portrait of Queen Saphronia, pale and dour in her fur-lined cloak, hung on the far wall in a gilded frame. Her expression—which had once conveyed serene authority to him—now seemed to radiate a lofty mixture of boredom and contempt.

Simon left the splendor of the lobby and made his way down one of the wide hallways. He paused to check his reflection in one of the full-length, silver-framed mirrors on the wall. He adjusted his collar. His gaze skimmed up and down his faded robes, making sure they were clean and straight before turning quickly away.

Simon avoided looking at his reflection as much as possible;

the sight of his own face stirred vague anxieties in the corners of his mind. He'd always disliked his mop of unruly brown hair—halfway between curly and wavy—and the dusting of freckles on the bridge of his nose. They made him look younger. Once, he'd tried cutting his hair short, but that just drew attention to his oversized ears. Even the color of his eyes was indecisive—they couldn't decide if they wanted to be green or hazel, and were forever shifting depending on the light and his mood.

As he turned a corner, someone's shoulder slammed into his. Simon lost his balance and toppled backward, landing on his bottom with a painful thud.

"Watch where you're going, Swoony."

He winced. *Wonderful.*

Slowly, Simon raised his eyes.

Brenner loomed over him.

Since Simon last saw him, he'd grown a patchy, reddish beard, but there was no mistaking that imperious tone or the tightly clenched expression on his face, which made him look as though he had a rather large, spiky tree branch up his bum and was determined not to show the pain. "Well, are you going to apologize? You ran into me."

Simon picked himself up and brushed his robes off. "You ran into *me*," he muttered.

"What was that now? Did I just hear you contradicting an officer?"

Simon blinked. "Officer?"

Brenner tapped the silver badge on his robes, which displayed a phoenix within a ring of stars. "I've been promoted."

Already? Brenner was sixteen, only two years older than Simon. His parents were high-ranking members of the Foundation, which probably didn't hurt. "Congratulations," Simon said woodenly.

"I heard they stuck you in the mailroom," Brenner said. "Is that true? I'd say you've disgraced your family name, but your parents did a fine job of that themselves."

Simon gritted his teeth. That was a low blow, even for Brenner. *Ignore it. Don't rise to the bait.*

When Simon had first started his apprenticeship, he and Brenner had been paired up for an exercise that involved summoning a wraith (a rather weak Eldritch entity, barely a step above an imp) and commanding it to attack a straw dummy. With a jar of summoning ash, Simon had conjured a wrinkled, pug-faced creature with batlike wings and an unsightly, hairless purple backside. Instead of obeying Simon's commands, the wraith had promptly urinated on both of them and then flew in loops around the room, spraying the other apprentices and their Masters with foul-smelling liquid, shrieking all the while. It had taken Simon several minutes to successfully banish it. Brenner had gotten the worst of the spray. His expensive, hand-embroidered robes had been permanently ruined, and the stench had clung to him for weeks; people would hurry past him in the hallways, noses pinched shut. Both he and Simon had received failing marks.

After that, Brenner had made it his personal mission to make Simon's life as miserable as possible.

"What do you want from me?" Simon asked as dispassionately as he could.

"Want?" Brenner sniffed. "I don't *want* anything. I just despise you."

Well, that was honest. "I'm not fond of you either."

Brenner put a hand to his chest. "Such a devastating retort! Your wit pierces me to my core. You may not have much physical presence or talent, but you make up for it with your scintillating intellect. No, wait—you don't have that. But your endearing personality shines through. No, wait, you don't have that either. Hm, why do you exist, again?"

"I need to get to work," Simon muttered. He strode stiffly down the hall.

Brenner called after him, "How's Master Neeta, by the way? Oh, I forgot, she dropped you. Can't seem to hold on to a Master, can you, Swoony? You're like a stale spice cake at Solstice. You keep getting passed around. No one actually wants you, but they're too polite to chuck you in the trash! Did you hear me? *You're a stale spice cake!*"

Simon's molars ground together. But he knew better than to respond. It always made things worse.

He wondered—not for the first time—if this was what his life was truly meant to be like.

And if so, if he was cursed.

Chapter Two

When Simon first began his training, at age twelve, he'd been apprenticed to a tall, strict woman named Neeta Daneel. She put him through a range of exercises: meditating while balancing a stack of flat stones on his head, meditating while sitting naked in an ice-cold pond, meditating while she tried to distract him by rattling off a list of his faults in her cool, dry tone.

"Soft," she said, poking his stomach. "No muscle tone. You stutter. You avoid eye contact. You let other people push you around. You lose your concentration easily. *Focus!*"

He dreaded training. Every night, he went to bed with his stomach churning with anxiety. But he kept coming back.

He learned to levitate a pebble, then to heat the water in a teacup, then to maintain a small flame while Neeta did everything in her power to disrupt his concentration. He spent a full week trying over and over to climb a sheer cliff near the edge of the sea, using Animism to help his hands and feet stick to the stone, but he never made it to the top. By the end of the week his body was mottled with bruises from falls.

"You lack *focus*," Neeta told him for perhaps the thousandth time.

To improve his concentration, she had him hold a live grasshopper in his mouth while channeling his power; he swallowed it by mistake, and she had him repeat the experiment with a fresh grasshopper.

He told himself that she didn't enjoy doing these things—that this was simply standard practice for all apprentices—until he talked to some of his former classmates, who assured him that *their* training was far more pleasant.

Neeta, it turned out, was infamous as a demanding and sadistic Master. She kept losing apprentices because they kept asking to be transferred. No one wanted to work with her, and no other Master wanted to work with Simon because of his notorious family history . . . or at least, that was what he told himself.

Perhaps in reality, he was just incompetent; in the preliminary group classes at the Foundation Academy, which were meant to prepare young Animists for their apprenticeship, he was always the one lagging behind, always the one lingering in the classroom for hours after the bell had rung, trying to perfect some simple task that came naturally to everyone else.

In any case, every other Master had turned down Simon's request for mentorship. And so he and Neeta were together.

He'd hoped this might create a bond of sorts. Instead, she just seemed endlessly impatient with his failures, which made him all the more desperate to please her. His goal in life was to win a single word of praise. But each time he managed to complete some impossible task, she would simply grunt or mutter, "Finally."

Once the first phase of his training was complete, he began accompanying her on missions . . . supposedly as her backup, though he was never of much help. At one point, he actually *fainted* in the midst of a battle—his crowning humiliation, and the source of his nickname, Swoony, which Brenner used often and with relish once he heard about the incident.

Simon still wasn't sure what had happened, exactly. Oh, he remembered what led up to it. An investigation had gone awry. He and Neeta had found themselves cornered by a muscular, bald thug with a nose ring the size of a door knocker. Simon could still see the behemoth running toward him, wielding a pair of stone swords he'd pulled from somewhere, veins popping out of his skin, mouth open in a berserker roar. Simon stood frozen, the terror rushing to his head like bubbles in a champagne glass.

Then . . . something had happened. A rush of prickling heat, a flash of green light, and a blast of pain, like an ax dividing his skull.

After that, blackness.

He was convinced it had been some bizarre medical fluke, a miniature seizure striking at the worst possible moment. What else would explain the strange light and pain? Or maybe that was just what he *had* to tell himself. The alternative—that he was simply weak of mind and body— was too shameful.

He'd woken up with Neeta standing over him, hands on her hips and an all-too-familiar look of disappointment on her face. Nearby, the criminal lay neatly trussed up, hands bound and a gag stuffed into his mouth. With cool reserve, Neeta had offered Simon a hand up, then asked, "Have you ever considered going into a different line of work? You'd make a fine tailor."

Before that, she'd always openly criticized him for his slip-ups, but in that moment, the pity in her eyes as she helped him to his feet was far more painful than any insult she'd ever hurled his way.

Shortly after, Neeta had resigned as his teacher. No one else stepped in to take her place. The Foundation had finally shrugged its shoulders and assigned him to the mailroom— to Master Melth, himself a failed Animist who had tumbled to the bottom rung of the Foundation's ladder.

It wasn't the life Simon had envisioned when he made the decision to become an Animist. But it was better than going home to Blackthorn. To his father.

Anything was better than that.

Simon opened the door to his office, if you could call it that: a stone-walled chamber, tucked away in a lonely corner of Headquarters, barely larger than a walk-in closet. Half the floor space was taken up by a hulking desk of cheap yellow pine.

A box, wrapped in plain brown paper, sat on the desk. When his gaze fell on it, his chest tightened. He didn't have to open it up to know what it was: another month's supply of Simon's medicine, courtesy of Dr. Aberdeen Hawking. Simon had stopped taking the pills when he began his training, but his father didn't know that. The packages continued to arrive like clockwork.

Simon carried the box into the hallway and kept walking until he spotted a plump sweeper imp waddling along. It blinked round orange eyes at him and swished its tail. He approached, holding out the package. "Medical waste," he said. "Can you handle it?"

The imp's mouth stretched open, distending to nearly twice the size of its head. Simon was never sure how they managed that trick. He deposited the package into the toothless cavern, and the imp swallowed it down with a quiet gulp. Its innards rumbled, and it belched out a purple cloud before trundling onward.

"Thanks," Simon called. He felt a twinge of guilt for wasting the pills but returned to his desk.

The mailroom was poorly insulated, icy in the winter, sweltering in the summer. For almost a year now, Simon had lived and worked here, sleeping on a cot that folded out from the wall, listening to the drip-drip of the leaking pipes and the scratch of mice in the walls as he drifted off each night, back and shoulders aching from the long hours spent bent over his desk.

Sometimes, he felt closer to forty than fourteen.

He could ask to be moved to a warmer room, he supposed, but he knew from experience that complaints would be met with a derisive snort and a lecture from Master Melth. He could imagine it easily enough: *If I had the power to request any office I wanted, do you think I would be working* here? *I put up with the cold when I was your age, boy. Just count yourself lucky that you have a roof over your head.*

Simon pulled out his chair and sat.

Another day, another pile of papers to sift through. Necessary work, he reminded himself, even if it was rather dull.

Tap-tap-tap.

Simon looked up from his desk in the mailroom, blinking blearily. Something at the window? He rubbed his eyes, which were dry and sore from a long day of reading by candle flame. The weak light of sunset, filtered through a square of dirty glass, was scarcely enough to see by.

Tap-tap.

He stood and approached the tiny window.

A bedraggled pigeon sat on the sill, peering at him with one pumpkin-orange eye. A folded piece of paper was tucked into an iron band on its leg.

Strange. Letters typically arrived through a chute in the ceiling above his desk. They came through in brick-sized bundles, bound with string, at odd moments throughout the day. Occasionally, if a letter was important enough, Master Melth would bring it to him personally. But never once had a message arrived by pigeon.

He opened the window. The bird stood placidly as Simon removed the paper and unfolded it. His candle had burned out; he held a finger to the wick and focused, and a golden flame leaped into being. He studied the letter in its flickering glow.

Good Sir or Madam,

It is with grave urgency that I write to the Foundation to request the aid of an Animist. Our humble town, Splithead Creek, is in danger. An unspeakable horror has taken up residence in our mountains. When we tracked the beast back to its lair and attempted to drive it out, it killed one of our men.

We beg you, slay this monster. If you succeed, you will have our eternal gratitude. (Though, I should note, you already have our taxes.)

Your Servant,

Mayor Jacob Umburt

"Splithead Creek," he murmured. He turned to study the faded map of the Continent spread across the back wall. His finger trailed along the edge, until he located a tiny dot near the edge. He glanced at the pigeon, which cocked its head. "You've come a long way."

The town's name tickled a distant memory, but he couldn't place where he'd heard it, or when.

The pigeon cooed and rustled its wings.

"You must be hungry," Simon said. A half-eaten slice of toast sat on a plate on his desk; he'd grabbed it from the kitchens earlier. He broke off a piece and offered it to the bird, who pecked at it greedily. A smile tugged at one corner of Simon's mouth.

A chilly wind gusted from the open window, bringing a few drops of rain. He shivered and rubbed his arms. The evenings were growing cooler as the autumn wore on. Simon warmed his hands over the candle and watched the pigeon pecking at the crumbs.

"Simon? Simon!"

He gave a start. The pigeon fluttered off, leaving a few dirty feathers behind, as Master Melth—round, mustachioed, and balding—bustled in, looking flustered and exhausted, as usual. "Have you filed those letters from Westerdale yet?" He squinted. "What is that thing you're holding?"

"It's a request for aid."

"Let me see." He plucked the letter from Simon's hand.

"Splithead Creek? Is that even under our jurisdiction?"

"Yes." Though just barely.

Master Melth studied it for a few seconds longer then frowned. "Monster? Highly dubious." He opened a cabinet drawer marked *Dubious* and dumped the letter inside. It fell atop a loose pile of other, Simon guessed, similar letters. "Now, I'll need that stack of requests sorted in order of importance by six o'clock. My superiors are breathing down my neck, and I can't keep telling them—*Simon!*"

He jumped.

"Kindly look me in the eye when I'm speaking to you."

Simon forced himself to meet his Master's watery blue gaze. There was a burst capillary in the left eye, a splotch of red against the yellowed white. It was distracting. "Sorry. I was—"

"Daydreaming. I know." His voice dropped to a mutter as he added, "I used to daydream, when I was your age."

"I wasn't, though. I was thinking about that letter. It seems like those people are in real trouble. Shouldn't we at least—I don't know—send someone to investigate?"

Master Melth sighed and ran a hand over his bald spot. His features sagged, irritation slipping away to reveal the weariness beneath. "I've been in this position for fifteen years, lad. I've seen hundreds of missives like this. Every so-called monster turns out to be an overgrown mountain lizard or a mangy bear. 'Unspeakable horror,' indeed. Those farmers and goat herders on the fringes of civilization are so bored, they invent things to be frightened of."

"They said it's already killed a man."

"People die every day. The Foundation can't afford to waste resources hunting down a rogue animal."

"But—"

"This isn't a debate." Master Melth strode out, shutting the door firmly behind him.

Simon turned his attention to the stack of letters on his desk. He shuffled through them numbly.

His gaze strayed to the file cabinet marked *Dubious*.

He glanced nervously at the door, then opened the cabinet, fished the crumpled paper from the pile, and set it on the desk, smoothing it out.

Splithead Creek. Where had he heard that name? After a moment, it clicked. His mother had gone to the mountains near Splithead Creek on her pilgrimage to visit the Gaokerena tree, long ago. His heartbeat quickened.

He knew it was a flimsy connection. It meant nothing. Mother had traveled to many places in her lifetime, before disappearing for good. Even so . . . he felt, in some vague way, that this letter had been meant for his eyes. That the pigeon had brought it to *him*.

We beg you, slay this monster.

They were asking for an Animist. Simon was an Animist, albeit of the lowest caliber.

But even if he *wanted* to answer the summons, he couldn't.

There was a protocol. A summons was filed and evaluated according to its level of danger and urgency, and a panel of Foundation officials chose who was best suited to the job. Simon didn't have the authority to make such decisions himself. He was still an apprentice, and there was a pecking order even among the Masters, less official, but still quite real. Even when he attained his title—if he ever did—he would be in the lowest tier of power. This was beyond his reach.

Reluctantly, he tucked the letter into the cabinet.

A pile of fresh letters dropped from the chute above his desk with a giant thud. He undid the string binding them. He'd no sooner opened the first one than another three bundles dropped onto his desk, spilling everywhere. A groan escaped his throat.

Maybe he could summon a helper.

He pulled a palm-sized silver jar of summoning ash out from his robe pocket and turned it over in his fingers. Simon had prepared it himself, several weeks ago, by burning a mixture of dead roses, a sheet of paper on which he had written a secret fear and a secret desire, and a piece of a prized possession—in this case, the amputated leg of his childhood teddy bear, Mr. Wubbles.

Summoning differed from other forms of Animism. It was more intuitive, more unpredictable. Moreover, the ability to control the summoned entity was dependent on the will of the summoner. You never knew what you were going to get. But this mixture was of a low enough potency that the results wouldn't be *too* disastrous, even if they went wrong. Nothing like the urinating pug-faced wraith.

He cleared a space on the desk, sprinkled the ash in a circle, and nicked the pad of his thumb with a letter opener. A drop of blood quivered and fell, landing in the center of the circle. "I call upon you, servant of the Eldritch Realm," he whispered. "Claim my toll and lend me your strength."

A puff of smoke filled the air, and a quivering ball of lavender fur appeared on the desk. The creature was scarcely bigger than a mouse, with mothlike antennae and round black eyes that seemed far too large for its body. The eyes blinked. "Koo-roo?" a tiny voice chirped.

"Hello there." Simon held out a finger, and the creature hopped on, clinging with tiny, sticky feet. "You're scarcely even big enough to be an imp, aren't you? Well . . . see if you can pick up that letter."

The impling hopped to the desk and scuttled to the nearest letter. It latched onto it with its forefeet, tugged it a few inches, its eyes squeezed into slits from the effort . . . then collapsed, panting. "Koo-roo," it mewled.

Simon sighed. "Don't worry about it. You can just keep me company for a while." He offered a hand.

The creature scurried up his arm, onto his shoulder, and nestled against the side of his neck. Its body vibrated, as though it were purring. A tiny smile tugged at Simon's lips. Well, he seemed to have made a friend, at least.

He skimmed the contents of a letter—a request from the fishing town of Narth, which had been buffeted by savage storms recently. The fishermen wanted help calming the weather. He sorted the letter into the high-priority drawer, feeling a twinge of shame as he did so. The Foundation was supposed to be objective, but when he started this job, he'd been given clear instructions to prioritize the wealthier cities, the ones that reliably produced goods for the Foundation and fattened the Queen's coffers with their taxes. Attempts to deviate from these orders had been met with lectures from Master Melth—*If you want to keep this job, boy, you'll stop playing around and do it like you're told. When you make a mistake, I'm the one who gets my ear chewed off, remember?*

He shucked off envelope after envelope, sorting the letters into piles.

He wondered what his mother would think, if she could see him now. No doubt she'd be disappointed.

He skimmed another letter—a request for funding from a library in the city of Goldorn, on the eastern end of the Continent. They received the same request every month: *Our history section is woefully meager. Our children know so little of our fair city's roots . . .*

Come to think of it, Foundation Headquarters' library didn't have many history books, either. At least, none that went back further than a century or two. What little he knew of Eidendel's deeper history, he had learned from his parents.

And with that thought his mind drifted, as it so often did, to the past.

~~~~~~

Simon was five years old and sitting in his mother's lap, enveloped in her comforting, familiar scent—bittersweet, like herbs and arcane powders. She was showing him a map of Eidendel in a picture book, with the streets marked and the buildings all drawn in extraordinary detail. "See, Simon?" she said, pointing. "Here's the Temple, and here's the library."

Simon snuggled into the crook of her arm. "Where is our house?"

"Blackthorn? It's right here, on the city's edge." She tapped a spot. "Do you notice anything unusual about Eidendel? About the shape of it?"

Simon scrunched his nose up. "It's round?"

"That's right. Eidendel was built inside a *crater*. Do you know that word?"

"A big hole. From a . . . a me-te-or?"

She smiled at his clumsy pronunciation. "A big hole, yes . . . but it wasn't a meteor that did this. It was a man. An Animist."

Simon's eyes widened. "Who?"

"No one knows his name. It's been forgotten, as many things have been. Eidendel was built over the ruins of the city he destroyed during the War of Ashes." She stroked his hair.

"You see, Simon, he used a forbidden type of Animism. It's said he transformed into something immense and terrible, and the few who witnessed the transformation went mad. Afterward, they could only babble about a storm with eyes and teeth. And the man himself died. But for a few brief hours, he held the power of a god."

"How?" Simon whispered, caught halfway between fascination and horror.

A shadow slipped over her pale green eyes. They grew distant, thoughtful. "You know how Animism normally works, Simon? We draw energy from this world. From Earth. Or we summon creatures from the Eldritch."

Simon nodded.

"Imagine both our own world and the Eldritch as tiny islands surrounded by a vast sea. There are other worlds, other islands, probably. But we only know of these two, so far."

"A sea? Could we take a boat to the Eldritch?"

"It's not that sort of sea. The Earth and Eldritch are not separated by space, but by . . . let's call it wavelength. Frequency. They exist in the same place, on different levels of reality. Do you understand?"

"Yes," he said, though he didn't. He just wanted Mother to think he was smart. To her—and to Father too—being smart was very important. To call someone *slow* was the worst thing.

Olivia was always so quick to understand things. Simon, not so much.

"Very good," Mother said, smiling. "So—there's the Earth and there's Eldritch, and other worlds, yet to be discovered. Islands, so to speak. But there is also a sort of space *between* worlds. This is all theoretical, you understand. And highly controversial. But the *sea*—the empty space that surrounds and separates our world and others—is what we call the Outer Realm. It's inhabited by entities more powerful and strange than any Eldritch creature. We call them the Elder Gods."

Simon listened. He understood less the more she spoke, but the rhythm of his mother's voice was calming, despite her words.

She wrapped one of his curls around her finger, playing with it. "Long ago, before the War of Ashes, the gods would sometimes visit our world. They would eat people, some- times whole cities at once—*gulp!*"

He flinched.

"They were dangerous, never doubt it. But they would strike bargains with humankind, as well. Sometimes, they'd protect chosen villages from other gods, in exchange for cer- tain favors or sacrifices. It was a dark and wild time." She smiled, almost fondly. "Of course, the Elder Gods have not made an appearance for many, many years. But they are not the only power that flows from the Outer Realm."

She fell silent for a few heartbeats, a small, pensive frown on her lips. Simon waited.

She took a breath. "You see . . . the realm itself is filled with—or perhaps composed of—a powerful energy. The Elder Gods, for all their formidable strength, are but fish swimming in this sea of power. You might say that it's around us all the time—that we are separated from it by only a thin veil. And every so often, a human is born who can penetrate that veil, who can draw water from that sea . . ."

"Veera?" said a deep voice. His father stood in the entrance to the study. "What are you doing?"

"I'm simply telling him about the history of our city," she replied coolly.

Father's eyes narrowed. "Go to your room, Simon."

Simon hesitated. His mother smiled, ruffled his hair, and said, "Go on, little scholar. I'll be up soon to kiss you good night."

Scholar, Simon thought as his chest filled with warmth. *That's a very good thing to be called.*

He crept out and closed the door behind him, but he lingered in the hallway, pressing his ear to the door, trying to make out what his parents were saying. The words were muffled; only the urgency in their voices came through.

"—only a child—can't possibly understand—"

"—always trying to hold him back—"

"If the Foundation found out—"

They were always arguing. He could never tell what they were arguing about, but somehow, he always felt like it was his fault.

Later that night, his father came up to his bedroom and knocked on the door. "Simon? I'm coming in." The door creaked open.

Simon sat up, clutching the covers. His father sat on the edge of the bed, his lips pressed into a thin seam. He scratched his stubble and cleared his throat. "Listen, Simon. Your mother, she's an amazing person, but she's a bit . . . abnormal. She's—" He paused, as if searching for words. "She's very smart. Smarter than me, even. And sometimes, smart people get restless. They like to poke at reality, like a child poking a badger with a stick. They can't seem to help themselves. But a poked badger will eventually bite. There are things about this universe that simply aren't meant to be understood by the human mind. Barriers that aren't meant to be breached. People like your mother . . . they have trouble accepting that. Sometimes, they're drawn to areas of study that are . . . risky. Unstable. Do you understand?"

"No."

"Oh, blast it. I'm no good at this." He rubbed the back of his neck. The lamplight reflected off his glasses. "All right, Simon, listen. There are rules that even powerful Animists like us have to follow. The rules are frustrating sometimes, but they're there to prevent people from getting hurt. Or worse. Your mother does not have much regard for those rules." He fidgeted. "Has she . . . has she ever mentioned the name Azathoth to you?"

Simon shook his head.

The tension eased out of his shoulders. "Good. Well, forget that name. I shouldn't have spoken it. But she was talking about Elder Gods again, wasn't she?"

Simon nodded.

"All right. Well. Here's what you need to know: the Elder Gods never existed. There are ancient stories, but they're no more than the fantasies of primitive and superstitious people, a sort of mass hysteria. When the Foundation imposed order on the world, they stopped human sacrifice and other cruel practices, and they swept away all those old, false beliefs."

"But . . . imps and wraiths are real. Aren't they?"

"Of course. Imps, wraiths, ghasts, shoggoths . . . there's nothing supernatural about them. They're simply creatures from the Eldritch that can cross over to Earth when summoned. But Elder Gods are not from that world. They're not from any world. Because they don't exist. Anytime your mother starts talking about that sort of thing, you just come to me. All right?"

"Um. All right."

"Good." He stood. "I'm glad we had this talk."

The next day, at the breakfast table, Simon sat with Olivia and his mother. Father was secluded in his laboratory, as he often was, working long hours on his research for the Foundation.

Simon glanced up from his bowl of porridge and said, "Mother, are the Elder Gods real?"

"Olivia, stop feeding that imp," Veera said.

Olivia had conjured a tiny creature resembling a spotted toadstool with legs and was giving it crumbs of her blueberry muffin. She glanced up. "Why?"

"Because they're not meant to eat human food."

As if to prove her point, the toadstool opened a fang-filled mouth and vomited a tiny puddle onto the table.

"So what *do* they eat, Mother?"

"Oh, lots of things. Plants and fungi from their own world. Other Eldritch creatures. Occasionally they'll eat human flesh."

Curiously, Olivia offered her finger to the toadstool. The imp sniffed it.

"Careful," Veera said, smiling. "It may get a taste for you." She clicked her teeth together, and Olivia giggled.

Simon asked again, louder, "Mother, are the Elder Gods real?"

"Hm?" She glanced up, just as Olivia's imp vanished in a wisp of green smoke. "What makes you ask that, Simon?"

"Father says they're just stories," he said.

She laughed. "Of course *he* says that. He only thinks something is real if he can weigh it on a scale or boil it in a test tube. I prefer to leave all possibilities open."

"But aren't the Elder Gods something bad? You said they used to kill lots of people. Aren't they evil?"

"'Evil' is just a word people give to things they fear," his mother replied. "A true Animist fears nothing."

Simon shifted in his chair, uneasy. Maybe Father was right: his mother *was* a bit abnormal.

Still, Simon couldn't help envying her. He was afraid of so many things.

When Simon glanced out the mailroom window, it was dark. He rubbed at his eyes. Sometimes, after hours of shuffling through letters and placing them in the proper drawers, he descended into a sort of numb haze where time slipped away. The impling had long since vanished, whisked back to the Eldritch Realm. He missed its warmth. Maybe one day, he could call on it again.

He doused his candle and unfolded his cot from the wall. Yawning, he changed into his sleep-clothes—he kept them in a wooden chest beneath the desk—and eyed his robes. They were due for a washing. He turned on the tiny, rust-stained sink in the corner of the room, added some soap, and let it fill up with water. Then he sat on the edge of his cot and began a series of breathing exercises designed to quiet his mind.

Be empty.

He imagined himself growing insubstantial, translucent, like glass. Then he expanded his consciousness outward, focusing on the meta around him. It was everywhere, floating in the air and slumbering far beneath the stones of the Foundation Headquarters. If he concentrated, he could *see* it faintly—a network of shimmering golden lines traced into the darkness behind his eyelids, like thousands of fireflies. That same energy glowed in the center of his chest. He breathed in rhythm with the pulsing warmth inside him, the energy that bound him to the web of life.

He crouched, pressed his palms to the floor, and slowly drew meta up through the floor and into his body. His skin tingled as the power filled him. His robe glowed a soft gold as it levitated into the air. Water from the sink levitated as well, sticking together to form wobbly, transparent globules laced with soap bubbles. They floated toward the robe, coalesced around it into a swirling sphere of water. The robe drifted within, turning around and around, slower, then faster.

It wasn't the most efficient method of washing clothes— if Simon's concentration faltered, the whole thing would collapse, soaking the floor—but there was no communal laundry in the Foundation Headquarters. Because most apprentices didn't live in Headquarters. They had their own homes, their own families . . . or, if they were old enough and well-off enough, their own rooms in the massive, stately apartment complex next door. (Such rooms were, Simon knew, well outside of what he could afford on the small allowance paid to him by the Foundation.) Master Melth was letting him live and sleep here as a favor. He tried to remind himself of that, when he started feeling resentful.

Once or twice, in desperate moments, he'd thought about asking for money from his father. But a mixture of pride and fear always stopped him. He wasn't sure his father had much to spare, anyway.

When the robe was clean, Simon let the water blob disperse slowly into the air, becoming droplets, then mist. Once the last of the moisture had been pulled from the fabric, Simon hung it up on the hook near the door and wiped the sheen of sweat from his brow. Channeling for that long always left him drained and shaky.

He settled onto the stiff mattress and pulled a thin blanket over himself. Faint moonlight crept in through the window.

His shoulders ached. His back ached. He shifted around, trying to find a more comfortable position, until sheer exhaustion weighed him down, and the warm darkness of sleep enfolded him.

The nightmares were waiting.

Chapter Three

"Care for a copy of the *Eidendel Underground*, sir?"

Simon looked up, blinking blearily. He sat on his usual bench outside Foundation Headquarters, eating his usual mincemeat pie, shivering in the damp cold. He'd slept poorly—he'd had *that* dream again, the one that had plagued him for the last four years—and a headache pulsed behind his left eye.

"The other papers are nothin' but Foundation propaganda," the voice said. "We've got the *truth*."

He turned his head to see the bedraggled woman, braids adorned with feathers, holding out a rolled-up paper. *Her again?* If he didn't know better, he'd think she was following him. Though there was no spark of recognition in her grimy face. "No, thank you."

She waved it under his nose, as if tempting a dog with a

biscuit. "Half a gilly?"

Buying one would probably be the quickest way to get rid of her, and he didn't feel like talking, so he fished a tarnished gilly out of his coin pouch, pressed it into her thin, dry palm, and took the paper. She handed him his change and smiled, showing several missing teeth. "You won't regret it."

She walked away, and Simon exhaled a soft breath.

In spite of himself, he felt a flicker of curiosity. He shuffled through the flimsy pages of the *Underground*, which was filled with exactly the sort of braying nonsense he'd expected. GRUNEWICK LABORATORY STILL IN OPERATION! GOVERNMENT LAB CREATES HUMAN-DEMON HYBRIDS AND UNDEAD SOL-DIERS. ABOMINATIONS!

Simon chewed another mouthful of his pie and used a sheet of the paper to wipe the grease off his hands. The cheap ink came off on his fingers, leaving them smeared with black.

Conspiracy mongers were obsessed with the now-abandoned Grunewick Laboratory, which sat on an island off the coast of Eidendel. It hadn't been in active use since the War of Ashes, centuries ago. Simon himself had been there, once, along with a class of other new apprentices; they'd been taken on a tour of the main floor, which was nothing but empty, dusty rooms and bed frames. He couldn't deny, though—there was something morbidly entertaining about all these baseless speculations, printed as news. He wondered how many of the

Underground's readers actually believed all this.

He flipped to another page. When his eyes fell upon the name *Dr. Aberdeen Hawking*, he froze. His mouth went dry.

Ever since Simon's father left the Foundation, he had been the tabloids' favorite chew toy. There was always some new rumor, each one more bizarre than the last. The allegations ranged from political corruption to romantic liaisons with demons.

He shouldn't have been surprised to see his father's name. He shouldn't care. He should just chuck the paper in the trash. But his eyes moved involuntarily, scanning the lines of blearily printed text: *Though the official story is vague, the consensus among our experts is that Dr. Hawking was expelled from the Foundation for grave-robbing and performing gruesome experiments on human corpses.*

Grave-robbing?

"Numerous bodies have disappeared from the city morgue, in a series of incidents over the past several years," says a source who chooses to remain unnamed for her own protection. "The Foundation has covered it up, of course, as they always do, but I believe Dr. Hawking is the culprit." Furthermore, these expert sources have reason to believe that Dr. Hawking may have experimented on his own daughter, the now-deceased Olivia Hawking. Was he, perhaps, involved in her mysterious death?

Simon wanted to violently crumple the paper until it was nothing but a microscopic ball.

Experts, Simon thought contemptuously. *What* experts? They probably found some crazy hermit living under a bridge, asked him to ramble for a while, and then called him an "expert source." Simon tossed the paper into the nearest rubbish bin. His hands were shaking.

He and his father weren't on good terms, to put it mildly. They hadn't even seen each other since Simon left home two years ago. But he still hated hearing those ugly rumors.

The clip-clop of hooves caught his ears.

He turned his head to see a patrol rounding the corner, two men and two women clad in green Animist robes and riding sleek, well-fed horses.

As the patrol drew closer, Simon's stomach clenched. *Brenner.* He sat astride his mount, his hand resting on the hilt of a thin, coiled whip.

Of course. The day was already off to such a splendid start—why *not* Brenner?

Simon stood, looking around for an exit route. The patrol hadn't noticed him yet; if he was careful, he could slip away before Brenner started his usual routine of sneers and insults.

"Who here seeks the truth?" The bedraggled woman wandered across the street, waving a rolled-up paper. "Who dares to look behind the curtain?"

Oh dear.

Brenner held up a hand, and the patrol halted. In one smooth motion, he dismounted, and his fellow Animists followed suit. Brenner drew his whip and tapped the hilt against his hip a few times. "What have you got there, woman? Let's see."

The woman froze—perhaps realizing her mistake, a little too late—and backed away. "Nothin' important, sir, nothin' a man of your station needs to trouble hisself with . . ."

Brenner snatched the paper out of her hand and squinted at it for a few seconds. He raised his eyes to the woman, who was fiddling with an amulet around her neck, muttering under her breath.

Brenner's fingers tightened around his whip handle. The whip uncoiled itself and flicked out, snapping the air. The cord glowed red, like the heart of a furnace, as he raised the whip high and brought it down with a *crack*.

Simon gasped. The woman fell to all fours, papers spilling from the satchel on her back, blood dripping from a gash on her arm.

A few passersby stopped, turned, and stared.

Brenner loomed over the woman and rattled the paper at her. "Libel," he said, "is a serious offense. Perhaps you don't appreciate *how* serious."

The woman curled into a ball, protecting her head with her arms. Several people averted their gazes and hurried past. Simon watched in stunned horror as Brenner raised his whip again.

"Stop!" The word burst from Simon's mouth before his

brain had time to silence it.

Brenner raised his head, eyes narrowed. The woman started to climb to her feet, but one of the other patrollers planted a boot on her back and forced her down again.

"Who said that?" Brenner called out.

Simon squeezed one hand into a fist. A voice in his head whispered, *He's a patrol member. He outranks you. You'll just get yourself into trouble.*

The woman squirmed, like a beetle impaled by a pin.

If Simon did nothing, what would happen to *her*?

Brenner raised his voice: *"Who said that?"*

Simon moistened dry lips with the tip of his tongue, and replied, his voice shaking, "I did."

Brenner blinked at him. His brow crinkled. "Swoony?"

Simon flinched. The other patrol members smirked.

Simon drew in an unsteady breath. "I . . . I think maybe you're overdoing things a bit? Perhaps you should . . . l-let her go."

Brenner glanced down at the woman, as if suddenly remembering her existence. He glowered at Simon. "And why should I do that?"

Simon's survival instincts were screaming at him to shut up *now*. The woman wriggled and clawed at the patrol member's boot. He couldn't see her face, but he could hear her rapid breathing echoing through the silence. "If you don't release her, I'll report you."

A short, harsh laugh, almost a bark, shot from Brenner's throat. "*Report* me? For what? Doing my job?" Brenner's whip rustled and hissed in his hand, as if sensing the potential for conflict. He raised one gloved fist, the paper crumpled inside it. "This is radical anti-Foundation propaganda, bordering on treason."

"It's just a gossip rag."

"It always starts with words, doesn't it?" Brenner tossed the paper to the ground. "I'd watch *your* words carefully. If you defend her lies, you are complicit in them."

"I'm not defending the *Underground*. I just don't think it's necessary to smash her face into the street."

Brenner snorted and turned away. "What would a mailroom clerk know about police work? Go home, *boy*." He drenched the word with all the lofty disdain of his two additional years.

Behind Brenner, the other patrol members watched coolly. One of them, a burly young man with a beard, kept his boot planted firmly on the woman's back. A strangled wail escaped her throat, a pitiful sound.

Simon realized he was about to do something stupid. He strode forward, dropped into a crouch and pressed his palms to the cobblestones. His palms tingled with icy-hot pinpricks as he drew meta in from the earth.

Brenner's smirk fell away. "What do you think you're—?"

Simon thrust a hand out. Yellow light crackled and

spurted from his fingertips, straight at the bearded Animist next to Brenner. The light was harmless, but it achieved its intended effect; the man stumbled backward, cursing and shielding his eyes against the flash.

The woman leaped to her feet and dashed away, heedless of the loose papers flying from her satchel.

Brenner's whip flicked out, lightning-fast, and seared into Simon's cheek. He fell, gasping, to the street. He pressed his hand to his face, and his palm came away glistening red.

Brenner's shadow fell over him. Simon stared up into his ice-blue eyes and felt a tickle of fear at the base of his spine. He looked around. People were inching away.

Brenner grabbed Simon by his robes, hoisted him up, and slammed him against the nearest wall. Simon's head bounced off the bricks. A burst of pain filled his skull, and his vision swam. "Swoony, Swoony, Swoony," Brenner said, smiling tightly. "You wretched little toad. You've always been a thorn in my side, but now you've *really* done it. A criminal escaped our grasp because of your interference. I should arrest you on the spot."

"Go easy on him, Bren." The patrol member who had spoken—a pretty blond girl—yawned and inspected her nails.

His head snapped toward her, and he scowled. "Why should I?"

"Look at him. Poor thing is shaking like a wet rabbit. Let him off with a warning. He won't do it again." She gave

Simon a syrupy smile. "You know better now, don't you?"

Brenner's scowl deepened. "Fine." His fists tightened in Simon's robes. "Say you're sorry. Say it like you mean it, and I'll consider letting this slide."

Simon gritted his teeth. He felt sick with terror. He wanted to say something witty or rebellious, but his head was a blank. His cheek throbbed.

Brenner's thumb pressed against the cut, grinding into the raw flesh. The pain was dizzying. *"Say it."*

An apology leaped into his throat, and he swallowed it. "Let me go." He squeezed the words through clenched jaws.

Brenner dug his thumb in harder. "One last chance."

Simon's vision had gone blurry. The pain stabbed through him, an insistent hammer, drowning out his thoughts. "I'm sorry," he gasped.

Brenner twisted his thumb back and forth, as though trying to drill a hole into Simon's cheek. "I can't hear you."

"I'm sorry! I'm sorry!" he cried out, hating himself.

The pressure relented, leaving him dizzy and shaking. Brenner wiped his bloodied thumb on the collar of Simon's robe, then leaned closer and whispered, too soft for the others to hear: "If you ever embarrass me like that again, I'll do worse than cut you."

He shoved Simon into a muddy puddle then turned to face his underlings, hands on his hips. "Let's go. We've got work to do." He mounted his horse, and it broke into a canter. His lackeys followed, disappearing around the corner.

Simon picked himself up slowly. His robes were stained with mud and blood. He didn't see the woman anywhere.

With a trembling hand, he touched the cut on his cheek. His fingers glowed yellow, and the wound sealed itself shut.

Brenner had gotten more arrogant—and more dangerous— since his promotion. He'd always been cruel, but this was the first time he'd injured Simon. Or threatened him. What would he have done to that woman, if Simon hadn't intervened?

He ought to report him. Of course, there was no guarantee it would do any good. Brenner's connections would provide him cover, and his underlings would back him up. Still . . . he *couldn't* keep quiet about this.

Should he tell Master Melth?

No. He'd go straight to Neeta.

His heart quailed a little at the thought. He hadn't seen her since his humiliating fainting spell. But she was the only person he knew with the power to do something about this.

As he walked toward Headquarters, he glanced down at one of the scattered newspapers on the cobblestones, now stained with mud and boot prints—the paper that had so enraged Brenner. When Simon peeled a page off the street and gingerly held it up to the light, he could just make out

the headline—OUR QUEEN: SECRETLY A REPTILE?
The illustration showed a toothy, scaled, many-eyed monstrosity wearing a dress and crown.

Simon sighed.

Chapter Four

Simon hurried through the lobby. The Queen's portrait glowered down, her eyes seeming to follow him. She might not be a reptile, but she didn't seem particularly warm-blooded, either.

The monarchy had been around since the Foundation's beginning, the crown passed from mother to eldest daughter. The Queen wasn't involved much in governing, these days, but she persisted as a powerful symbol. Simon had only seen her once, from a distance, at a public gathering. The sight of her standing on a high balcony, peering down at the crowd, was still imprinted in his mind, though he'd been a small child at the time. Her sour expression had been precisely captured in the painting.

Neeta would be teaching her class around this time. He headed into the east wing of Headquarters, where most of the classrooms were located, and lingered outside a set of doors, peering in at the cavernous lecture hall. Rows of stadium seats surrounded a podium, where Neeta herself stood, holding a long wooden pointer.

She looked more or less as he remembered. Her long, glossy dark hair was tied back in a severe tail. A pale scar bisected the amber-brown skin of her cheek. She wielded the pointer like a weapon, tapping it against the tapestry-sized map on the wall. Her voice echoed through the room: "So, as you may recall from our previous lesson, it was Akeera Vel-Jeer, from Delga of the Sunari peninsula, who first discovered the existence of the Eldritch Realm. Incidentally, he also coined the term 'meta' in reference to the living energy that flows through all things, and which Animists must harness in order to—*Brown!*"

A red-haired girl, who'd been slumped in her seat, jerked upright.

"This *will* be on the exam, so I would advise you to pay attention," Neeta said. "Quickly, now. What are the classes of Eldritch creatures, ranging from least to most powerful?"

"Erm . . . imps, wraiths, shoggoths . . . ghasts, demons . . ."

"Ghasts are a *species* of demon, Miss Brown. And demons, as you may know, are among the most powerful and dangerous entities to summon. Ghasts cannot speak, but some demons can. They have their own language, and can learn human tongues, as well."

A boy's hand shot up. "When will *we* get to summon demons?"

"Not for a very long time, and perhaps not ever. Only Animists who achieve the rank of Master may do so, and it's risky even for us, if we don't make proper preparations."

The boy groaned and slumped in his seat.

Neeta raised an eyebrow. "Getting bored?" Her lips curved in a tiny, grim smile. "Perhaps you'd like a demonstration?" She withdrew a vial of summoning ash from within her robes and sprinkled a circle on the floor to her left. She pulled a knife from a sheath on her wrist and methodically slashed her arm—Simon winced. A splash of blood fell into the circle.

She took a deep breath, pressed the palms of her hands together, and closed her eyes.

Simon—along with the roomful of students—watched as the air above the ash shimmered, then solidified into a semitranslucent, luminous green sphere, slightly taller than a person. The sphere's bottom rested on the floor, encompassing the ash circle.

Neeta murmured a series of words. Smoke exploded within the sphere, swirling. A low growl rippled from inside the smoke. When it cleared, the students leaned forward.

Simon couldn't clearly see the creature inside—only its outline, which resembled that of a person, but twisted. Wrong.

The ghast shrieked and rammed itself against the translucent sphere, pressing its hands and face against the inner surface so it bulged outward.

"Be glad for the barrier," Neeta said. "Ghasts are hard to control. If the Animist's will is weak, the creature may turn on its summoner. Its jaws are strong enough to crush a human skull in one bite. Its talons can disembowel an enemy with a slash."

The ghast pressed harder against the wall of its prison, clawed hands scrabbling against the sphere. Through the semiopaque bubble, Simon glimpsed a pale, wrinkled, skull-like face, gaping mouth crammed with fangs. The students sat pale and sweating, backs rigid.

"You might notice it has no eyes," Neeta said. "It doesn't need them. It can locate you by your heartbeat, or by your smell. During my days as an apprentice, I had a talented and overambitious classmate called Andren who laughed off his mentor's warnings and attempted to summon a ghast in his second year of study, just to prove that he could. They found his remains—what little there were—scattered across his room. A dash of brains on the bedpost. A bit of entrails in the washbasin. The rest had been eaten. His death is listed as a 'summoning accident' in the library's obituaries."

The ghast rammed its head against the barrier. The sphere quivered like a soap bubble on the verge of bursting, and the students recoiled in their seats.

Neeta made a waving gesture with one hand. "Dismissed."

The ghost vanished in a puff of smoke. The barrier wobbled and disappeared with a pop, leaving only a smear of bloody ash on the floor. Neeta crouched and wiped it up with a hand towel, then straightened. "Now, as I was saying. The Eldritch Realm was discovered nearly five centuries ago, shortly after the formation of the Foundation—"

She kept talking for several minutes. The class remained silent, backs rigid.

The bell clanged. The fledgling apprentices, all between the ages of ten and twelve, hurried out, whispering among themselves. Simon caught a few snatches of conversation.

"Did you *see* that thing?"

"Hundreds of teeth—"

"—thought it was going to break through that bubble—"

"Is she even allowed to *do* that inside the school?"

Neeta's teaching methods, it seemed, had not changed much.

Simon waited until the last of them had filtered into the hallway, then entered the classroom.

Neeta sat at a hulking desk, a pen in one hand, scratching busily away at a notebook. A polished bronze plate, engraved with the name *Master Neeta Daneel*, had been set into the wood of the desktop. Simon swallowed, mouth dry. He hadn't seen his former Master in months. "Er . . ."

"Yes?" she said without looking up.

"It's Simon. Simon Frost."

Neeta froze. Her fingers briefly tightened on the pen . . . then she raised her head. Her dark eyes swept up and down the length of him in that cool, assessing way he remembered. "Your robes are filthy. What happened?"

Simon found himself straightening his back and squaring his shoulders, trying to look a little taller. "I, uh. I have something I need to report. It's important."

"Let me finish this. I'll be with you in a minute." She bent her head and resumed writing.

Simon's gaze wandered to the bookshelf standing against the back wall, the rows of leather-bound volumes with titles like *The Subtle Art of War* and *Ethics of Interrogation* in gold letters. He noticed a thick green tome titled *The Foundation: A Complete History*.

Like all apprentices, Simon had been required to read it as part of his training. The book was as dry as month-old bread, the words tiny and densely packed. They told a thorough (yet somehow still vague and unsatisfying) account of the last five hundred years, ever since the War of Ashes ended and the Foundation was established. Historical records from the prewar era were spotty. There was a brief passage at the beginning, though, that he had been required to memorize word for word:

Before the Foundation rose to power, the Continent was composed of warring tribes and feudal states locked in constant,

bloody conflict over territory and resources. Animists were mer-
cenaries without honor, employed by the feudal lords to keep
their subjects in line. The lords themselves were brutish thugs,
exploiting the peasantry for their labor; those ordinary folk who
were not blessed with the gift of Animism were defenseless, often
treated as an expendable resource, worked to death, and then
buried in mass graves. For much of human history, this was life.

Our first queen, an Animist of great strength and intellect,
was repulsed by this cruelty and resolved to put a stop to it. The
feudal lords were subjugated and united under a single banner,
and a system of rules was established to prevent Animists from
oppressing the ungifted or using their powers for crass personal
gain. Thus, the Foundation was born.

Simon sometimes wondered if the world could possibly have been as bad as the book made it out to be. But he kept his doubts to himself.

Neeta set her pen down, closed her notebook, and nodded to a chair. "Sit."

Simon obeyed.

She tapped her nails—neat, unpolished ovals—against the desk. "Well?"

She'd never been one for pleasantries. "It's about Brenner. I saw him being rough with a citizen. He and his patrol. They threw her to the street and whipped her, just for selling a newspaper they didn't approve of."

"Which newspaper?"

"Does it matter?"

"Just answer."

"Er . . . it was the *Underground*. It contained a rather . . . unflattering illustration of the Queen. There were some unpleasant rumors about my father, too." He fidgeted. "I don't approve of it. But still, the way they acted . . . it was wrong."

She sighed. One finger continued to tap slowly against the desk. "Brenner can be overzealous. This wouldn't be the first time he's stepped over the line. But you must understand, Simon. Ideas are potent weapons, more dangerous than steel or Animism. A malicious falsehood is like a plague. It must be contained or it spreads. I've seen what happens when such plagues are allowed to rage unchecked."

"Master Neeta. Believe me, if you had *seen* this paper . . . no sensible person could take it seriously."

"You might be surprised. The uneducated among us can be gullible."

"Even so—"

"Let me ask you this, Simon. Do you believe that the Foundation is good? That it is necessary?"

"Well. Yes. Basically." He worked for the Foundation. How could he say otherwise?

"Then trust it."

"It's Brenner I don't trust," he muttered.

"He will be disciplined. I'll see to it myself. Occasionally, a swollen ego must be lanced and drained." Before he could say anything else, Neeta spoke again: "I heard you'd been transferred to the mailroom. Does the work suit you?"

"It's . . . tolerable. A little dull."

She smiled—a strange, sad, wry smile this time. Her smiles were never fully happy. "The most important work is rarely the most exciting."

"I don't feel very important." He hesitated. He'd come here to tell her about Brenner, not to plead his own case. Still, now that he was here . . . "I know you don't think much of me. But . . . I really believe I'm capable of more, if you would just give me another opportunity. I want to be an Animist. A real one. Perhaps I could train as a Healer, or—"

"Healers need extraordinary levels of focus and mental clarity. Two things you don't possess. Remember the rabbit?"

Simon remembered, though he tried not to think about it. "Then put me on patrol."

She arched an eyebrow.

"I know I'm young, but Brenner's not much older than me, is he? Patrol members don't *have* to be like him. Let me prove that. I can do better."

"Is the mailroom really *so* awful? Most common folk would consider the job prestigious. Many would feel *honored* to be in your shoes."

His hands were balled into tight fists in his lap. "I know. Sorting letters is necessary, I understand that, but . . . I don't feel like I'm *helping* anyone. Is it wrong, to want more?"

Neeta breathed in slowly, let it out through her nose, and interlaced her long fingers. For a few heartbeats, she simply stared at him. He always had the uncomfortable sense that she could peer straight through his skull, into the gray matter within. It reminded him of his father. "There's an old story," she said at last, "about an ant who climbs to the top of a wheelbarrow. Have you heard it?"

He shook his head.

She settled back into her chair. "Once, there was a hardworking little ant. She spent each day in an anthill at the base of an old wheelbarrow, carrying grains of sand, building tunnels alongside her friends and family—part of a harmonious whole, unaware of anything outside the colony. But eventually, she grew restless. Curious. She began to wonder what lay beyond her little world. So she left home and—slowly, agonizingly, over the course of hours—she climbed alone to the top of the wheelbarrow. For the first time, she looked out at the greater world. The wheelbarrow stood perched atop a high hill overlooking a village, so she could see far and wide. She saw houses and stores, the roads, the ocean beyond. She saw humans, dogs, and horses. She could see other anthills, too . . . how very small they were! For a long time, she watched in fascination, amazed at the sheer size of reality. But the more she saw, the more an oppressive sense of dread crept over her.

"Then a human child appeared. A boy. She watched him approach one of the other anthills and crush it with a foot, carelessly, the way children will do. She saw a civilization extinguished at the whim of this enormous, incomprehensible thing. The child laughed as thousands died beneath his boot.

"For the first time, the little ant realized fully what it meant to *be* an ant. For what could she do, against creatures like that? She looked down at her brothers and sisters below, and she envied them for not knowing the truth. She bowed her head, put her face in her forelegs, and wept. And then she climbed down and she never, ever told anyone what she had seen."

Simon felt a curious, squeezing sensation in his chest. Neeta had never been one for riddles or cryptic allegories. What was this about? "I don't understand the point of that story."

"There's no need to understand. Just keep working in the mailroom, and you'll be fine." She picked up a stack of papers and began shuffling through them. "Take care, Simon."

He left the classroom.

As he walked, he found himself thinking about a conversation he'd once had with Neeta during a mission, while she was still his Master. They'd been preparing to arrest a young woman in Eidendel, an unregistered Animist who used her skills as a Healer to treat those who couldn't afford a professional. Allegedly, the law was there to stop amateurs and charlatans from harming the public, but the woman's clients seemed satisfied.

"Can't we just leave her alone?" Simon had asked.

"She isn't registered. Which means she hasn't been properly trained. Which means she's not a *true* Animist. Which means she probably isn't skilled enough to do what she's doing."

Either that, Simon thought, or she couldn't afford the entrance fee, which was steep even for Animist families. "But she hasn't hurt anyone."

"That we know of. In any case, the law must be consistent. If we started allowing exceptions, looking the other way, people would take the Foundation's rules less and less seriously. Eventually, the entire system would collapse. And then where would we be?"

He'd watched as Neeta arrested the woman, who'd submitted tearfully, head bowed, hands held out for manacles. As punishment, the Healer had been steeply fined and forced to take daily doses of vinculum root, a strong sedative that dampened an Animist's power. It was often given to criminals to keep them under control.

There were many things he didn't understand, he reminded himself. High-level Animists like Neeta dealt with problems far beyond anything he'd experienced. Was he really in a position to judge her?

Still, the doubts burned inside him, prickling and itching, like some sort of spiritual rash.

He touched the healed cut on his cheek, where Brenner's whip had bitten into him. It would likely leave a scar.

Chapter Five

Back in the mailroom, Simon pulled out his chair, sat down at his desk, and surveyed the three-foot-high pile of letters in front of him.

His gaze strayed to the file cabinet marked *Dubious*. He retrieved the letter, the one carried by pigeon, and read it again, then again.

His mother's voice came to him.

Sometimes, she had said once, *there are currents that pull us. We can choose to resist, or to surrender and let the universe take us where it will. But when you feel that tug, pay attention.*

He looked around at the four barren stone walls of the mailroom, then down at his robe, stained with mud and blood and torn in several places.

What was he doing with his life?

Following the rules hadn't gotten him anywhere. If he

stayed here, playing his part, nothing would ever change. He had become an Animist in order to prove to his father—and himself—that he was competent, that he was worthy. He'd wanted to accomplish something. And here was a chance to do just that. A call for help, delivered to him on a silver platter. Why was he wasting time sitting in this room?

Before he could lose his nerve, he folded the letter and slipped it into his pocket. He rummaged through his drawer and fished out the small pouch of gillies he'd tucked away for an emergency, then hastily packed a bag. He hesitated, then opened the bottom drawer of his desk. A glass bottle glinted inside, tucked between stacks of papers.

Though he'd been throwing away the shipments of medicine for a while now, he still kept a few pills in a bottle tucked in the drawer. Just in case. He bit his lower lip and thought about leaving it there . . . then grabbed the bottle and shoved it into his pocket.

As he stepped out of the office, he found himself face-to-face with Master Melth's scowl.

"Where do you think you're going?"

Simon took a breath. He couldn't falter; not now. "I'm sorry. I know this is short notice, but I have some business to take care of. I'll be back in a few days."

"A few *days*? Are you joking?"

"No." He resumed walking.

"If you leave now, don't bother coming back."

Simon froze. For a moment, he wondered if he'd lost his mind. Was he really going to throw his job away? His *home*? For what? A bunch of faraway villagers he'd never even met?

Yet there was more to it. An instinct, perhaps. A faint whisper of hope—absurd, childish, but *there*—that if he went to Splithead Creek, he would find some clue to his mother's current whereabouts. She had visited the village once, after all. Maybe someone there would remember her and be able to tell him something. Something he was destined to discover.

He looked into his Master's pallid, pinched face and suddenly felt a wave of pity for him. He saw himself in this man . . . or rather, a shadow of his own future. Unless he changed it. "All right," Simon said. "Goodbye, then."

Master Melth's jaw dropped. Simon kept walking. A bubble of exhilaration rose in his chest.

He could catch the three o'clock train out of Eidendel.

But once he arrived, what then? If there *was* a great beast terrorizing the people of Splithead Creek, he'd need some way of dealing with it. Simon didn't know enough combat Animism to trust in his own strength. His best bet, he decided, would be to summon an Eldritch creature. Not a demon, no—that was too perilous—but he could probably manage a wraith. For that he'd need summoning ash.

He strode toward the Chamber of Sacrifice.

The cavernous, stone-walled room was unlocked, as usual. He'd been inside several times, first during his group classes and then in his apprenticeship to Neeta. Animists, even apprentices, could more or less use the Chamber as they needed. Simon just needed it less than most.

The room smelled like bird droppings. Feathers littered the floor. A wall of wire cages lined with hay stood against the back wall. Chickens paced inside, scratching and pecking. They were imported weekly from local farms. In the center of the floor was a stone altar next to an iron-grated drain, stained dark from years' worth of blood.

Simon lingered in the doorway, stomach squirming. He'd always hated coming here. But summoning anything stronger than an imp required a living sacrifice. He crept in, easing the door shut behind him. The chickens stared at him with their bright, blank eyes. Their faces remained as inexpressive as ever, but some of them began to pace faster and shift restlessly in their cages.

A silver ax hung from a hook on the wall, next to a blood-stained leather smock.

He opened one of the cages and, with both hands, lifted out a plump white bird. "I'm terribly sorry about this," he whispered. "I'll make it quick."

The chicken didn't even struggle, just gave him a bleak stare. A lump rose into Simon's throat.

He carried her toward the altar.

When it was over, he brushed the ashes into his silver summoning jar. The gazes of the remaining chickens needled his back as he walked out of the room.

If the hen hadn't been sacrificed, he reminded himself, she would've just ended up on someone's dinner table. This way, at least, she would help save innocent people.

On the way toward the main doors, he passed Neeta's now-empty classroom and paused, lingering. He didn't owe her an explanation. She wasn't his teacher any longer.

But he wanted to tell her, anyway. He wanted her to know he was leaving—if for no other reason than to show her what he thought about her mysterious warnings and ominous fables.

He took a step toward the door . . . and froze.

Behind the door, he heard Neeta speaking in a low, urgent voice: "I told you not to visit me here."

A deep voice replied, "I won't be long. Any word on the stolen bodies?"

Bodies?

"We've increased security in the morgue, but we still haven't located the corpses," Neeta said. "We have no idea who took them or why."

"Then you will need to investigate more aggressively."

"Is this really a priority? Aren't there more important matters in need of our attention?"

"It's not our decision. The order comes from the top—from the Queen herself."

There was a brief silence. "The Queen has not issued a direct order in over twenty years."

"Do you doubt her judgment?"

"No. Of course not. It's just . . . Why would she break her silence for *this*? A few missing bodies? It seems a bit . . . beneath her notice."

Simon leaned in closer, pressing his ear to the door.

"The culprit isn't just stealing random corpses from cemeteries," the deep voice said. "They're stealing fresh, well-preserved bodies. Do you understand what that implies? We're dealing with an Animist, dabbling in things that no human should dabble in. We need to find the culprit and stop them before they do real harm. If that happens, someone will be held accountable, and that someone will be *you*. Understood?"

"I . . ." Neeta cleared her throat. "I'll do what I can." Another pause. Then: "What was that?"

Simon's chest clenched. Had he breathed too loudly? He dashed away, down the hall, through the lobby, and out the main door. He stumbled and nearly fell down the steps, then paused to catch his breath, hands on his knees.

He had the clear sense that he'd just heard something he shouldn't. A line from the *Underground* flashed through his head: *Numerous bodies have disappeared from the city morgue, in a series of incidents over the past several years . . .*

Apparently, that part of the story was true. And the Foundation really *was* trying to keep it quiet.

But still, he didn't believe for a moment that his father was responsible.

Whatever this was about, it had nothing to do with him. He couldn't allow himself to get distracted—not now. If he hesitated, he might lose his courage.

As he hurried down the street, breathless, he spotted a disheveled figure approaching. The woman he'd rescued.

She bared her stumpy teeth in a smile. "Care for a copy of the *Underground*, sir?"

She'd already forgotten his face. He hadn't really expected gratitude, but still, it stung a bit. Was her mind that addled? Or was he just that forgettable? "No, thank you." He started to turn away when a glint of green caught his eye. There was a jeweled amulet around her neck—a silver tentacle coiled around a smooth, oval-shaped green stone, which looked spectacularly out of place amidst her dirty rags. Despite his distraction, he found himself staring at it. It looked familiar. "What's that you're wearing?"

"This?" The woman's hand strayed to the amulet. "Why, it's the emblem of Our Lord and Uncreator, Azathoth, the most powerful of all the Elder Gods."

He should have guessed. Conspiracy theorists, anarchists, and other oddballs flocked to the Cult of Azathoth like stray cats to a rubbish heap. Simon's late paternal grandfather had apparently been a devotee, as well. His father had always been keenly embarrassed by this fact . . . at least, Simon assumed he was. He'd gotten tetchy anytime someone mentioned the name *Azathoth*.

"You should come to one of our meetings," she said, her eyes shining feverishly. "We have 'em every Saturday in the Gregor Temple."

"No thanks. I was curious about the necklace, is all. If you'll excuse me, I'm in a bit of a hurry, so—"

She took a step closer. A whiff of something sour and cabbagey emanated from her mouth, and Simon shielded his nose with one hand. She removed the amulet from around her neck and held it out, cradled in both palms. "Take it," she said.

"That's very kind, but I don't—"

"Take it." She pressed the amulet into his palm, curling his fingers around it.

He stared into her eyes, caught off guard by the strange intensity in her expression. Did she remember him, after all? "Thank you."

She smiled again, a secretive, closed-lipped smile. Then she turned and slipped into the shadows. He watched her retreating back, bewildered.

Well, he wasn't going to wear the amulet. He didn't want anyone assuming he was a cultist. But it seemed ungrateful to throw it away. He tucked it into his pocket.

At the station, he bought a train ticket—depleting his already meager funds—and left the city. Outside the window, green hills and forests rolled past as the wider world unfolded. A little bubble of giddiness spiraled up from his stomach. He was on his way.

Eidendel receded into the distance behind him, a labyrinth of gray stone. Near the city's edge, where land met sea, he could just make out the finger of rock upon which Blackthorn, his childhood home, was perched.

He wondered if his father was there now, hiding away in his laboratory. These days, if the gossip was to be believed, Dr. Hawking rarely left the house. And he had certainly never come for Simon, either to visit or to bring him home. Just as well.

At age twelve—two years after Olivia's death—Simon had left home with the vow that he'd never return, that the tomb-like chambers and shadowed halls of Blackthorn would remain buried in his childhood, along with the memories of what had happened there. Even before the loss of his sister, that place had been a beacon for tragedy.

The mansion had been in the Hawking family for over a hundred years. Simon's great-grandfather had built it—or rather, had summoned a small army of imps to build it for him—and after marrying and producing a single child, had hanged himself from the rafters of the dining hall. His bones were buried somewhere on the property.

Simon's grandfather had grown up in that house. He, too, had killed himself . . . as a matter of fact, had done it exactly one year before Simon's birth. Apparently hanging was too banal for him; he had summoned a ravenous ghast from the Eldritch Realm and commanded it to feast on his flesh. The housekeeper who found the remains had been thoroughly traumatized. After that, the rumors began to circulate.

The Hawkings were all powerful Animists (well, except for Simon), but their lives were short and plagued by melancholy and madness. Ever since he was a small child, Simon had overheard gossipers whispering that Blackthorn—or perhaps the entire Hawking lineage—was cursed, either by mystical forces or hereditary insanity.

As a child, he'd asked Mother if it would happen to Father, or to him.

"There's no curse," she'd replied. "Your grandad and great-grandad chose to die before their time. You can choose not to. It's as simple as that."

He wanted to believe her. He wanted to very much.

Chapter Six

The train snaked through hills and hamlets, stopping several times to disgorge passengers, until only Simon remained, alone in his cabin, watching the brass lantern sway back and forth on the ceiling, throwing shadows against the walls. He dozed fitfully as the hours dragged by.

When he woke and looked out the window, he saw an empty, white world. Woolly clouds blanketed the sky, and fog covered the flat, open land, so the train seemed to be sailing through a cotton sea. A single leafless tree loomed out of the mist then was swallowed again as the train swept past.

Simon had never been this far from the city of Eidendel. He felt as though he were approaching the edge of creation.

The whistle keened. The train ground to a halt.

When he stepped outside, lugging his single suitcase, it was raining—a steady, spiteful drizzle.

He sneezed and drew his heavy woolen cloak tighter around himself.

There *was* a village, though calling it that felt generous. A few dozen ramshackle houses and barns huddled together like frightened children. Congregations of crows perched on the tin rooftops, looking warily about. A pasture of drenched, miserable-looking sheep shivered nearby.

He was surprised that such an isolated place even had a train stop. There was no station, just a sign with the words *Splithead Creek* carved into the weathered wood.

He watched the train proceed and vanish into the fog.

There was no one outside that he could see. Given the weather, that wasn't surprising. At the far end of the village's single long road stood a stone building, larger than any of the others, though still no bigger than an average house in Eidendel. A Foundation flag, rather tattered and ill-kept, hung limp and wet from a pole out front.

He trudged down the wet road, mud sucking at his boots, and climbed up the sagging wooden steps to a pair of oaken doors. He knocked three times. "Hello?"

No response.

Simon waited, shifting his weight. His boots were already filled with water, and his socks squished. He was about to knock again when he heard the thump of approaching footsteps.

The door creaked open to reveal a towering, muscular

man with a curly black beard and a shaved head, wearing deer-hide pants and a sleeveless vest of scruffy brown fur. The man squinted at Simon and wrinkled his nose, as if he'd found a smashed bug on the bottom of his boot. "Haven't seen you around these parts," he rumbled. "If you're trying to sell something, we probably can't afford it."

Simon supposed he didn't look very impressive, soaked and bedraggled as he was, dragging a suitcase almost as large as himself. He cleared his throat. "My name is Simon Frost. I'm from Eidendel. I work for the Foundation?" It came out sounding like a question; he winced. "You—the mayor here, that is—sent a request for aid." He removed the wrinkled letter from his robe pocket and held it out.

The man took it with one meaty paw. He held it with a strange delicacy, pinching the corners between his thumbs and forefingers as he studied the words. He looked from the letter to Simon and back again several times, then scratched the shiny dome of his head. "You?"

Simon withdrew a bronze compass from his pocket and showed him the bas-relief phoenix on the front: the emblem of the Foundation, proof of his registration. For good measure, he tapped the phoenix-shaped clasp on his cloak.

The man grunted skeptically, but shoved the letter into his pocket and opened the door. "This way."

Simon followed him into a wide hall. Fires blazed in two large hearths on opposite walls. The head of an elk was mounted over one, a great, spotted cat over the other.

The man led him to a door, knocked, and called out, "Mayor Umburt, sir? The Animist's here."

"Ah, excellent!" boomed a deep voice. "Come in."

They entered a wood-paneled office filled with yet more trophies. Stuffed quails hung suspended from the ceiling on wires, as if frozen midflight. In one corner, a stuffed rattlesnake hissed silently at a snarling bobcat, and in the other—surreally—a pair of squirrels seemed to be having an animated conversation over acorns. One had its paw on its chest and its head tilted back, as if it were laughing.

Simon wondered if the mayor was a bit mad. He supposed living in this dreary, isolated corner of the world could have that effect on people.

Behind a hulking desk sat a bearded man in a billowy scarlet shirt. Everything about him—his hands, his face, his build—was stout and blocky. He blinked at Simon. "You're a child."

"I'm fourteen. But I *am* an Animist."

The mayor stared for a moment then sighed. "You may go, Brock." He nodded to the guard—butler?—who bowed his head and ducked out, closing the door quickly behind him. Umburt folded his hands and frowned, causing his broad face to crinkle up like a bulldog's. "You don't have a partner. Don't Animists usually work in pairs? Master and apprentice?"

"Usually, yes."

Umburt paused, as if waiting for an explanation. When it became clear that none was forthcoming, he massaged his forehead with short, blunt fingers. "All right. Let's see a demonstration."

Simon blinked. "Pardon?"

"Of your powers. Show me what you can do. Let's see . . ." He rubbed his hands together. "Ah, yes—summon a demon!"

"Er . . . I'm not at that level yet." Quickly, he added, "I *could* summon an imp or a wraith. They're not as powerful, but—"

"Whatever."

Simon rummaged through his robe pocket and withdrew the small jar of summoning ash. He hated to waste something this potent on a demonstration, but he had enough of it for at least two summonings. And if he didn't prove his power now, he might lose his chance.

He cleared his dry throat. "It's a little harder to perform Animism indoors." *Stop making excuses*, he thought. But his traitor mouth rambled on. "I suppose it would be inconvenient to go outside now, since it's raining, but when I'm standing on the soil, I can channel larger amounts of meta—"

"What?"

"The Earth's energy. It flows through all living things and exists in the atmosphere as diffuse particles." At Umburt's blank look, he continued, "It's what Animists use. For power."

The mayor grunted. "Get on with it."

Sweat trickled down Simon's back as he emptied some of the ash into his palm and sprinkled it in a circle on the floor. He nicked his palm with his pocketknife, pressed his spread hand to the floorboards within the circle, and focused. The cut on his palm pulsed.

This was the moment he'd been waiting for, the chance to prove himself.

"I call upon you, servant of the Eldritch Realm," Simon whispered. "Claim my toll and lend me your strength."

The ash glowed a smoky green. The glow brightened until a column of solid green light shone up to the ceiling. Simon leaped to his feet, heart pounding. Umburt sat up straighter, staring intently.

A puff of smoke filled the room. When it cleared, a three-foot-tall form stood in the center of the circle. The creature was squat and nearly neckless, with a wide, flat, froglike face and moist olive-green skin splotched with purple. It looked around, its bulging eyes rolling independently of each other, and opened its mouth to reveal a set of bare gums.

The mayor's expression went blank.

A sickly heat crept up Simon's neck and spread across his face. All right, he thought. It didn't *look* very impressive, but that didn't matter. He just had to demonstrate that he had control over it. "Servant," he said. "Bow to me." After a half beat, he added, "Please."

The imp waved its short, pudgy arms, hands flapping, and shrieked like an irate parrot. It ran into a wall, staggered back, then ran into the same wall again.

Simon stood stiffly, his ears burning.

The imp fell on its back and lay there, squealing, its stubby limbs flailing.

The mayor removed a small brown glass bottle from his desk drawer and took a swig. "I think I've seen enough."

Simon clapped his hands together, and the imp vanished in another puff of smoke. Awkward silence filled the room.

He cleared his throat. "I can demonstrate some basic fire techniques, if you like."

"No, that won't be necessary." Umburt leaned back in his chair, which creaked under his girth. "I should have expected this," he muttered. "I don't suppose the Foundation takes our complaints very seriously. We're just a bunch of illiterate yokels, stinking of manure. That's how you think of us, isn't it?"

"I can't say I've ever thought much about you, sir."

"Precisely."

There was a small, dark stain on the mayor's left breast pocket. Simon couldn't quite tell what it was. Maybe sauce or coffee or a bit of crusted porridge . . .

"Why are you staring at my shirt?"

Simon forced himself to meet the mayor's eyes. They were a watery brown. "Sorry."

"Never mind," Umburt said. "We won't be requiring your

services. I'll send another letter to the Foundation tomorrow. They can't insult us like this and expect us to take it quietly."

Simon could feel an invisible rope cinching around his neck, pulling tighter and tighter.

He raised his head, forcing himself to maintain eye contact. "Sir . . . if I may speak bluntly, you're not in a position to be picky."

Umburt's eyes narrowed. "Excuse me?"

"Frankly, you were right. The Foundation doesn't consider your village worth its time. If you send another letter, it will end up shoved in the back of a file cabinet and forgotten. They didn't send me here. *I* decided to come. I'm all you've got."

Umburt muttered something under his breath and slammed the brown glass bottle onto his desk. "Bloody parasites," he growled. "They're more than happy to take our taxes, but what do they do for us?"

Simon waited, hoping his robe hid the way his legs shook.

Umburt rose from his chair and walked over to the window. He interlaced his fingers behind his back and stood there for a moment, gazing out at the landscape, as if contemplating the cruel unfairness of his lot. Then he turned and glowered at Simon. "All right. You're here. You may as well try."

A giddy mixture of relief and anxiety swept over him. But he managed to keep his tone calm. "Yes, sir." He cleared his throat. "So. This . . . monster. How big is it, exactly?"

"See for yourself." He opened his drawer and removed a large wooden box. With a grunt, he slammed the object down on the desk.

Simon leaned closer. Inside the box was a plaster cast of a reptilian footprint, twice the size of a lion's paw. The four toes were elongated, like fingers, each tipped with a talon as long and sharp as a pocketknife. A fifth talon jutted out from the side like a thumb.

A web of chills spread across Simon's skin. "Where did this come from?"

"Near a stream in the mountains. A hunter first encountered the beast there. He barely escaped with his life. Funny thing—he insisted that it *spoke* to him. Or tried. He couldn't make out what it was saying."

"It's intelligent?"

The mayor shrugged. "Or the hunter was drunk. Who knows? In any case, we sent a group of our men into the mountains with weapons and torches, hoping to drive the beast out. They tracked it down to its hiding place, an abandoned house in the forest. They managed to wound it, but at a high cost. Two men were badly injured. One died."

"I'm sorry to hear that." He gulped. "Did anyone get a clear look at it?"

"Only glimpses, but it was enough to give them nightmares. And we know it's still there. Just yesterday, another hunter found the remains of a kill in the mountains—the hindquarters of a deer, with bite marks too large to belong to a bear." He met Simon's gaze. "So tell me, Animist. What are we dealing with here?"

"It doesn't sound like any natural animal I know of," Simon admitted.

"A demon, then?"

"That wouldn't make sense." He paced. "Eldritch creatures don't just wander between realms. They only appear when they're summoned, and only remain for a few hours before they vanish. There've been a few cases of summoned entities remaining for a full day, if the summoner is very powerful, but—"

"Speak up, boy. You're muttering."

"Sorry." He took an unsteady breath. Maybe deep down, he'd believed Master Melth's claim that this monster was just an overgrown bear. "Listen, I . . . I may be out of my league here."

"So you're running away, then?"

"I didn't say that." He looked again at the massive footprint. "This abandoned house . . . where is it?"

The mayor pointed out the window. "See that mountain range?"

Simon peered through the glass. Beyond the village, grassy, windswept plains sprawled, their foggy monotony broken only by the occasional scraggly tree. Mountains loomed against the cloudy sky—a dim, humped shape, like the back of a sleeping dragon.

"The house stands on the leftmost peak," Umburt said. "Just follow the trail. It's easy enough to find. Though considering you don't have a weapon, a Master, or the ability to summon a proper servant, I wonder how you plan to stop this monster."

That was an excellent question. "You said it's capable of speech. Maybe it can be reasoned with."

"You can't be serious."

"It hasn't gone out of its way to attack humans."

"I told you, it killed one of our men," Umburt snapped.

He'd also said that they stormed the house with torches and weapons. Most beings, earthly or Eldritch, didn't react very well to that. "I know. But if it could be persuaded to leave . . ." When Simon saw the look on Umburt's face, the words died in his throat. "Well. I'll figure something out. Er . . . is there an inn here?"

Umburt waved Simon toward the door. "There's a spare room at the end of the hall. I recommend staying the night and leaving at first light tomorrow. You don't want to be out in the mountains after dark."

Simon nodded, uneasy. He started to turn then paused. If he was going to ask, now was the time. "By any chance, is there a woman named Veera Frost living in this village?"

Umburt frowned. "Who?"

"She would be in her late forties. Medium height, thin, with blond hair and green eyes. She has a small mole here." He touched a spot on his own left cheek.

The mayor shook his head. "Never seen her. Why?"

Simon turned away. "I just wondered."

Chapter Seven

Brock, the guard-slash-butler-slash-live-in-companion, led Simon to the small, sparsely furnished guest room. With its black iron frame and granite slab of a mattress, the bed resembled a torture device. Though it was probably no worse than the foldout cot in the mailroom.

"You want something to eat?" Brock asked. "There's mutton stew, mutton stew, and mutton stew."

Simon gave him a half-hearted smile. "I'll have the second option, please."

Brock left and returned with a bowl of brown sludge, a wooden spoon jutting out. He set it on the nightstand. Simon eyed the globby mixture and took a bite. It was lukewarm and gristly, but edible.

Brock stood, muscled arms crossed over his chest, his expression inscrutable. "I overheard some of the talk in there.

Seems like you don't have much of a plan. If it were up to me, I'd burn down the lair with the monster still inside."

"That seems . . . drastic."

"Seems good and simple to me. But after what happened, the mayor didn't want to risk any more men. Said matters of magic were best dealt with by magic."

"Animism isn't magic," Simon replied automatically. "It's a manipulation of natural energy through focused human will."

Brock gave him a flat smile. "Magic is a common word for the common folk, eh?"

Simon froze, a spoonful of stew halfway to his mouth. Come to think of it, Neeta had once said something similar. *Never call it magic. That's a vulgar term used by uneducated people. We aren't performing card tricks, here.* "It doesn't matter what you call it, I suppose." He cast an uncertain glance up at Brock. "I, um. I get the impression you're not fond of Animism."

"Well, there *are* some here who see the Foundation as a bloated tick on the arse of the people, sucking us dry. Animists give us crumbs, then go back to their soft, cozy lives in the city and expect us to be grateful."

Simon thought about the tiny, drafty office where he spent most of his waking hours. He opened his mouth to tell Brock he was wrong then shut it. He was suddenly, acutely conscious of how Brock towered over him. He could see the veins standing out on his muscular arms. "I, um. I think that's a bit—well, I'm not saying you're wrong, but that's not entirely fair. I mean . . . certainly, the Foundation has its problems. But—"

"Don't get nervous, lad." Brock chuckled and clapped Simon on the shoulder, hard enough that he flinched. "We called you here, didn't we? Might as well do your job."

He nodded and took another bite of meat sludge, hoping Brock would leave.

"That man the mayor mentioned," Brock said, "the one who was killed . . . he was my brother."

Simon drew his breath in, nearly choking on the gristly stew. Brock's expression was stony, but there was a subtle tightness around his eyes and mouth. Simon swallowed. "I'm sorry," he said quietly. "I truly am."

"I don't want words," he said. "I want the monster's head."

"I—that's not something I can promise. I may not have to kill—"

"Bring me its head, Animist. If you're worth anything, that is."

Brock gave him another bone-jarring clap on the shoulder, then walked out, shutting the door behind him. Simon rubbed his shoulder, wondering if there'd be a bruise.

The situation crashed down on him all at once: the enormity of his mission, the stakes, and the consequences of failure. This was real. He could die. In fact, that possibility seemed overwhelmingly likely. He started to shake. The space inside his chest was shrinking down to the size of a postage stamp. He could barely draw a breath, and the harder he fought, the more his chest constricted. Dark fog crept in around the edges of his vision.

Oh, Spirit. Not now. He hadn't had a fit in *months*.

Simon plunged his hand into the capacious left pocket of his robes. Panic jabbed at him when his fingers encountered nothing but a hankie and a few crumpled bits of paper. The medicine. Where was the medicine? Had it fallen out of his pocket?

He pushed deeper, groping through the loose paper scraps, until he touched smooth glass, and the terrible pressure in his chest eased, just a little. He fished out the tiny, clear bottle, undid the rubber stopper, and shook its contents—two shiny black capsules—into his sweat-damp palm. There they lay, like fat, oblong droplets of pure night. If he looked very closely, he could see glistening swirls of purple moving inside.

These were his last two pills. He'd been holding on to them for a while now, saving them for an emergency.

He started to lift his palm toward his mouth then stopped.

He'd made up his mind. No more.

It took all his willpower to slip the pills back into the glass bottle and set it on the nightstand; his fingers trembled so hard, he almost dropped it.

Don't think about the future. Just get through the next minute. The next few seconds.

Little by little, the invisible boulder on his chest lifted, at least enough for him to breathe, though a lingering pressure remained. He let out a quiet sigh. Rain ticked against the window.

He'd made a mistake coming here. It wasn't too late to admit that, was it? He could slip away and leave the village on the next train. Maybe if he pleaded, he could get his old job back. By tomorrow night, he could be back in the mailroom with a cup of hot tea . . . and the knowledge that he had failed. Again.

No! He'd chosen this. These people needed help. If he backed out now, it would mean that Brenner and Neeta and everyone else was right about him: that he was a useless coward, fit only for a life of drudgery. He wouldn't accept that.

Simon glanced at the bed. He should probably at least *try* to rest before heading out to the mountains tomorrow.

After changing into his sleep-clothes, he crawled onto the rock-hard mattress and pulled the thin blanket over himself. But his eyes didn't want to click shut; it was like trying to close an overstuffed suitcase.

He clung to the memories of his mother—her bittersweet scent, like dried flowers and herbs, her cool fingers absently stroking his hair, smoothing curls away from his brow.

Would he ever see her again?

His gaze strayed to the tiny glass bottle, which he'd placed on his bedside. One pill would numb him. Two would plunge him into a merciful void, empty even of dreams.

He'd first gotten the medicine a few months after the Incident, when his father realized that Simon's misery wasn't a passing phase, that Olivia's death had broken something inside him. Father had taken him to a Healer, a minuscule, wizened Animist with a pair of gold-rimmed spectacles perched on her hawkish nose. Simon recalled, word for word, the instructions she'd spoken as she handed him his first bottle: *Two before bedtime, to ensure that you sleep through the night. They can be taken during the day, too, to stop the fits, but don't take more than three in twelve hours . . . and keep in mind, they'll dull your senses and reflexes.*

Those little capsules had kept him afloat through the darkest time of his life. But an Animist couldn't be reliant on drugs. During a battle, sharp reflexes meant the difference between life and death. When he'd started his training with Neeta, he'd weaned himself off the medication, enduring the sleepless nights, the fits of shaking and sweats.

After a few minutes, he shook a capsule into his palm. Being sleep-deprived wouldn't help his chances. Maybe one would be enough.

He dry-swallowed it, feeling the slight flutter as it passed down his throat. The world went soft and fuzzy, and he felt himself sinking.

Most of the time, he didn't allow himself to think about Olivia. It did no good. But during unguarded moments, the thoughts slipped in.

Where was she now? Was her soul wandering somewhere far from this world? Or had she simply winked out like a candle?

Animism was in some ways a religion as well as a discipline—or at least a branch of metaphysical philosophy, with a bit of austere spiritualism thrown in. It had its temples and services. But it had never offered much in the way of answers. Animists were a little vague on what happened after death; as a child, he dimly remembered listening to temple sermons about drops of rainwater merging back into the ocean and decaying things giving life to new grass and trees. Death as transformation, death as rebirth. Maybe Olivia was in everything now, her essence spread thin, particles of her consciousness clinging like dew to spiderwebs and robins' feathers. There was some comfort in that, he supposed. But it was a cold, distant comfort.

He started to drift off. A girl's voice whispered in his head: *Simon.*

His eyes snapped open. He lay still, every muscle rigid, holding his breath. "Who said that?"

Silence. He waited, counting his heartbeats, but there was no response. He let out a shaky breath.

Olivia was dead. He couldn't allow himself to lose sight of

that reality—couldn't let himself start backsliding.

In the months after her death, before he started taking the pills, he'd heard her voice often. A few times, he'd even *seen* her—a brief glimpse, a face in a crowd. But each time he chased her down, it turned out to be some girl who shared her hair color or height, but who otherwise looked nothing like his sister. Even without Animism, the human mind could weave illusions.

But what if . . .

He slammed that mental door shut. Still a faint uncertainty lingered, like a question mark etched into his brain, as he sank into blackness.

Chapter Eight

Simon stared down at the tiny figure in the casket.

Olivia wore a bright yellow dress. Her face had been made up with pink lipstick and blush, but it couldn't hide the pallor of death. Her hands were folded over a bouquet of white lilies. Simon's father stood stiffly beside him, his face a mask, his eyes unfocused and faraway.

Simon knew he should be crying, but none of this felt real.

Whispers floated on the edge of his awareness:

"Tragic, isn't it?"

"They say she was attacked in her own home."

"A burglary gone awry, an unregistered criminal Animist—"

"Some story."

"*Shhh.* Not here."

Simon's mother stood beside him, silent. Her hand

tightened on his until he squirmed with pain. Then she released him and stepped forward. The room fell silent as she stood in front of the casket, hands clenched into tight fists. She spun around, glaring at the roomful of people. "All of you. Get out."

The crowd shifted uncertainly. The priest cleared his throat. "Dr. Frost . . ."

"Get out!" She raised both arms into the air, and crackling yellow light wreathed her palms.

The onlookers let out cries of alarm and rushed for the exit, tripping over each other in their eagerness to escape. The priest waddled after them, stumbling on the hem of his overlong robe. Simon stood frozen, not breathing.

Panting, his mother leaned over the casket and started to lift Olivia. His father caught her arms and pulled her back. "Veera." His voice was low and firm. "Put her down."

"I won't let them bury her," she said, wild-eyed. "I won't let her *rot*."

"For Spirit's sake, pull yourself together!" he hissed. "Our son is watching."

She pulled free of his grasp and stood glaring at him, chest heaving. Wisps of blond hair had escaped their tight bun and hung loose around her face. "And what about our son, Aberdeen? What *about* him?"

Dr. Hawking's jaw tightened. "Simon," he said quietly, "go wait outside."

Simon's eyes darted from his mother to his father.

"*Go!*"

He bolted out the door and into the hallway. Trembling, he slammed the door shut and pressed himself against it. But he could still hear the raised voices of his parents.

"Veera. You need to let go."

"Let go? You mean give up on Olivia?"

"Olivia is *dead*! There's nothing we can do."

There was a long pause. Then his mother spoke again, in a sharp whisper. His father replied, just as quietly. Simon couldn't make out the words. They spoke for several minutes like that, in frantic, hissing, barely audible voices. Then Father raised his voice again: "Enough. Stop this madness at once, or I will make it stop. Do you understand?"

There was another pause. Then, softly: "Just give me a few minutes alone with her. I want to hold her before they put her in the ground."

Simon slid down the wall, to the floor, and hugged his knees.

The door opened, and Simon gave a start. When he looked up, his father was standing over him. He was pale, his face sagging like an old man's. "Simon," he said. "How much did you hear?"

"I heard yelling. Is Mother angry?"

He looked away. "No. She's just sad."

He imagined her cradling the tiny body, rocking it back

and forth, her tears falling on Olivia's cold, still face.

She should have lived, he thought. *She should have lived, and I should have died.*

Later, when they lowered Olivia into the ground, his mother's expression was empty. The priest droned on about the cycle of life and death. When Simon took her hand again, she clutched it without looking at him.

The next morning, Mother was gone.

Simon woke to the feeble crow of a rooster.

Outside the window, the sky was awash with hazy gray light. With his knuckle, he rubbed grit from the corner of his eye. He climbed out of bed, moving in slow motion, drugged sleepiness still clinging to his thoughts like webbing.

Someone—Brock, probably—had left a bowl of cooling porridge and a hunk of bread for him outside the door. He ate the porridge, though when he tried to bite into the bread, he nearly chipped a tooth. Not wanting to seem ungrateful by leaving it in the room, he slipped it into his pack. Maybe he could use it as a projectile weapon, if it came down to that. It certainly seemed hard enough to crack a demon's skull.

He dressed. Once he'd laced up the boots, he stood and looked himself over in the room's tarnished mirror. He looked young and small and utterly unprepared.

Still, he was an Animist. He would do everything in his

power to live up to that role.

Even if it kills you? a cowardly voice in his head whispered.

Yes, he replied. But the hollow ringing in the pit of his stomach remained.

If you don't have a realistic chance of defeating the monster, you're just throwing your life away. And for what? These people don't like you. You're not even supposed to be here. What are you trying to prove?

Sometimes, his cowardly side could be disturbingly logical. Still, he presented his counterargument: *If I don't help them, no one will.*

Or maybe, deep down, you actually want *to die. Maybe you're looking for an excuse.*

He gritted his teeth. No. He wasn't that person—not anymore. He had a purpose. He was stable—

Oh yes, very stable. Standing here, staring into space in a walleyed stupor while arguing with yourself in your head. You're the picture of sanity.

Oh, shut up.

Simon left his suitcase in the room, taking only what he could carry in his lightweight pack: some bread he'd purchased in Eidendel, his bronze compass, and his one remaining pill. The house was empty and silent. His footsteps echoed through the entrance hall. The animal heads on the wall seemed to track his progress with their glassy, unseeing eyes.

He stepped out through the front door, into the crisp morning air. A few villagers were out. An old woman swept her yard with a straw broom. A few barefoot children ran about, shrieking with laughter. None of them seemed to take any notice of Simon.

He trudged toward the mountains, through fields of autumn-brown grass, past a lone scarecrow with a withered pumpkin for a head, until he reached a wooden post jutting out of the ground. It marked the beginning of a barely visible trail—little more than a deer path—that wandered up through the pine-covered foothills. A short distance ahead, it vanished into a thick maze of pine trees.

Had his mother followed this same trail? Was this the route she'd taken to the Gaokerena tree where she'd spent a week meditating, seeking knowledge in its sacred presence?

The trail sloped steeply upward. Before long, he was puffing for breath, his clothes damp with sweat despite the chill. The forests enveloped him, a mixture of dense pine and knobby deciduous trees, their leaves gone dry and brown. The sprawling branches blocked out the sun, so it felt almost as though he were moving through a tunnel. A few weak beams of light trickled through gaps in the canopy, and motes swirled within, glimmering like fireflies.

Dust in sunlight had always fascinated Simon. As a small child, he'd mistaken those shining specks for meta—the diffuse form of it that existed in the atmosphere—until his father explained to him that meta particles were too small to be seen with the naked eye.

Ahead, two huge, moss-covered boulders blocked the path. Light trickled through a narrow space between them.

What now? Go around? The forest was too dense.

Simon had to wriggle like a worm, but he was small enough—just barely—to squeeze himself through the gap.

When he emerged, breathless, he found himself standing in a spacious clearing—a little round valley tucked away in the forest. Pine trees towered around the valley's rim, their gnarled roots lacing its earthen walls. Rising up from the clearing's center was a single tree. A soft gasp escaped Simon's throat.

He'd seen the Gaokerena tree in Eidendel, the one in the Gregor Temple, but this one was easily twice its size. Had the tree been on level ground with the pines, it would have dwarfed them. Ten people could have stood around its circumference, hands joined. Scaly bark covered the fat trunk, and a mass of squiggly branches sprawled outward from its top, sprouting long plumes of moss-green leaves. The light filtering down through those leaves had an eerie green quality, giving Simon the feeling that he was underwater. There was no wind, but the branches swayed slightly, creaking.

Gently, he touched the rough bark.

His mother had once told him that the trees spoke to those who knew how to listen. There was an old story about a sage whose daughter died of sickness. He buried her beneath a

Gaokerena, and the next morning he found her awake and smiling, sitting under the branches.

Just a legend, of course. Over the years, countless grieving people had attempted to duplicate the results, with no success.

Simon circled around to the other side of the tree . . . and froze. There, nestled in the fork formed by two thick roots, was something round, pebbly, and roughly as large as himself—a sort of pod—with a dark, lustrous sheen that looked greenish or purplish, depending on how the light hit it. A ropy stalk ran from the tree's trunk to the top of the object, like an umbilical cord, spreading thin roots over the surface.

With a single finger, Simon touched the pod. It was cool and hard, like stone. A long, jagged crack ran down the center, as though it had split open, revealing a hollow interior caked with some dense, stringy matter that had dried to a crust.

Simon crouched, examining the ground near the base of the tree. Glittering, dark fragments littered the mossy earth.

Mysteries within mysteries.

He cast one last glance at the pod, then left the clearing, pushing his way through the wall of pine boughs, back to the trail.

By noon, he reached his destination—a dilapidated cabin sitting at the base of the peak, sheltered by trees, its back to the sheer rock wall. A small well stood out front, a glossy raven perched on its stone lip. Simon wasn't a believer in bad omens, but the sight still made him unreasonably nervous.

"Shoo," he said, waving his hand. The raven ignored him.

The windows were dark. No smoke came from the brick chimney. But he could feel . . . something. A presence, like a dark aura. The hairs on Simon's neck tingled and stiffened.

He would need a light.

A small golden glow, like a candle flame, flickered to life above his palm. He cupped it carefully, sheltering it as he made his way to the front door. The wood was gray and ancient, peeling in places, like a snake shedding its skin.

If the monster *was* intelligent, negotiating was Simon's best chance. *Don't think of it as going into battle,* he told himself. *You're just paying someone a visit.* That being the case, maybe he ought to knock. So he did. "Hello?" No response.

He pushed the door open. Hinges squealed.

The smell of rotting flesh hit him like a moist, meaty slap in the face. He gagged and pressed a hand over his nose and mouth, staring into the darkened hallway.

Breathing through his mouth, he entered, leaving the door open behind him. The floorboards groaned beneath his feet as he crept down the hall. Aside from that, a deep hush hung over the house.

The door slammed shut, and he jumped, letting out an undignified yelp.

Just the wind.

To his left stood a half-open doorway. Beyond lay the remains of a kitchen, its walls streaked and spattered with some dark substance. Simon took a cautious step inside; he raised his hand, still cupping the tiny light. The room was empty, save for a rusted sink, but the dark liquid was everywhere. Blood. Flies buzzed around a congealed puddle on the floor.

In the corner of the room lay the partially eaten body of a deer. There wasn't much left except its head and front legs. Yet its eyes seemed to be *moving*. When he stepped closer, he saw that its sockets were filled with squirming maggots.

Simon turned away, his stomach shifting queasily. Dry-mouthed, he reached into the pocket of his robe and withdrew the jar of summoning ash. It hadn't worked out so well the first time, but it was worth another shot. At least he wouldn't be alone.

He sprinkled the remaining ash on the floor, added a few drops of blood, and whispered the ritual words. There was a poof, and when the smoke cleared, a wrinkled, pug-like face stared up at him. Reddish eyes bulged. A pair of veiny wings rustled and spread.

"Oh, Spirit," Simon whispered. "Not *you*."

The wraith's tiny, hinge-like jaw flapped open, and a hellish shriek sprang from its throat. Its wings flapped, and it rose into the air, spraying out an arch of foul-smelling liquid. Its body spun in circles, splashing the walls. Simon thrust out a hand. "*No!* Go away! I dismiss you! *I dismiss you!*"

In a poof, the wraith vanished.

So much for that. He'd lost the element of surprise. And now the air smelled even worse.

In the darkness of the hall, something creaked. He spun around. "Who's there?" he called.

No response.

He took a cautious step into the hallway. "I'm not here to hurt you. I just want to talk." Another step.

There was a jolt, and a sharp tingling swept over his skin, like a thousand icy pins pricking him at once. He sucked in his breath and looked down. His boot rested on the edge of a summoning circle, no larger than his hand, daubed on the floorboards in messy rust-colored lines, a mixture of ash and—blood? It looked more black than red.

He recognized the symbol within. A trigger symbol. This was a special type of summoning circle, designed to unleash a summoned entity upon contact. He'd stepped into a trap.

The tiny golden flame winked out, drowning him in darkness. His rapid breathing echoed in his ears.

Well, that answered the question of whether the monster was intelligent. It wasn't just smart. It knew Animism.

A ghostly green light penetrated the gloom, slowly brightening as the circle lit up, lines of emerald fire etched into the wood. Pale smoke rose up out of the floor. Simon watched, rooted to the spot, as a whitish, gelatinous mass materialized.

A dozen glistening eyes protruded from its skin at odd places, blinking. Its mouth opened and closed, a red cavern lined with rows and rows of teeth.

A shoggoth.

Gasping, Simon backed away. Neeta's voice echoed in his memory: *Shoggoths are stupid but strong. They have no capacity for fear or pain, just mindless hunger. If you see one, don't try to fight it.*

What should I do, then? he'd asked.

Run.

The shoggoth's eyes blinked wetly, with a sucking sound like boots in mud.

Simon kept backing away, stumbling over his feet. The shoggoth slithered toward him, leaving smears of greenish slime on the floor, its mouths opening and closing. It had several of them, all filled with sharp teeth.

Think, think. What could he do? There had to be *something.*

He thrust out both hands. A pathetic spurt of yellow light shot out, fizzling harmlessly in midair.

A pseudopod whipped around his legs and yanked them out from under him. He hit the floor with a bone-jarring thud. Panting, he looked up into a gaping mouth bristling with needle-like fangs. The throat was a slimy dark tunnel—a vision of nothingness.

This is how I die, he thought.

Time slowed. The shoggoth's mouth descended. Simon's vision blurred, colors bleeding together into a swirl.

 ℰ⌒

For a while—it could have been a few seconds, or a year—he floated. A thin, warbling whine filled his ears, like the keening of distant flutes. A faint light pierced the blackness and spread. Slowly, his surroundings took shape.

He was standing in a desert. Hard, cracked earth sprawled under a night sky strewn with stars. They glowed with feverish fairy-light.

He blinked a few times, dazed.

Before him loomed a set of arched stone doors, three times his own height. They stood alone, unconnected to any wall or building. The doors were smooth and solid, aside from the vertical crack running between them. If he looked closely, he could see dim greenish light seeping through the crack. Baffled, Simon took a few steps forward and peered around the edge of the doorframe, at the other side. But there *was* no other side. When he looked at them from behind, the doors simply weren't there.

He circled around to the front once more and stared at the impossibility in front of him. He had never been here before, and yet there was something eerily familiar about it.

"Hello," said a tiny voice.

Simon spun around. "Who's there?"

"Look down."

He lowered his gaze, but saw only his shadow stretching out from his feet—another impossibility, since there was no sun. The shadow rippled, peeled itself off the ground, and stood.

Detached from its surface, it had a rough, sketchy look, like something scribbled by a child. As it moved and shifted, its edges flickered, blurring. Only its eyes remained clear—two blank white circles. "We meet again, Simon Frost."

"We've never met."

"Oh . . . you wouldn't remember. Most humans don't remember meeting me. So sad, that. I feel awfully unappreciated. But it isn't their fault, of course—I just spill through the cracks in their minds. Like sand from a broken hourglass."

"Who are you? What *is* this place? Are we in the Eldritch? Are you a demon?"

"So many questions! No and no. This is somewhere else. Somewhere between and above. And below. All over the place, really. Your concept of *place* is so limited; it's rather hard to describe in your language where we are. It isn't exactly a 'where' at all."

It seemed like he should be panicking. But a dreamlike calm had settled over him. "Am I dead?"

The shadow-thing tilted its head. "Not yet. Do you want to live?"

He had a sense that the question was not rhetorical.

He realized—somewhat to his surprise—that he *did* want to live. There were too many books he hadn't read, too many foods he hadn't tried. Far, far too many unanswered questions. "Yes."

"Then open the doors," the shadow said.

"And where do they go? Back to my world? Or to another not-place place that you can't possibly describe?"

"The second. But you must go through them to return."

Simon placed his hands against the doors and pushed. They didn't budge. He faced the shadow. "They're locked."

"I can help you unlock them. Of course, I would like something in return. A bit of your essence, please. Just a taste."

"My . . . essence?"

"Yes. How to describe it?" The shadow's head tilted the other way. "You humans are rather like those wooden nesting dolls . . . have you seen them? One inside the other, down to the middle. But the funny thing is, you don't even know about the other people inside you. A few of you learn to see beneath the first layer, but there is so much you'll never grasp. What I want is a chip off the innermost doll. You won't miss it. You won't even notice. Though . . . I can't say for sure. The thing you call your sanity might wobble a bit, and it's already wobbly." The shadow leaned forward. Despite its expressionless face, Simon detected a hint of hunger. "Tell me. Those ghosts inside. Do they ever whisper?"

Simon frowned. "I don't have time for riddles."

"As you wish. What will it be, then?"

A chip off the innermost doll. It sounded ominous. But he wasn't in a position to bargain. Give up one thing, or give up everything—if that was the choice, the answer seemed self-evident. "All right. Go ahead."

The shadow-thing stretched out a fuzzy-edged hand and touched his chest.

A faint chill, like a cool breeze, passed over him. The shadow-thing rippled. The dark hand withdrew, cradling a tiny silver light. Its fingers closed around it, snuffing it out like a candle flame. Its face split open in a jagged crescent smile. "Thank you."

The doors flew open. Beyond lay a hazy green light.

Simon entered, and the doors slammed shut.

He was in a cathedral. At least, that was his first impression. The off-white walls soared up to a vaulted ceiling, where a massive chandelier hung. There were no windows, but a sickly green glow suffused the air.

There was something unsettling about the walls and ceiling. At first he thought they were made of ivory, or some pale, washed-out wood—countless interlocking pieces, some long and narrow, some broader. Then he looked more closely.

Bones.

Thousands of them—some human, some animal, some he couldn't identify. The chandelier was an elaborate concoction of femurs and skulls. Garlands of spines and pelvic bones were strung from the ceiling, stretching outward from the chandelier like the spokes of a wheel. More skulls stared from the curved walls in rows, forming ledges. The beams supporting those walls, he realized, were the ribs of some impossibly huge beast.

At the front of the cathedral, suspended high on the wall, hung a complete human skeleton—human, that was, save for the horned skull and the pair of skeletal bat wings arching from its back. In one hand, it held a bone-scythe; in the other, a pale chalice.

Beneath the suspended skeleton stood a well built from circular rows of skulls. He approached. When he peered in, he saw that the well was filled with swampy green light.

He dipped a hand into it, and it swirled around his fingers, lapping at them, warm and cool at the same time. A tingling, prickling sensation crept up his arm and spread through his body. He yanked his arm back.

He heard a faint creak and looked up to see the skeleton's arm moving—slowly, but definitely *moving*—extending the chalice toward him. Offering it.

Was this a good idea?

Did he have a choice?

Simon grabbed the chalice and—before he could change his mind—plunged it into the well. The green light flowed in, filling the vessel. He raised it to his lips and drank.

It was like drinking cool air. Like nothingness.

The cathedral vanished.

Time unfroze; the shoggoth's dripping maw descended. Simon screamed and thrust out a hand, felt his fingers sink into cold, moist flesh. There was a jolt, like silent thunder, and the world vibrated.

The shoggoth stopped. Twitched. Its fishlike eyes bugged out, and a low groan rose up from the depths of its throats. He felt more than saw its bulk quiver, rippling like a mass of gelatin.

And then it exploded. Gobbets of pale ooze spattered the walls and floor. A chunk of something warm hit Simon's cheek and slid down.

"What." The word escaped him as a breathless squeak.

The hallway was covered in still-twitching chunks, already dissolving into luminous goo. The puddles shrank as clouds of steam rose from them, flesh dissipating into air.

Shakily, Simon climbed to his feet. What had happened? The memories were hazy and slippery in his head, like a dream. There was a fleeting image of a desert, a shadow, and . . . a cathedral?

He leaned against the wall, wincing as he put his hand in a dollop of slime. It came away sticky.

Had *he* done this?

The pale glow of the shoggoth's body faded as its remains dissolved.

Ahead, he heard a low rustling sound, like someone

dragging a leather bag across the floor. His eyes snapped into focus just in time to see something resembling a tail—*several* tails—vanish around the corner. His heartbeat sped. He'd almost forgotten he had another enemy here.

But why had it summoned a shoggoth? Why hadn't it attacked Simon directly?

Umburt's voice echoed in his head: *We sent a group of our men into the mountains with weapons and torches, hoping to drive the beast out. They managed to wound it . . .*

Simon took a few wobbly steps forward, hugging the wall, and looked down. A long smear of blood marred the floor. It wasn't red, but a shimmering black. Eldritch creatures healed quickly, but they were vulnerable to certain types of metal. If the wound had been inflicted with iron, it wouldn't heal on its own, at least not for a long time. Of course, he didn't know for sure that he was dealing with an Eldritch being. But he didn't have any better theories at the moment.

"Hello?" he called out quietly.

No response. From around the corner, he heard breathing, heavy and labored. And then a moan—low, pained, and unexpectedly human.

The sound reached down into Simon's chest and pulled. A strange, confusing mixture of emotions swept over him.

Simon's heart thudded against his sternum and in the hollows of his wrists. It wasn't too late to turn back. But somewhere deep inside himself, he sensed that if he left now, it was over; he would forever lose his will to remain an Animist. Not because he had failed his mission, but because he had abandoned someone in pain.

"I don't know if you can understand me," he called. "But if you can, please believe me—I don't want to hurt you." Still no response. His heart seemed to have lodged itself beneath his jaw. "I'm coming in now." He inched forward.

When he turned the corner, the hallway opened into a large room. Dim light filtered in through the single grimy window. A huge form crouched before him, its sides heaving. Simon's stomach gave a sharp lurch.

The creature before him was twice . . . no, three times the size of a horse, and four-legged. It barely fit into the room. In the faint light, he could only see its outline, the arched, spiny back, the long neck and angular reptilian head. A mass of writhing tentacles surrounded its body. It seemed to him like a thing born out of a fever dream—part dragon, part octopus, yet strangely human in shape. Purple eyes glowed in the darkness.

And then Simon spotted the wound—a long, ugly gash split the skin of the monster's shoulder, crusted with dried blood.

Simon took another small step forward. The monster tensed; sharp teeth glinted, and a low growl rippled from its throat. "It's all right," Simon said. He kept his voice low, soft. "You're scared. Aren't you? I'm scared, too. But I can help."

Slowly, he stretched out a hand.

The monster arched its neck, bumping its head against the ceiling. Its forelegs tensed, claws gouging into the wooden floor.

Simon gulped. "Please." He took a step closer and laid his hand against the monster's side. Its scales were smooth, metallic. They fit together like interlocking pieces of a puzzle. The swell of flesh heaved under his palm. With wonder, he realized he could feel a great heart beating.

He looked up, into the shining purple eyes. "Can you understand me?" He stretched a hand upward to touch the smooth curve of the monster's neck.

Something lashed out and whipped the side of his head. Stars burst behind his eyes. The world spun. He hit the floor, and everything went dark.

Chapter Nine

Simon woke with his skull full of slushy red pain. He moaned and opened his eyes, exchanging one darkness for another. When he tried to sit up, a wave of vertigo rolled over him, pinning him to the bed.

Bed?

He lay still for a moment, breathing shallowly. A sour smell pervaded the air. Straw poked out of the thin mattress, scratching his cheek. His shoulders ached; his arms were twisted into an unnatural position behind his back, and he couldn't move them. As hard as he strained his eyes, he could see nothing.

His memories lay scattered all over the floor of his brain; he tried to collect them, to line them up in the proper order.

Focus. He counted backward from ten. His mind seemed to be working more or less normally.

Light. If he could summon a light . . .

He tried again to lift his hand and realized that his wrists were tied. Rope dug into his skin, chafing. His legs, too, were tightly bound at the knees and ankles.

To his left, clothes rustled. Someone was in the room with him. "Who's there?" he called out, his voice cracking.

And then another sound—the crunch of teeth chewing.

Simon's eyes had finally begun to adjust to the near darkness. He was in a small, bare, windowless room. Sunlight filtered in through cracks in the ceiling—the only illumination. Simon's pack lay in the corner, its contents spilled across the floorboards.

"You were trespassing, you know." The voice was young and female. She sounded as if she were talking through a mouthful of food. "It's not nice to break into other people's houses."

Who . . . ?

His gaze jerked toward the small form in the corner, which he hadn't even noticed until that moment. She was sitting, legs crossed, her back against the wall.

More crunching noises broke the silence.

"You're eating my bread," Simon said.

"It's dry." Her ragged cloak looked as though it had been patched together from the remains of several outfits; it hung in loose folds around her thin frame. A hood covered her head, hiding most of her face in shadow.

Again, Simon tried to sit up, but the nausea slammed into him, leaving him dizzy and shaking. "Who are you? Where is the monster?"

She raised her head. Within the hood, her eyes glowed a dim purple. "I am the monster."

He blinked.

Simon had been prepared to find the unexpected when he came here. He'd heard, too, that some demons could change their shape. Even so, he'd never imagined that he would find himself facing something as befuddling as this—a girl his own age.

He squirmed, trying to loosen his restraints. "This is unnecessary," he said, struggling to keep his voice calm. "I'm not your enemy."

Floorboards creaked as the girl stood and approached. Her breathing rasped in her throat, as if just standing were an effort. "You were sent by those villagers, weren't you?"

"Well, yes. But I'm not one of them. I'm an Animist."

"I know what you are."

He twisted his wrists. "What are you going to do with me?"

"I'm asking the questions here." She circled around the bed. "How did you kill that shoggoth?"

Hazy memories flitted through his head then slipped away into darkness. "I don't know. I don't think I *did* anything. It just exploded."

Something touched his throat, and he jerked. It felt like a snake—dry, warm, and sinuous. He couldn't pull away; he could only lie there, helpless, as the snake-thing wrapped around his throat and gave it a squeeze—not enough to hurt, just enough to remind him of his own helplessness. As if he needed a reminder. "Don't lie to me."

Simon swallowed. It was difficult. "Something happened. It was like time slowed down. Then I . . . I don't know. I had this dream. Or I think it was a dream. I can't remember."

The snake-thing squeezed his throat. "Do you take me for an idiot?"

"I'm not lying!" he gasped. "I swear!" It hurt to breathe.

She leaned closer, and for the first time, he got a good look at the face under the hood. She was gaunt, with disheveled, shoulder-length dark hair and hollow circles under her eyes, which glimmered purple. Her skin was grayish with dirt.

A bead of water—sweat?—landed on Simon's face. The feverish heat of her breath puffed against his skin, the sickly smell filling his nostrils.

Then she straightened; the snakelike thing loosened and slid off his throat, and he gulped in air. "Never mind," the girl muttered. She turned away.

Something moved behind her, protruding from under the hem of her patchwork cloak. He blinked, unsure if it was some trick of the light. *A tail?* Not just one . . . two, three, four, *eight* of them. Except they weren't tails. And suddenly, he knew what he'd felt around his throat.

Even in human form, she had tentacles. He could see them moving, shifting restlessly beneath the cloth.

She shot a glare at him over one shoulder. "It's rude to stare at a girl's behind, you know."

He averted his gaze. "Sorry."

She picked up Simon's bag, slung it over her good shoulder, and walked toward the door.

He blinked. "You're leaving?"

"Well, I can't stay here."

"I—I thought you were going to kill me."

"Sorry to disappoint you, but I don't kill for fun. And you aren't much of a threat. You can probably work your way out of those ropes if you keep at it long enough."

He could hardly believe his luck. Once again, he had narrowly evaded death. Being left tied up on a bed in the middle of nowhere wasn't the ideal situation, but it was better than being eaten alive.

Still . . .

"What about you?" he asked.

She stopped. "What *about* me?"

The sickly smell still lingered in the air. He recognized that odor. "Your wound is infected, isn't it?"

Her shoulders stiffened.

"You're too weak to fight, which is why you summoned the shoggoth."

"What's your point?"

"Let me treat your injury."

She turned to face him, eyes narrowed. "You think I'm going to fall for a cheap ruse like that?"

"I want to heal you. That's all. I swear."

She fell silent. A shadow of uncertainty flickered across her expression; a crack in her armor. "Why?"

He wondered, for a moment, how to answer that. He had no particular obligation to help her, and every reason to fear her. He didn't even know what she was. And yet he couldn't shake the feeling that they were alike in some way. He *couldn't* just leave her. "Because you're suffering," he said. "Isn't that reason enough?"

They stared at each other in silence.

With her free hand, she drew a long, rust-flecked knife from beneath her cloak. In two swift strides, she closed the distance between them, and the knife descended.

Snick, snick. The ropes fell away from Simon's wrists and legs. His hands tingled as blood began flowing freely again.

"One wrong move, and I'll gut you," she said.

A cold bead of sweat trickled down his spine. "I used up my stores of meta. I have to draw in more first, which will take a few minutes. It will help if I can put my hands on the floor. Most meta-receptors are on the palms and fingertips—"

"Go on."

He crouched, pressed his palms to the floorboards, and

closed his eyes. He was keenly aware of her looming over him, knife in hand. It was hard to shut out the thought, but he forced himself to focus. He experienced a brief, unexpected flash of gratitude toward Neeta for forcing him to channel with that grasshopper in his mouth. Once you'd learned to ignore wriggling legs against your tongue, you could ignore anything. His palms warmed and tingled as meta flowed up through the Earth, through the foundation of the house, into his body. The wood was rotten and riddled with worms, spiders, and roots, which helped; they had their own bits of meta to contribute and surrendered it without complaint. A few died, and he felt a pulse of remorse.

Animists took what they needed from the Earth, as all creatures did. It had always been so; energy flowed and changed form. That was nature. Still, he wondered if Umburt was right, in a way—if there was something parasitical about Animism.

He stood slowly—the pain and vertigo had passed, leaving him a little woozy, but otherwise normal—and faced her, heart pounding. "Ready."

The girl curled one of her tentacles around the knife's handle. She held the blade against his stomach as she opened her cloak. "Make this quick," she said.

It was difficult to see, in the dimness. "I'm going to summon a light." He cupped his right palm, and a golden flame sprang into place, casting its soft glow. Beneath her cloak, her clothes were little more than rags. She'd bound her left arm in a makeshift sling, with a dirty bandage tied around the shoulder. The bandage had already soaked through with blood.

"This will hurt," Simon said.

"Do it."

Slowly, Simon peeled off the bandage, which seemed to be fashioned out of a torn shirt. She flinched, but made no sound as he inspected the deep gash. The flesh around it was red and swollen, clotted with pus. Crimson lines of infection had crept down her arm, like tiny rivers under the skin.

He pressed one hand against the wound. Her skin burned fever-hot under his palm.

His mind leaped back to the test he'd taken back at the Academy. He'd tried to heal an anesthetized rabbit with a ruptured spleen. He'd failed then; the rabbit had died on the table. Neeta's voice echoed in his head, telling him he lacked the necessary focus for serious healing. He shoved the memory away.

He could sense the infection, a sort of dark greenish sludge congealing under the flesh. He visualized the sludge coalescing, clumping together. Then he *pulled*, coaxing it to the surface with his mind. The girl grunted with pain.

"Almost done," he murmured. Sweat trickled down his brow.

The infection didn't let go easily; extracting it was like

fishing a hairy, greasy clog out of a sticky drain. It clung as if it had a will of its own. "Come on," he muttered through clenched teeth. He pressed down a little harder. At last, he felt something give.

Thick yellow pus ran from the wound, dripping to the floor. The redness in the surrounding flesh faded as the swelling went down, and the lips of the wound closed, forming a thin pink line of scar tissue.

Simon exhaled softly and he wiped one sleeve across his sweat-drenched brow. The meta-flame in his other hand went out. A tiny balloon of triumph swelled in his chest. He'd healed a serious injury. Neeta had been wrong about him, after all. "How does it feel?"

She flexed the arm and squeezed her hand into a fist. She gave Simon a suspicious look, then shoved the knife into a sheath at her hip, beneath her cloak, and crossed her arms. "Better."

"I'm glad." The room was a little spinny. He sank to the edge of the bed.

"Are you—?"

"Fine." He gave her a wobbly smile. "I don't suppose there's any water left in there?" He nodded to his pack.

She rummaged through it and fished out his canteen. "I drank most of it."

He drained the last few swallows. "I'm Simon, by the way. Simon Frost."

She kept her arms crossed over her chest. "Alice," she muttered.

Such a normal name. Yet it suited her. "Pleased to meet you, Alice." He held out a hand. When it became clear she wasn't going to take it, he lowered it awkwardly.

His gaze wandered to the tentacles poking out from beneath the hem of her cloak. He tried not to stare, but there was something hypnotic about them; the way they constantly moved, curling and flicking. "I don't understand," he said. "How is it that you're able to stay in this world?"

She gave him a blank look.

"I mean . . . most demons can't remain long on Earth."

She scowled. "I'm *human*."

Simon wasn't immediately sure how to respond to that. He could point out that most humans didn't have tentacles, but that seemed a bit condescending. "So then . . . how . . ."

"I'd like to know, too."

"You don't remember how you got this way?"

She stared down at her hands. Her fingernails were a deep green, with the dull luster of water-polished pebbles. "I can't remember anything from before a few months ago. I just woke up in this forest. All I know for sure is my name."

"But you know how to talk. You knew how to make that trigger circle."

"I don't know *how* I knew that. I'm not even sure I could do it again, if I needed to." She crossed her arms over her chest again and studied the floor, looking suddenly younger. "Things just . . . come into my head. Words, pictures. As soon as I saw you, I recognized the symbol on your cloak"—she pointed to the silver clasp, which was shaped like a phoenix, the emblem of the Foundation—"and I knew what it meant. I knew you were an Animist. But I can't remember anything about my own past."

"Then what makes you so certain you're human?" She tensed, and he realized that he'd asked a cruel question. "I mean—"

"I feel it," she replied, quietly but firmly.

Who *was* this girl?

Simon cleared his throat. "In that case, you must be under some sort of curse. Or maybe someone transformed you, and the shock of it made you forget your past?" At her skeptical look, he added, "People do block memories sometimes, when they've had a trauma. I've never heard of someone forgetting *everything*, though. I suppose there could be some other cause. Anyway, why don't you come with me to Eidendel?"

"To the city? Are you joking?" She pulled down her hood. "Look at me." His eyes had adjusted to the dimness, and he saw that the grayish tone to her skin wasn't dirt: she *was* gray. Dolphin-gray. Dove-gray.

"Well, all right, you're a little . . . unusual. But the citizens of Eidendel are accustomed to unusual things. They aren't like these villagers. The people of Splithead Creek, they're . . ." He paused, searching for a nonjudgmental term.

"Backwoods yokels?" Alice supplied.

"I was going to say 'sheltered.' They have little experience with Animism, or demons, or anything of that nature. It's rare for an Animist to even be born in this part of the world; it tends to run in families, and the families tend to flock to the cities. Of course they'd see you as a monster. People always fear what's unfamiliar to them."

"So you're saying in Eidendel, there are other people like me?"

"Well, not exactly. But they wouldn't be shocked by you, either." At least, he didn't think so.

She frowned. He could almost see the gears in her head turning as she considered his words. Then her eyes lost focus. She tilted her head, as though she were listening to something.

"Alice?"

"Shh." Her gaze snapped toward the wall.

Simon blinked. "What are you—?"

"*Shh.*"

For a long moment, there was silence. Then, faintly, shouting voices—many of them, mostly male—reached his ears. Dogs barked, adding to the chorus. His stomach tightened.

Alice spun to face him, teeth bared. She grabbed Simon, hands fisting in his shirt, and slammed him against the wall. Simon's head bounced off the wood. She was breathing hard and fast, her eyes wild and white-edged. The purple irises glowed. "You planned this!"

"No!" Simon gripped Alice's wrists, trying to push them away. Tentacles shot out from under her cloak, snaked around his forearms, and yanked them back, pinning them against the wall. Another grabbed his throat, squeezing. "I swear," he said, voice choked, "I didn't know they were coming!"

"You're lying." Her voice shook. "I was a fool to trust you."

"Alice." He held her gaze. "Do you really think I would heal your injuries just to stall for time? If I wanted you dead, I would have just let you walk away. The infection would have finished you off."

Uncertainty flickered in her face.

"I told you before, I'm not your enemy," he said. "*They* are."

She drew in an unsteady breath. She loosened her grip but didn't release him. Her nostrils twitched. "I smell oil," she muttered.

Simon went cold inside. Brock's words came back to him: *If it were up to me, I'd burn down the lair with the monster still inside.*

Apparently, Brock was going to make good on his threat.

Chapter Ten

The angry voices grew louder. "They're here," Alice said.

All at once, her tentacles released Simon, and he slumped against the wall, his bones like rubber.

She dropped into a crouch. Beneath her cloak, he saw movement—things bulged and shifted, as if her muscles were rearranging themselves. She began to swell. Then she cried out. She gripped her recently healed shoulder, shaking, her form dwindling back to normal. "Can't shift," she said. "Not yet."

Outside, the dogs had gone into a frenzy of snarling and barking. "They're closing in," she said. "They've already surrounded the house." Her eyes were wild, frantic. "I have no choice. I have to fight them."

"There are too many. There's no way you'll be able to fend all of them off."

"Even if they kill me, I'll take a few of them with me."

That, Simon thought, seemed like a bad outcome all around. "Let me talk to them," he said.

"You really think they'll listen to you?"

"Just give me a chance." The smell of oil was so strong now, even Simon could detect it. They didn't have much time.

He ran, stumbling, out the room and down the hall to the front door. He flung it open.

A crowd of people stood outside. Torches burned in the shadows of the forest. Several burly men in the back held pails filled with black, glistening oil. At the front of the crowd loomed Brock, wearing an open jacket, exposing a chest matted with black hair.

"Uh—hello," Simon said. "What are you doing here?"

Brock crossed his arms over his chest. "After you left, the men and I talked among ourselves. Decided we'd lend a hand."

Meaning, they hadn't trusted him to get the job done and had come here to kill Alice, with or without the mayor's approval. Simon bit the inside of his cheek.

Brock leaned forward, peering over Simon's shoulder, and grimaced. "Bloody hell, what a stink. Is the monster still in there?"

"It's been dealt with."

There were a couple of half-hearted cheers from the crowd, but mostly confused silence.

"Show me its corpse," Brock said.

"Er—that isn't—"

Brock shoved Simon aside and stomped into the house.

"Wait!"

The other villagers crowded into the doorway, but Brock called, "The rest of you stay out here." He flashed them a toothy smile. "If I don't come back in five minutes, burn the place down."

Simon's jaw hung open. Dear Spirit, this man was a lunatic.

Brock strode down the hallway, shoved open the door at the end, and vanished inside. Simon ran after him. The room appeared empty. Brock squinted, holding his torch aloft. Its light reflected off a pair of purple eyes under the bed. Brock lunged.

"No!" Simon cried.

The struggle was brief; Brock hauled a thrashing, snarling Alice out from under the bed and pinned her to the floor with one boot on her back. Her tentacles thrashed, but in human form, she was too scrawny to put up much resistance. "What is this thing?" he said, lip curled in disgust. "Looks almost like a human girl, but clearly you're no girl. A shape-changer? Folks tell tales of witches transforming themselves into cats or wolves. But you . . . you're a special one, aren't you?"

She panted, glaring up at him, but she'd stopped struggling.

Brock glanced at Simon. "Didn't think you had it in you, Animist, but I was wrong. Seems you've subdued the creature." He lifted his foot and aimed a kick at her ribs. She flinched.

Simon tensed. "Stop that. Can't you see she isn't dangerous?"

Brock ignored him and aimed another kick at her rib cage. *Crack.* Alice cried out and scrambled away, toward the corner of the room, fingernails scratching at the floorboards. Brock advanced toward her.

"I said *stop*!"

"Why are you protecting her?" Brock growled.

Simon hesitated. He knew he had to be careful with his words. "There's no point in beating an enemy who's already defeated. It's cruel."

"Cruel? You call *this* cruel? I watched this *thing* throw my brother around like a rag doll. I heard his skull crack. I saw him *die*." He grabbed the back of Alice's cloak, hoisted her up, and slammed her against the nearest wall. Alice glared at him, teeth bared—but still, she didn't speak, didn't struggle. "Not so powerful now, are you?" He drew a long knife from a sheath at his belt. "Time to finish this."

Something dark rose up within Simon. His fingertips prickled as he instinctively drew in meta. Tiny darts of lightning crackled and arched within the cups of his palms. *I could kill him.* The thought came to him with surprising calm. Brock was totally focused on Alice, blinded by his own rage; the back of his neck was exposed. Simon could walk up behind him and deliver a short, sharp jolt of meta to his brain stem, stopping his heartbeat. He would be dead before he even felt anything. It didn't take much skill or strength to kill someone in that way. With the right opportunity, any Animist could do it.

He *wanted* to do it.

Slowly, he raised his hand, two fingers extended. Time slowed as he reached out toward Brock's unguarded nape. A strange humming filled his head, and a dark filter slid over his vision.

Just one quick touch.

He took a step forward—then froze. His insides turned cold with shock. What was he doing? If he killed Brock, the villagers would kill *them*.

Brock raised the knife.

Simon lunged and grabbed his wrist.

Brock turned burning, bloodshot eyes to him. "Don't make me go through you," he said through clenched teeth.

Simon managed to keep his voice level, despite the way his heart thudded against his ribs. "That isn't necessary. I'll take her with me. Back to Eidendel."

"*We're* the wronged party here." He wrenched his wrist from Simon's grip. "We don't need your courts. We do these things quick and clean."

Alice rose to her hands and knees, head downcast, hair hanging around her face. Her fingers twitched and arched like claws. Brock planted a foot on the back of her head, forcing her face against the floorboards. "Stay where you are, witch."

"Let her go," Simon said firmly. "She's my responsibility."

Brock's eyes narrowed. Simon flinched as one massive hand came down on his shoulder and gripped, *tight*. "Maybe I didn't make myself clear. This isn't your decision, boy." His fingers dug in with bruising force. "Last warning. Stand aside. Now."

Simon struggled to keep his breathing steady, even as panic clanged in his head. His gaze darted to Alice. Beneath the hood, her face had started to change, the muscles shifting beneath her face in disconcerting ways. Her tentacles lashed behind her.

Outside, he could hear the villagers talking in low voices, growing restless. Even now, were they pouring oil around the foundation of the house?

He closed his eyes. What would his father do in this situation? He visualized the man's expressionless face, his cool gray stare.

Simon opened his eyes. The fear fell away, replaced by a peculiar, icy stillness. "Tell me, Brock. What's your full name? You do have a family name, I assume?"

Brock's fierce expression went blank. "What's it matter?"

"When I return home empty-handed, the Foundation will demand an explanation. And when I tell them what happened, I'll have to let them know who the responsible party was."

His face darkened. "You trying to intimidate me?"

Simon forced himself not to drop his gaze. "I'm just telling you how it is. I admire your courage, actually. Defying the Foundation in order to satisfy your own sense of justice . . . considering they could crush your entire village like a beetle? It's a bold move. But if you're willing to take *full* responsibility, I can at least guarantee that your kinsmen won't suffer for your actions."

The corner of Brock's eye twitched.

"I hope you're not thinking about threatening *me*," Simon said. "Have you forgotten that I was able to take down the monster single-handed?"

"Maybe you got lucky."

"Don't be stupid. The reason she didn't struggle, even when you beat her, is because *I'm* here. She isn't the least bit afraid of you. Even now, in her weakened state, she still has the power to kill you. But I made her promise to behave."

Alice huddled on the floor, motionless, her face hidden by her hood.

Cords of tendon stood out in Brock's neck. His face had grown shiny and taut; a vein in his temple strained against the skin. It seemed in real danger of bursting. A thin line of sweat snaked down the back of Simon's neck and under the collar of his robe. *Don't look away.*

For a long moment, neither spoke; neither moved. Simon's knees were quivering like jelly, but he kept his face carefully neutral. "Now," he said, "kindly take your hand off my shoulder."

A few seconds passed . . . then Brock pulled his hand back. He shoved his knife back into the hilt. "You little snake. I should have seen through that bumbling coward act of yours. This is all a game to you, isn't it?" He spat on the floorboards.

Simon said nothing.

"Do whatever you want with the witch," Brock muttered. "Just get out of our village and never show your face around here again." He strode out, slamming the door behind him.

Chapter Eleven

Simon waited, afraid to move or breathe. Outside, the dull murmur of the villagers' voices receded and faded into silence.

Alice sat up, cradling her ribs. With her thumb, she wiped a bit of blood from the corner of her mouth. "They're gone," she said. "I can't smell them anymore."

Simon sagged against the wall, light-headed. "Thank the Spirit," he murmured.

Alice started to stand and winced, clutching her chest. She crumpled back to the floor.

He dropped to his knees beside her. Gently, he touched her shoulder; she flinched, and he pulled away. "Anything broken?"

"A few bruised ribs."

"Let me heal them." He reached out.

She waved him away. "It's nothing."

Her nose was bleeding. Her lower lip had split, and there were bruises on one cheek where Brock had shoved her face against the floor.

"I'm sorry," he said. "I should have done something sooner."

"No." She spat blood and wiped her mouth with a sleeve. "I *had* to let him knock me around. Make him think I was helpless. Lucky he fell for your bluff." She paused. "It *was* a bluff, wasn't it?"

He let out a shaky laugh. "I'm amazed he didn't see through me." His smile faded. "For a moment, I thought we were both going to die."

"You know, you could have just walked away."

"And let him kill you? No. I couldn't do that."

Alice was staring at him, her expression strangely intent. She leaned forward to touch his throat, and he tensed.

"Um . . ."

"*You're* bruised, too." Her fingertips ghosted over his skin, tracing a sore spot. "Did I do this?"

He'd been too preoccupied to notice until now, but his neck did ache where she'd grabbed it earlier. "Well, you've got quite a grip." He smiled.

A shadow of unease lay over her expression. "That man . . . he said I killed someone."

"You don't remember?"

"I remember them storming into the house. It happened

so quickly, after that. It's all a blur." She looked down at her hands, curling them slowly into fists. "I just know I was angry. And afraid."

"It wasn't your fault. You were defending yourself."

She sat curled into a ball, knees drawn to her chest. "Maybe. But I can't really blame that man for wanting revenge either. I killed someone important to him. If I were him, I would probably feel the same."

He opened his mouth to say something—what, he wasn't sure—then closed it again. What was there to say? He couldn't pretend to understand what she was going through; he had never killed anyone, in self-defense or otherwise. Had never even entertained the thought.

Until today.

Awkwardly, he stood and dusted off his pants. "We should go."

She hugged her knees. "Where?"

He glanced out the window. Judging by the slant of the light, it was midafternoon. "There's a train arriving in a few hours. If we hurry, we can make it."

"Will they even let me on a train?"

"You can hide your tentacles beneath your cloak," he said. "We need to get away from Splithead Creek. Brock may change his mind."

She huddled in the shadows, arms folded over her bent knees.

"Alice?"

"Why do you keep trying to help me?" she whispered. "What's in it for you?"

"I'm an Animist. Animists are supposed to help people."

She watched him warily, like a wild animal through the brushes. "That's not a real answer."

She was right. But he wasn't quite sure *how* to answer. He looked away, picking at a loose thread of his sleeve. "Most of my life, I've felt pretty useless. I mean, I'm just . . . you know. This." He gestured vaguely toward his own unimpressive form. "I don't have much talent, as an Animist or anything else. I'm passable at healing, but not good enough to make a career of it. And when it comes to everything else, well . . ." He gave her a strained smile. "Back at the Academy, my nickname was Swoony, because I once fainted during a battle. I would have been killed if my teacher hadn't been there to rescue me."

He expected her to laugh, but she didn't.

"I'll probably always be a mediocrity, at best," he said. "But if I can help at least one person, my life won't have been a total waste." Out loud, it sounded even more pathetic.

"You killed a shoggoth," she said. "If you're really so useless, how did you do that?"

"I don't know." He still couldn't clearly recall what he'd seen after he blacked out. There were only faint flickers, fuzzy images, and none of them made sense; they had the quality of a fever dream. "If you don't believe me, I don't blame you, but it's the truth."

"Hm."

"So . . . will you come with me, or . . ."

"Well, I don't have anywhere else to go, do I?" She massed her tentacles beneath her, pushed herself to her feet in a fluid, serpentine motion, and strode toward the door.

When they stepped outside into the cold mountain air, a light snow was falling like ash. It settled over the trees and into Alice's dark hair as they walked. Her bruises, he noticed, were already starting to fade.

Her tentacles shifted restlessly under her cloak, the tips peeking out from under the hem. They were gray, a few shades darker than the rest of her skin, smooth and rubbery looking. As he watched, one of them stretched out, plucked a dead leaf from a bush, and twirled it idly before flicking it into the woods.

"You're staring again," she remarked.

"Sorry. I'm trying not to, honest. It's just—before this, I've never known a girl with tentacles."

"Really? I'm astonished."

Dead leaves crunched under their feet as they walked. Hers were bare, toenails the same lustrous dark green as her fingernails. If the cold ground bothered her at all, she didn't show it. "I'll get on the train with you," she said, "to get away from here. But I'm not going to Eidendel."

"I really think the Foundation could help you."

"I don't trust the Foundation."

"Why?"

"They're tyrants. Isn't that reason enough?"

"You've never dealt with them before," he pointed out. "Not that you know of, anyway."

"No. But I know that the Queen controls the whole Continent . . . pretty much the entire civilized world. There are a few island nations in the southern sea too small for her to bother with, but everything else the Foundation has conquered over the past five hundred years."

"For someone without memories, you know an awful lot."

"It's like I told you. I have all these images and facts in my head, but they don't feel like *my* memories. They're more like pictures in a book, if that makes sense."

"I see." He frowned. "Well . . . the Queen hasn't had absolute power for a long time. She's more like a figurehead. The Primary Council runs things. Its members are voted in by citizens, and the Council members select people to be on the subordinate boards and panels. It's a republic. More or less."

"Whatever you want to call it, it still smells like tyranny to me." A mossy, half-decayed oak lay fallen across their path, mushrooms sprouting from its trunk. She crawled nimbly over, like a spider, her tentacles doing most of the work. It was uncanny. "Rules, rules, and more rules. You'd have to study for decades to learn them all."

Simon followed, awkwardly hoisting himself up and swinging his leg over the log as if it were a horse. He winced as he slid down the other side. "The rules exist for a reason, though. I mean—for instance, it's against the law to try to bring someone back from the dead using Animism. Which seems sensible enough. It's probably not possible, anyway, but imagine if someone did it wrong and created something horrible."

She grunted, which could have been agreement or disagreement.

"And it's forbidden to transform a person into something else," he continued, "or to . . . combine two living entities."

Alice stopped. "Is that something that . . . Has anyone tried it?"

"A long time ago. During the War of Ashes, Animists created these sort of . . . human-demon hybrids as weapons. They were stronger and faster than humans, and they could stay on Earth indefinitely, but they were . . . unstable."

They continued on a few paces in silence. It occurred to Simon, of course, what Alice was thinking. She herself had both human and demon traits.

"But the techniques have been lost!" Simon insisted. "Even researching it is strictly forbidden."

"Are there any of these hybrids left?" she asked.

He shook his head. "The last of the Abominations—that's what people called them—died off hundreds of years ago. Judging by accounts of the war, those creatures weren't anything like you, anyway. They couldn't talk. The process of transformation warps the human mind beyond recognition."

"So I'm alone," Alice muttered. "There's nothing else like me in this world."

"Not that I know of."

She lifted a tentacle and gripped it in both hands. "If these—what did you call them?—these Abominations are illegal, does that mean *I'm* against the law, too?"

"We don't know that you're part demon. There's probably some other explanation. And in any case, the Foundation can't punish you just for existing. Even if you *were* transformed through illegal Animism, they'd be more interested in finding the person who did this to you."

She squinted. "What makes you so sure they wouldn't just kill me?"

"They aren't like that. They don't go around murdering innocent people."

"But if they don't see me as a person—"

"But you clearly *are.*"

She crossed her arms over her chest and raised an eyebrow. "Thanks, but that doesn't answer my question."

He raked a hand through his hair. "I don't know how to prove it to you, but I've lived under the Foundation's laws my whole life. I know what they're like. They have their flaws, I realize. But, I mean . . . they aren't *evil* or anything."

She rolled her eyes. "You should have that as a motto on your crest. 'The Foundation: We're Not Evil or Anything.' It really inspires confidence."

"I see your point." Simon wasn't sure how to feel about this whole conversation. He'd never quite trusted the Foundation either. Yet now, somehow, he felt the urge to defend them. He *was* an Animist, after all; what business did he have wearing these robes if he didn't think there was anything good about them? His hand drifted to the silver phoenix clasp near his throat. "I believe in what they stand for. What they're *supposed* to stand for."

"And what is that?"

"Protecting the weak. Upholding justice. Making sure that Animists use their powers for good, and that the ones who hurt others are held accountable. There has to be *some* kind of organization to prevent evil people from just doing whatever they want . . . doesn't there? If not the Foundation, then what? Who?"

"I don't know. But that's not the point." Alice strode forward. "I'm not going to ask the Foundation for help. Don't try to change my mind."

The snow had turned to a despondent drizzle. Wet gray slush sloshed beneath their feet. The clouds formed an unbroken, oppressive wall overhead.

Simon hurried along behind Alice, puffing for breath. Even walking, she was fast. "Then where will you go?" he asked. "What will you do?"

She shoved a branch aside; when she let go, it sprang back and nearly whipped him in the face. "I'll find some answers on my own," she said.

"How? You don't even know where to start. You're all alone—"

She stopped, so suddenly that he almost ran into her. Her shoulders were stiff, drawn in under her cloak. "Don't you think I know that?" Her hands, bunched into fists at her sides, trembled.

"I'm just trying to help," he said softly.

Still facing away from him, she wiped at her eyes with the heel of one hand, then scowled over her shoulder. "Well, if you've got any other ideas, I'm all ears."

Simon hesitated. He hadn't wanted to bring this up, but if going to the Foundation wasn't an option, this was the only thing he could think of. "Have you ever heard of Dr. Aberdeen Finius Hawking?"

Her eyes briefly lost focus, as if she were consulting some mysterious encyclopedia within herself. "He's a powerful Animist. He published some research on . . . artificial body parts? Mechanical limbs and organs, powered by meta. He used to work for the Foundation, but there was a scandal. He left, or he was expelled, or maybe a little of both. The details are fuzzy. So, what about him?"

"He's my father."

She stared. "*You're* the son of a famous Animist?"

He tried not to be insulted by the incredulity in her voice. "Yes."

"You told me your last name is Frost."

"Frost is my mother's name. Here, look." Simon pulled his compass out of his pocket and pried it open. Inside the lid was a hidden compartment, sealed shut with a minor security spell, the sort that would respond only to his touch. He brushed a forefinger against it, and the compartment snapped open, revealing a small picture tucked into the compass's lid—a grainy, sepia-toned family photograph of a six-year-old Simon, his parents, and his twin sister Olivia. His mother smiled, her hand on his shoulder. His father stood stiffly off to the side. It was the last photograph of the entire family together.

Simon handed it to Alice, who examined it closely. Simon squirmed and felt a familiar heat creeping up his neck, into his oversized ears, which had an unfortunate tendency to turn bright, glaring red whenever he was the slightest bit self-conscious. He never showed that photograph to anyone.

Alice clicked the compass shut and tossed it back to him. Fumbling, he caught it. "So, I take it he's clever, your father."

"The cleverest person I know."

"Do you think he could . . . make me normal?"

"Is that what you want?"

"Obviously. Would you want to spend the rest of *your* life looking like a monster?"

"Well, no. I guess not." And yet . . .

Alice was strong. That much was obvious. And while her tentacles, purple eyes, and gray skin took some getting used to, they were more fascinating than repellent. The thought of her becoming an ordinary human was oddly disappointing. "I mean . . . *maybe* he could do something about your condition. I can't promise. My father is brilliant, but he's also unpredictable. And ill-tempered. And reclusive. There's no guarantee that he'll be willing to help. Really, it's probably a bad idea . . ."

"Are you going to take me to him or not?"

Simon gulped. He was the one who'd brought this up, he reminded himself. "Yes. I'll take you."

Around early evening, they reached the foothills. Splithead Creek lay before them, a smear of brown on the soggy, yellowish-gray plains.

"The railroad is over there, just beyond the houses." Simon pointed. "If we go around the village, we can avoid notice."

"Let's hope," she muttered.

They crept down the foothills, through the autumn-yellowed fields, to the tracks. There, they waited, shivering at the edge of the village. A few faces peered at them through the windows, but no one came out.

A whistle pierced the silence. Simon looked up. He could see the train in the distance, chugging along the tracks, belching clouds of blue-gray smoke into the air. It pulled up with a screech of brakes. As they boarded, Simon reached automatically for his suitcase and then remembered that he'd left it in Mayor Umburt's house. Oh well. There was nothing there he really needed.

The door whisked shut behind them.

Chapter Twelve

The porter gave Alice an odd look. Simon mumbled something about her being a long-lost cousin he was taking home for a family reunion. Fortunately, the man didn't ask questions.

Simon and Alice sat across from each other in the creaky leather seats. Simon couldn't afford a private cabin, so they were exposed to the aisle. Her tentacles remained hidden beneath her baggy cloak as she huddled against the wall. Outside the window, forests rushed past.

Alice's stomach gurgled.

"Do you want something to eat?" Simon asked. "They have sandwiches."

She perked up. "Coffee, too?"

"Probably. Do you like coffee?"

"I think so."

"I've never cared for it. Too bitter. But I can order some for you, if you like."

When the porter came around to check on them, Simon ordered a coffee and two ham and cheese sandwiches. The food arrived shortly, on a small wheeled cart, which the porter left for them to use as a table. The sandwiches smelled a little suspicious. Simon picked at the stale crust and limp lettuce without much enthusiasm. Alice wolfed hers down in two bites then said, "Are you going to eat that?"

He pushed it toward her.

She shoved it into her mouth and washed it down with a swig of the steaming black beverage, and sighed, wiping her mouth with one sleeve.

Simon smiled a little. "Better?"

"Much." She leaned back, hands resting over her stomach. "It's been so long since I've had anything except raw meat." She scrunched up her nose. "I can't believe I ate that deer carcass."

"It *was* a bit rank."

"I was so hungry, I didn't care. When I've been in my other form for a while, I start to think differently. It becomes harder to remember certain things."

"Like?"

"Like how to talk. Or why I shouldn't eat people. Meat is meat, after all."

He shifted in his seat.

"And before you ask, no, I've never actually eaten a person. But I thought about it, while you were passed out on the floor. You smelled delicious."

"Well, thank you for restraining yourself. I appreciate it."

The corners of her lips twitched. It wasn't *quite* a smile, but it was something. She picked a few crumbs off her plate. "You know what I'd really love right now? *Bacon.* Juicy, thick bacon. Not too crispy."

"You remember eating bacon?"

A tiny crease appeared between her brows. "That's the strange thing. I *don't.* I just know what it tastes like." She resumed staring out the window. The hazy sunlight painted a bright stripe down the side of her cheek. A curl of dark hair lay against her temple. "It's frustrating. If I don't think about it too hard—if I just let my mind go fuzzy—it feels like my past is all there. Like I know who I am. But I can't latch onto anything. It slips through my fingers when I try to hold it."

"What if I asked you questions? Would that help?"

She shrugged.

"Where are you from? What were your parents like?" No response. He kept trying: "Do you think you trained as an Animist? You made that summoning circle, after all. With a trigger symbol, no less. Do you know any other forms of Animism?" A pause. "Nothing?"

She shook her head. Simon let out a little sigh.

The train's wheels rattled. Outside, endless, mist-covered

countryside rolled by.

"As long as we're asking questions," Alice said, "there's something I'm curious about."

"Oh?"

Her gaze focused on him, suddenly sharp and intent. "Who's Olivia?"

The words hit Simon like a punch to the gut. "Wh . . . what?"

"When I knocked you unconscious, in the cabin, you were dreaming. You cried out in your sleep. You kept saying the name 'Olivia.'"

There were a few crumbs scattered atop the wheeled cart. He studied them intently, as if trying to read the future in their pattern.

He could dodge the question, he supposed. But how could he expect her to trust him if he wouldn't trust her?

Besides . . . it had been so long since he'd actually *talked* about this with anyone. He'd never had any close friends. Even during his session with the Healer, he hadn't said much, because his father had already filled her in on the most pertinent details; Simon had simply answered a few brusque questions while she jotted down notes in a ledger. An untold story was a heavy weight. Maybe it was time he shared it with someone.

"Olivia was my twin sister. When we were ten years old—on our tenth birthday, actually—she was murdered." He was surprised at how calm the words sounded. "Apparently I witnessed the whole thing. I was the *only* witness. But I blocked the memory of that night to protect myself from the trauma. At least, that's what the Healer said."

Alice was silent, listening.

"When I came to, the whole room was torn apart. No ordinary person could've done that, so the killer was probably an Animist, or else a demon summoned by one. But we never learned his identity or motive."

"So what makes you think it was a 'he'?"

Simon hesitated. "Sometimes, I have bad dreams. I see her body on the floor, and . . . there's a faint image. A man's shadow. I can never see his face. I don't even know if he's real or if I invented him. It could've been a woman, I suppose. Could have been anyone, really."

"The girl in the picture . . . that was her? Your sister?"

"Yes." His gaze wandered to the window. "I think you would have liked her. Most people did." A faint smile touched his lips. "She was amazing. Brilliant. By the time she was four years old, she was using meta to animate her toys. They walked around the house and had tea parties on their own. And she was kind. She would bring injured birds into the house to heal. Once, when we were out in the city, she saw a man whipping a horse. She used Animism to make the whip handle red-hot, so he was forced to let go—she could do that, channel heat or cold through the air. Then she marched over and gave him a scolding, and he was so stunned he just stood there. She was seven."

He could only imagine what a force of nature she would've been if she'd had a chance to grow up.

"After she died . . . my mother left. Packed up and vanished. I still don't know where she is or what she's doing, or if she's even alive." He stopped, breathing in slowly. "There *must* be a reason. She wouldn't have just abandoned us. I think maybe she's trying to find the person who killed Olivia. To find answers."

He knew one thing for sure: Olivia had been the glue holding their odd little family together, and once she was gone, that glue had dissolved.

"I can't imagine," Alice said quietly. "I don't even know if I *had* a family."

"You must have," Simon said. "Everyone has a family. Even demons have families. Mother always told me that they raise their young."

"I'm not a demon."

"I know. I'm just saying."

He wondered, again, where she'd come from. His mind strayed to the mysterious pod in the mountains. He thought about mentioning it, but something held him back.

The train ran through the night and into the morning. Several times it stopped to let passengers board, and people bustled past, dragging bulky suitcases up and down the aisle. At one point, a thin, white-haired man in Animist robes lingered near their seats, frowning at his pocket watch. A gray-furred imp crouched on his shoulder, tail coiled around his arm. Its lizard-like face turned toward Simon, eyes flaring yellow, and a long, sinuous tongue licked the air. Its gaze flicked toward Alice, and it began to growl, fur bristling. Its lips pulled back from snaggled yellow teeth. Simon tensed, and Alice drew her cloak tighter around herself.

"Hush!" the Animist hissed.

The imp growled louder, eyes flashing red, then purple.

The porter approached and cleared his throat: "Sir—sir, I do apologize, but there are no Eldritch creatures allowed on this train. Please dismiss your servant."

With a sigh, the Animist flicked a hand, and the imp disappeared in a poof. Both Simon and Alice let out whooshes of breath.

Once the Animist had moved on, Alice whispered, "I don't like how crowded this train is getting. How many more stops are there before Eidendel?"

"Four, I think. Five? There are more stops the closer we get. But we aren't far. Another two hours, maybe."

"Maybe we should get off at the next stop and walk the rest of the way."

Simon couldn't deny he was feeling pretty tense himself. But they were so close. "Most Animists know better than to bring imps or wraiths onto a train. I don't think that will happen again."

"And if it does?" She fidgeted, arms crossed over her chest. "If we're caught, there's nowhere to run or hide. It feels like we're in a cage."

He glanced at her fingers, digging into her bicep. Her nails had sharpened into claws. "Um. Your hands—"

"I know." She balled them into fists. "I'm trying. It's harder to control when I get nervous."

Whispered conversation caught Simon's ear. Across the aisle, he could see a pair of older women glancing surreptitiously at Alice. One leaned toward the other and spoke, covering her mouth with one hand. He couldn't hear what they were saying, but they weren't being terribly subtle about their suspicion.

Maybe departing this train *would* be a good idea. "Right. Next stop is a farming town called Heedrith. We'll get off there." Already, he could see the town's steeples on the horizon. A patchwork of farmland and fields rolled past the window.

With a hiss of brakes and a belch of steam, the train pulled into Heedrith.

Unlike Splithead Creek, it had an actual station. The wooden building echoed with the din of countless overlapping footsteps and voices. A curved ceiling arched overhead, supported by huge oaken beams resembling the rib cage of some titanic beast. Briefly, the association sparked a memory of another, similar thing he had seen somewhere, but what? It faded quickly. Something from a dream, perhaps.

They followed the stream of passengers out of the train. Alice hunkered down, as if trying to disappear, as they walked through the station's door, into blinding sunlight.

Heedrith was considerably larger than Splithead Creek (not saying much) but was still tiny in comparison to Eidendel. The cobbled streets and brick buildings had a quaint, rustic look. Simon saw no signs of Animists or their work— no imps flitting about, no men and women in robes—but a flag bearing the Foundation's phoenix emblem snapped atop a pole outside the station. Horse-drawn carts clattered through the streets.

Alice crept along at Simon's side, head down. No one glanced twice at her; she was only a small, thin form swallowed up by a ragged cloak. She resembled an old woman, with her posture and cautious, shuffling gait. The tentacles, currently hoisted up and massed under her cloak, resembled a hunchback's hump.

"I don't think we need to linger here," Simon said.

Alice nodded. They followed a wide dirt road along the outskirts of the town, past pens full of bleating sheep. Only when Heedrith had disappeared behind the slope of the hill, when they were surrounded by miles of empty countryside, did Alice relax. Her claws dwindled back to blunt fingernails. She pulled down her hood and shook out her hair. A breeze stirred her dark curls. She uncoiled her tentacles and stretched them out. "Much better." She breathed in deeply. "Fresh air. Thank the Spirit. That train smelled awful. Like oil and smoke."

"It didn't smell like anything to me."

"Well, if you grow up surrounded by the stink of civilization, you're probably used to it. *I* felt like I was sucking on a dirty pipe the whole time. Not to mention all the passengers. Packed together like that, they smell worse than cows. Did you get a whiff of that woman in the fur coat? Phew. Like dead flowers boiled in sewer water."

"I think that was her perfume."

"Well, whatever it was, it was ghastly." She walked with the easy, ground-eating stride of an experienced traveler.

Simon half jogged alongside her. "Maybe we should've stocked up on food in Heedright. On foot, it might take us a full day or more to reach Eidendel. I mean . . . if we had horses, it would be a different story."

Alice tilted her head. She flexed her arm. "You know, I think I've healed enough to shift by now."

Simon froze. "You mean—"

"I could carry you. I can run a lot faster in my other form."

"Er . . ."

"I won't eat you. I swear. Those sandwiches took the edge off. And it looks like there's barely a mouthful of meat on you, anyway, so you won't be *that* tempting."

It was hard to say whether she was joking. "You're not worried someone will see you?"

"There's no one nearby. Out in the open like this, I can smell someone coming from a mile away. I'll have plenty of time to shift back, if necessary."

Simon bit his lower lip. He had to admit, the idea of walking all the way to Eidendel didn't appeal to him. Already, his feet hurt. Still, this felt . . . risky. In more ways than one.

Alice averted her gaze. "If you'd rather not, I don't blame you. It's just an idea." She fingered the edge of her sleeve. "You've seen my other form. It's horrifying, I know."

"No. It's not that." He stopped, taking a breath, and scanned their surroundings. Nothing but rolling hills and fields of waving grass, with the occasional tree standing sentry over the peaceful countryside. Simon pulled a folded map from his pocket and studied it. This wasn't one of the main roads; it would still lead them to Eidendel, but ahead it grew narrower and grass-choked, according to the notes jotted next to it. It wasn't often used, except for local foot traffic. If Alice really *could* smell someone coming a mile away, they'd probably be safe.

Simon folded the map and slipped it back into his pocket. "All right." He wondered if he'd gone mad. "Let's do it."

Alice undid the clasp of her cloak and let it fall to the ground, then stopped. "Well?"

"Well what?"

"Well, *obviously* I have to take off my clothes before I shift, or I'll rip them to pieces." The gray of her cheeks darkened a little. "Are you going to stand there gawping the whole time?"

"Oh." He ducked his head. "Sorry."

Cloth rustled. He kept his gaze firmly fixed on his shoes.

"Here, catch." She lobbed her wadded-up clothes at him. Fumbling, he caught them.

"Don't look yet."

"I'm not."

"It takes me a minute or two to change. It's a bit messy. Promise you won't look until it's over."

Simon nodded, clutching her clothes against his chest. A moment of silence passed—then a moist, meaty sound erupted, like a dog ripping into a raw steak. The sound continued, punctuated by crackles and pops as bones rearranged themselves. At last, the sounds stopped, and he tentatively raised his eyes. Alice stood before him.

In darkness, her Eldritch form had been terrifying. In full sunlight, it was awe-inspiring. Her scales shone like dark gems, greenish black with undertints of purple. Her amethyst eyes blazed. Her hind legs were as thick as tree trunks, her tentacles an ever-writhing fan sprouting from her lower back, spread out like a peacock's tail. "Oh," he breathed.

Alice sat back on her haunches, like a dog, and lowered her dragon-like head. Even now, armored in dark scales, her body had a vaguely human shape, her forelegs more like arms—something between animal and human.

Simon took a tentative step toward her. "Can you . . . talk?"

She placed one massive, clawed hand against her plated

chest and spoke in a deep, growling voice: "Ah . . . riss." The syllables were distorted, made by a mouth not meant to pronounce human speech. She pointed at him. "Shy . . . un."

Simon. The tension eased out of his shoulders. She'd said it was more difficult for her to think in this form, but if she remembered his name, that probably meant she wasn't currently viewing him as a juicy steak.

He took another step toward her. With her clothes still tucked under one arm, he reached up and laid a hand against the bulge of her cheek. She was warm. Her eyes shone like fire behind stained glass—the light within them seemed to move and shift, brightening and dimming. As he stared into the narrow slits of her pupils, they widened and grew rounder, making her eyes look a bit more human. Her jaws opened in a smile, showing rows of serrated teeth.

Then one tentacle dipped down, looped around his waist, and hoisted him into the air.

Simon let out a sharp cry, legs flailing. "Hey! Wh-what—"

The tentacle dropped him onto Alice's back. He sat astride her, her sharp spine digging into his groin. He gulped. "Hold on. Just a moment." By draping Alice's folded clothes over her back, he was able to create a sort of makeshift saddle—it gave him a bit of cushioning, at least.

In this form, Alice had a mane of short, bristly black hair running from between her ears, down her sinuous neck, ending at the spot between her powerful shoulders. Bracing himself, he gripped the mane in both hands. "All right. I'm ready."

Alice's visible eye rolled back toward him, and she grinned.

His stomach tightened.

She sprang forward and broke into a gallop. Muscles bunched and surged beneath him.

As a child, he'd read stories about Animists summoning huge demons and riding them across land, sea, or sky. The tales always made it sound so romantic—the stars and wind, the excitement and freedom, the sense of absolute power and mastery over a majestic, dangerous creature as they moved in perfect tandem, like a single being.

Alice bounded down the road with all the grace and poise of a puppy outdoors for the first time. Each stride jarred Simon to the bones. He bounced like a rag doll atop her back, the impact flinging him back and forth, up and down as he clung with all his strength to the wiry strands of hair on her neck. He tried to yell for her to slow down, but he couldn't catch his breath long enough to get a word out. The scenery flew past in a dizzying blur. Alice leaped over a stream. His bottom briefly lifted off her back, and for the instant they were airborne, he felt a brief flash of exhilaration—

—then her feet struck the bank on the opposite side, and once again he was holding on for dear life. After losing his grip on her mane for the second or third time, he gave up and flung both arms around her neck, burying his face against her scales.

When Alice finally *did* slow down, his body ached in places and in ways he hadn't thought possible. He tumbled off her back and onto the grass, groaning.

She nudged him with her snout and rumbled with concern. He managed a wobbly smile. "Time for a rest?"

She settled her massive bulk onto the grass, while Simon tried to hold on to the contents of his stomach. Gingerly, he picked himself up and stared off into the distance. He could see the iron-gray sea through gaps in the hills. They'd covered a great deal of distance in a short time. She was faster than a horse. Far faster.

A rustling broke the silence—something moving in the grass. Alice's ears twitched, and she raised her angular head, nostrils flaring. She rose into a crouch, tentacles twitching, like the tail of a cat about to pounce.

Before he could say a word, she lunged. Her head shot forward like a snake's; her jaws clamped down on something small and fast. There was a squeal and a crunch. Alice raised her head, a dead rabbit dangling from her teeth. She tossed her head back and swallowed it whole, bones and all.

Simon stared. Alice smiled at him with bloody teeth. "Er . . . maybe you should change back," he said. "Eidendel's not far, and the closer we get, the greater our risk of being seen. We can probably walk the rest of the way." He set her clothes on the ground between them.

She tilted her head then gave a low grunt. Simon turned away, trying to ignore the meaty crackling sounds as she shifted back.

"You can look now."

When he turned, she was in human form, clad in her ragged, patched cloak once again. He smiled. The expression faded when he saw the way she was grimacing. "Does it hurt you to change shape?"

"Would it hurt *you* if someone wrenched apart your bones and muscles, squeezed them down to a fifth their size, and then reassembled them?"

"That bad?"

She flopped down on the soft grass next to the road. "The pain doesn't last long. I can deal with it. Mostly, it's just exhausting. I feel like I could sleep for a day." She sighed, then let out a small burp and clapped her hand over her mouth.

"We can rest here, if you like. It should be safe enough." He paused. "Thank you. For giving me a ride."

"You look a bit green."

"I'll survive. Really—it was quite an experience."

She looked at him from the corner of her eye. "You think it's ugly. My other shape."

"Actually, not a bit. It's . . . majestic. I wouldn't mind the ability to change into a gigantic dragonish version of myself. Would've come in handy when I was being bullied in school."

She let out a soft laugh. It was the first time he'd heard her laugh, and the sound gave him a pleasant flutter, like moth wings tickling the inside of his belly. Then she yawned and curled up on the grass. "The sun is making me sleepy." Heavy-lidded eyes blinked at him, then slipped shut.

Simon settled next to her, folding his arms across his knees. The sun-dappled countryside lay all around him, cloud-shadows moving over the hills. "Another few hours of walking and we should have a clear view of the city. We can make it there before nightfall, anyway." No response. "Alice?"

She remained huddled into a ball, tentacles wrapped around herself like a blanket, snoring softly. A thin line of drool ran from the corner of her mouth.

Already, she was asleep. Not surprising, considering all she'd been through. She hadn't napped on the train. Hadn't dared to let down her guard at all, he supposed.

A lock of dark hair lay across her forehead. He reached out on impulse to brush it aside, then stopped, his fingers inches from her head. What right did he have to touch her so casually? They barely knew each other.

He started to pull away; a tentacle flicked out and curled around his arm. He gave a start. "Sorry, I thought you were—" The words died in his throat. Alice's eyes remained closed; he could see them rolling beneath the lids as she dreamed.

He looked at the dark appendage wrapped around his

forearm. There were suckers on the underside; they gripped him with surprising force, sticking to him like a briar. He'd never had a chance to look at them this closely. When she was awake, staring felt rude, and touching them was out of the question. Cautiously, holding his breath, he brushed a finger over the tentacle's surface. The skin was shiny, slightly rubbery, and surprisingly soft.

She shifted restlessly and murmured. He shouldn't be doing this—poking and prodding her without her awareness, as though she were some exotic curiosity.

With a twinge of regret, he tugged his arm free. Her tentacle curled and uncurled in midair, as if searching for something to hold on to, then drooped to her side.

After an hour or so, Alice stirred herself awake, and they set off. They walked side by side, climbing over roots and boulders that littered the trail. It led them steadily uphill, the path growing steeper and narrower. When they finally reached the hill's rocky crest, Simon was panting, robes drenched with sweat. He wasn't used to traveling such distances on foot. *Too much time sitting at a desk*, he thought.

He brushed damp curls from his forehead and raised his head.

Eidendel lay before them. They stood on the edge of the massive, circular crater, and the city covered its bottom from end to end. Simon had never seen the city from this angle before. He gazed down on the intricately carved stone temples, the arched doorways and pillars of gray-veined white marble, the domed copper roof of the library, now a rusted mossy green. From this distance, the people moving through the streets looked like ants. A ring of cliffs surrounded the city, like a towering natural wall. Beyond sprawled the iron-gray sea.

"Well," he said, "here it is. My home."

He expected some sort of reaction from Alice. Eidendel was, after all, the largest, oldest, and grandest city on the Continent, the stronghold of the Foundation. But her expression remained neutral, guarded. Earlier, when they were alone in the countryside, she'd seemed far more relaxed. Now her mask was back in place. "How do we get down there?"

"There's a road." He pointed. "It cuts through the cliffs and dips down into the city, see? We just have to go around and follow that through the main gates."

Alice nodded, arms crossed over her chest, fingers digging into her biceps. A bead of sweat gleamed on her temple.

She was afraid. Of course. She had every reason to believe that human beings were her enemy, and here he was, dragging her into the heart of civilization. She hadn't *wanted* to come here.

He reached over and gently squeezed her shoulder. She gave him a startled glance. "I won't let anything happen to you," he said.

"You promise?"

The question, soft and unsure, caught him off guard. But he answered readily. "I promise."

She nodded and breathed in slowly through her nose. "Then let's go."

Chapter Thirteen

The salty smell of sea spray filled the air as they approached the city's main entrance. The towering gates stood open; a steady flow of traffic moved into and out of Eidendel.

Alice clutched Simon's sleeve, pressing close to his side as they entered.

The hubbub engulfed them. Vendors stood at carts, ringing bells and hawking their wares. Trays of meat dumplings steamed. Passersby rode down the street on horseback, in carriages, or on bicycles with enormous front wheels. No one gave Simon or Alice a second glance.

"See?" Simon whispered. "As long as you keep your tentacles covered, you're fine."

"I'm *gray*, remember? If anyone sees my face . . ."

"Look around you." He gestured toward the streets. A pale woman in flowing red robes walked past, her face swirled with painted black and white stripes. A bald, brown man rode past on an animal resembling a leathery-skinned bull; the man's head bore tiny golden horns. Above, an emerald-furred wraith swooped through the air on feathered wings, a mail-scroll clamped between its teeth. Three yellow eyes burned above its muzzle. "People from all over the land come to Eidendel. And they summon Eldritch creatures for all sorts of tasks. City dwellers aren't so easily surprised. Or frightened."

A line of sweeper-imps trundled past on their stubby little legs, muttering their chant of *"gubble, gubble."* Their fishy mouths sucked up crumbs and dirt. Alice watched them with a bemused frown. "They eat garbage?"

"They'll eat anything. Good for sanitation, not so good if someone drops jewelry or money on the ground by mistake. But I guess all conveniences have drawbacks."

Gradually, the tension eased out of her shoulders. She lifted her head tentatively and looked around, taking in the sights. "What *is* that thing?" She pointed.

In the stall ahead of them, a tiny clown doll with a painted wooden head walked about on its own, performing jumps and somersaults on a miniature stage. Children watched, clapping and squealing. The clown took a bow.

"Oh. It's a golem—a doll controlled by Animism."

"It's creepy."

"They're harmless. Quite common, actually. For certain

tasks, they're more convenient than imps because they don't have to be summoned, and they don't vanish back into the Eldritch Realm. My father keeps a bunch of them in his house to do the cleaning." He scanned the streets. No patrols in sight, thank the Spirit. Despite what he'd said, he knew he couldn't afford to let down his guard.

"Who here has the courage to peer into the abyss?" a voice brayed, distracting him. A man in a purple suit and top hat stood in front of a covered wagon painted with images of snarling, demonic figures. He waved a striped cane around as he barked at the crowd, "Right here, right now! Come see a gen-u-ine portal to the Outer Realm, birthplace of the Elder Gods and all their unspeakable kin!"

Alice scrunched up her forehead. "That *can't* be real."

"It's not. Just tourist stuff. No one really believes in the Elder Gods anymore . . . or at least, no sensible person."

The huckster turned toward them. "Oho, a skeptic!" He smiled and twirled his slick black mustache around one finger. "Perhaps you'd like to take a peek for yourself . . . if you dare to brave the horrors?" He gestured to the entrance of the wagon with a flourish of his cape. "Come and hear the tortured screams of the damned—only two gillies! Can your sanity withstand—" He stopped, mouth frozen open in a gape. He was staring at Alice . . . or rather, at something near her feet.

Simon glanced down and saw the tip of one tentacle

poking out beneath the hem of her cloak, twitching back and forth. His eyes widened. Alice noticed, too late, and the tentacle shot back under her cloak.

The vendor's face had gone sheet-white.

Simon linked arms with her, positioning himself between Alice and the vendor, and muttered, "Just keep walking."

They hurried forward. Simon steered her down a narrow side street.

"Sorry," Alice muttered. "I—I got distracted. I was careless."

"It's all right. He only saw it for a second or two. He probably has no idea *what* he saw. In any case, he has no reason to tell anyone, and even if he did, no one would believe him." Simon realized he was babbling and snapped his mouth shut.

"Maybe we should stick to the side streets," Alice said.

"Maybe. It'll take a little longer, but there are fewer people."

"Dare you seek the truth?" a voice croaked. He raised his head to see the newspaper seller wandering through the crowd, waving a rolled-up copy of the *Underground*.

Simon groaned. Why did they keep running into each other?

She walked toward him with a stump-toothed grin. "You, boy! You look like a clever lad. Have you ever wondered—?"

"No," he said, "I haven't."

"But surely, the unanswered questions must eat at you.

The world is an onion, layer upon layer of secrets, each more pungent than the last!"

"I'm not interested in pungent secrets, thank you." He leaned closer and whispered, "Haven't you learned your lesson after what happened last time? It's dangerous to wave those things around. What if a patrol saw you?"

"I fear nothing, for I am shielded by the indifferent hand of my Uncreator, the Lord of all Elder Gods."

"If his hand is indifferent, then how is it shielding you?"

"Contradictions, my boy. The world is full of them. Here." She thrust a paper at him and winked. "First one is free."

"Fine!" He grabbed it. "Just go, please. We're in a hurry."

The woman wandered away, vanishing into the crowd.

"She was . . . unique," Alice said. "Do you know her?"

"Sort of. It's a long story." He glanced down at the paper in his hand. The front page bore an ink illustration of a dozen bulging, reptilian eyes under the headline THE FOUNDATION IS WATCHING YOU!

Alice leaned over his shoulder as he skimmed the text.

The Foundation's invisible imps are hiding in your kitchens, your bedrooms . . . yes, even your lavatory! They're listening to everything. The Foundation keeps meticulous records of every citizen's private conversations, secret phobias, and washing habits . . .

"Washing habits?" Alice asked, arching her eyebrows. "Why would they want to know about that?"

"This is nonsense," Simon said. "I promise you."

"You don't have to convince me. There's an ad for 'dried frog pills' right beneath the story. 'They'll cure all, restore youth and vitality!'" She smirked. "Doesn't exactly inspire a sense of credibility."

A smile tugged at Simon's lips. "No, it doesn't. But you'd be surprised at what some people believe." Absently, he shoved the paper into a nearby bin and kept walking. "You know, that woman gave me an amulet the other day." He removed it from his pocket. It sparkled in the sunlight. "I saved her from a patrol, so this was a sort of thank-you, I suppose. I'd almost forgotten I had it."

"It's pretty," Alice said. "Can I see it?" He placed it in her hand. She studied the silver tentacle. "This looks familiar."

"It's the emblem of Azathoth, apparently. That's the 'Uncreator' she was babbling about."

"An Elder God?"

"The most powerful one. Though he doesn't actually exist, of course."

Alice gave him an inscrutable look. "You're sure about that?"

"Well, it sounds rather ridiculous, doesn't it? Like a fairy tale to frighten children. Huge, terrible beings that live in the dark spaces between worlds and show up on Earth to snack on humans . . . I mean, really? If they exist, why have none of them been seen for centuries? Why do we only have spotty historical records and vague legends?" Alice was silent. "Er . . . do you believe in them?" he asked uneasily.

"I don't know." She handed the amulet back to him. "It does seem strange that people worship them, if they're so terrible."

His fingers closed around the amulet. "I should probably just throw this away. I don't want anyone assuming I'm a cultist."

"You should keep it," Alice said.

His brows knitted together. "Why?"

"It was a gift, wasn't it? You said you saved her. It's a reminder that you helped someone. Even if she *is* a nutter. Who cares what people think?"

He stared at the amulet a moment longer. "I hadn't thought about it that way. Maybe you're right." He draped the amulet around his neck. "I'm sure my father would be appalled if he could see me wearing this. He has a lot of contempt for Chaos-worshippers. Even if his own father was one." Maybe *because* of that, come to think of it. Dr. Hawking didn't talk about Simon's grandfather very often, and when he did, it wasn't exactly in glowing terms.

And yet he'd married a woman with similar beliefs. Or at least, one who was open-minded about such things.

Alice walked alongside him. "Speaking of your father, I've been wondering. Why *did* they kick him out of the Foundation?"

"That was blunt."

She shrugged. "If I'm going to meet him, I want to know what sort of person he is."

"Fair enough. But I don't know why, exactly. My father—both of my parents—are scientists. They always wanted to push the boundaries of what Animism could do, so naturally they didn't always get along with the Foundation. Actually, my father is probably the more conservative of the two. After Olivia . . ." He stopped, taking a breath. "After we lost her, he just sort of . . . pulled away. Focused on his own research." Simon cleared his throat. "Also, he might have showed up drunk at a Council meeting and blasted a hole in the wall."

"Huh." Alice seemed to take the revelation in stride.

Simon stared at his feet. "Do you still want to meet him?" A part of him hoped she'd say no.

"I have nothing to lose and no other options. And we're here now. I may as well. Are we almost there?"

"A few miles. Blackthorn is near the shore, but you can only reach it by going through the city." At her questioning look, he added, "Blackthorn is the name of my father's house."

"Sounds a bit . . . ominous."

"A bit." Simon kept walking, though his steps had grown numb and mechanical. Dark memories stirred and rustled in the back of his head, like a nest of serpents poked with a stick.

He saw Olivia crumpled on the floor like a broken doll,

blood pooling beneath her.

He forced himself to keep walking. *One foot in front of the other*, he thought. *Just keep moving.*

The months after Olivia's death spread out in his mind like a dark, barren landscape: he saw himself lying alone in his bed, staring at the ceiling, unable to move or speak through the fog of grief, as though he were a broken doll himself. He had stopped eating. Even the smell of food had repulsed him. Eventually, he grew so weak that he couldn't leave the bed. He recalled—hazily—one of his father's mechanical spiders sitting beside him, spooning porridge between his lips with one segmented metal limb as another wiped away the dribbles that escaped down his chin.

He had slept little, during those months. Every time he drifted off, the nightmares were waiting. He existed in a numb haze halfway between sleep and waking.

There had been a hospital, briefly—beds with straps, a leather-padded bar between his teeth, cold jelly rubbed onto his temples, and a blinding flash of lightning inside his skull. And then the Healer, and the pills that brought sleep, and a slow, slow climb from the dark pit inside his own head. Only after he'd left Blackthorn, several years later, had the fog of grief finally cleared enough for him to start living again.

And now, after all this time, he was going back home. *Home.* The word tolled like a death knell.

His chest hurt. He stopped, one hand pressed to his

sternum as he fought for breath.

A hand touched his shoulder. "Simon," Alice whispered, "what's wrong?"

"Nothing," he murmured.

His chest heaved. One hand slipped into his pocket and gripped the glass bottle inside. But he couldn't take the medication. Not in front of Alice. The last thing he wanted was to explain his shameful affliction.

A tentacle lightly touched his cheek. "You look like you're about to pass out. Maybe you should sit down—"

"I'm *fine.*" The words came out sharper than he intended. She pulled back.

"Sorry. Just . . . give me a minute." He leaned against the nearest wall. The world swam and warped around him. Blackness ate at the edges of his vision.

If he could just stay on his feet . . .

Sweat dripped from his face, onto the cobblestones. When the worst of it had faded, leaving him shaky with vertigo but still standing, Alice was staring at him wide-eyed.

He wiped his brow and murmured, "Just a bit of indigestion." He forced his lips into a smile. "It's gone now."

She said nothing.

Simon kept walking, gaze fixed straight ahead. For a while, neither spoke as they made their way down a narrow residential street, between rows of drab brick buildings.

"What's that?" Alice said.

"What?"

"Listen."

The clatter of hooves on cobblestones caught his ears, and he tensed. Someone was coming. Surely not a patrol—not on this sleepy side street—but still. The fewer people saw them, the better.

"Hide!" Simon whispered.

Alice didn't hesitate. She darted into a nearby alley, then skittered up the wall like an enormous cloaked beetle, hauling herself up with her tentacles. They stuck to the bricks with their numerous suction cups, pulling her up with remarkable ease and strength, until she disappeared onto the rooftop.

Simon's gaze swept over the street, and he spotted a tall, slender woman riding a meta-powered horse of black iron. She wore a smartly tailored, immaculately fitted green Animist's robe. Simon's heart clenched.

Neeta. His former Master. Why was *she* here?

The horse trotted up beside him, joints clanking, and stopped, steam streaming from its nostrils. Neeta held the reins in her elegant, gloved hands. "Simon Frost," she said. "I've been looking for you." Her dark eyes drilled into his. "You quit your job in the mailroom. Master Melth said you ran off without warning. Is that true?"

No point in denying it. "Yes."

"Do you mind telling me why?" Her tone made it clear that the *do you mind* was just a formality.

He wet his lips. He couldn't tell her the full truth, but an outright lie was too risky. "I got restless. I'd been cooped up in there for so long, just sorting reports, day after day. I started to see those reports in my sleep. I realized that nothing would ever change unless I took matters into my own hands. So I left."

She arched a skeptical brow. "That's all?"

"Yes. That's all. Was that the only reason you tracked me down? To ask why I quit? I hadn't realized you were so worried about me. You've never shown much interest in my life before."

She frowned. "You've gotten bolder."

The words caught him off guard, but it was true—even a few days ago, he wouldn't have dared to speak to her in that tone. "Well, you were the one who kept telling me to grow a spine. To stop being a timid mouse."

"Perhaps I was wrong to push you so hard. Being a mouse is not always a bad thing. Mice can live long and comfortable lives, if they're careful."

That, he thought, *was an odd remark.* He remembered her cryptic story about the ant and the wheelbarrow and wondered what Neeta was hiding from him. She seemed almost to be hinting at something, but he had no idea what, and he didn't care to guess. "Thank you for your concern," he said. "But I'm fine."

She gave him another long, measured look. "What will you do now, then?"

"I don't know. I'll figure something out."

Neeta made a noncommittal sound. She started to turn her horse then stopped. "What is that around your neck?"

Simon touched the silver chain. "Nothing. A street peddler gave it to me."

"Show me."

He hesitated, then lifted the chain, pulling the amulet out from under his robe. Neeta tensed, almost imperceptibly. "I would advise you not to wear that."

"Why?"

"It could give people the wrong idea." She turned her mount. "Be careful, Simon."

"Of what?"

"Just be careful." With a kick, she galloped away.

Chapter Fourteen

"Alice?" Simon peered at the rooftop. "It's safe now. You can come down."

A few seconds passed then her head appeared over the edge of the roof. "Are you sure?"

"Yes. She's gone."

She skittered down the wall in her uncanny, spiderlike way. Her feet touched the ground, and her tentacles vanished beneath her cloak. Her eyes were wide and uncertain. "You're all right?"

"Yes, of course I'm—*oof!*"

She tackled him in a hug, squeezing him tight. Before he even had a chance to catch his breath, she released him and stood, crossing her arms over her chest, her gaze downcast. "Sorry," she muttered. "I just . . . I thought she might take you away somewhere. I was worried you would leave me."

"I wouldn't do that."

She took a deep, unsteady breath, then gave her head a shake. "That was your teacher? That woman?"

"Former teacher." They stood in awkward silence in the empty side street. A flock of pigeons flew by in a rustling flutter of wings, silhouetted against the pale sky. He bit his lower lip. "I feel like I owe you an explanation for the way I acted earlier. Before she arrived."

Alice waited, listening.

Simon opened his mouth, but the words stuck in his throat. He had never told anyone about this—not Neeta, not any of his classmates. At last, he removed the glass bottle from his pocket, pulled out the stopper, and shook the single black capsule into his palm. Inside, a wisp of iridescent purple glimmered.

Alice leaned down, sniffed once, and wrinkled her nose. "What is it?"

"It's medicine."

"You're sick?"

"Yes. Though not in the way you're probably thinking." He gave her a small, mirthless smile. "The Healer calls them 'fits.' They started after Olivia's death. The first time it happened, I believed I was dying. It *feels* like dying. But there's nothing wrong with my body. It's my mind that's broken." His fingers slowly curled around the pill. "The drugs were never meant to be permanent. It was just to get me through the worst of it. Except I never stopped." He swallowed, throat tight. "If you think I'm weak, I don't blame you."

"For what? Being sick, or taking a drug for it?"

"Both, I guess."

For a few heartbeats, she was silent. "I'm the one here with something to be ashamed of," she said. Her tone was low and tight, almost angry. "Not you."

He raised his head. "What do you mean?"

"For Spirit's sake, a man is *dead* because of me."

"That wasn't your fault. You were defending yourself—"

"I panicked," she snapped, "and I lashed out. And now he's buried in the ground."

He stared, taken aback. In the rush of everything that had happened, he had almost forgotten about Brock's brother. It hadn't occurred to him that Alice was probably still thinking about it. But of course. It made sense. It wasn't easy to forget that you had taken a life.

The fire died from her eyes, and she turned away. "Just . . . don't burden yourself with pointless guilt. Not over a thing like this."

Except it was more than that. The pills had become intertwined, in his head, with Olivia's death—with Simon's own inability to prevent it, and his helpless descent into the fog of grief afterward. They'd become symbolic to him of his own weakness. Maybe Alice was right; maybe the shame was his real enemy. But it wasn't that easy to untangle the threads. "I'll try not to," he said. "But . . . only if you promise to try, as well."

She tensed. "It's different for me."

"Not *that* much different." The words felt bold, and warmth crept into his cheeks, but he kept going. "The past is the past. Blaming yourself doesn't bring back the dead. All we can do is try to move forward. Right?"

She looked away and nodded. "I'll try."

He started to slip the pill back into its bottle, but Alice caught his wrist. He gave her a questioning look. "May I see it?"

Puzzled, he handed her the pill. She sniffed it again. "Do you know what's in this?"

"Just some common medicinal herbs. I don't think I ever asked the Healer about the exact ingredients. Why?"

"It smells strange." She handed the pill back to him.

"Your nose must be more sensitive than mine." He slipped the pill back into the bottle. "Anyway, it doesn't matter now. This is my last one."

They resumed walking. She glanced at him sideways. "Your eyes change color. Did you know that? They're hazel now. They were green earlier."

"They look different depending on the light."

"No. They changed," she insisted. "They were *bright* green."

"When?"

"When you were having that fit."

He stared, baffled. "I—I don't know."

She shrugged. "It might have been the light, I suppose." Her gaze searched his face. "You know . . . if you're having second thoughts about this . . ."

"About what?"

"Going back. To where it all happened."

He shook his head. "I made my decision." And where else *could* they go?

⁂

Blackthorn stood atop a stark, rocky cliff overlooking the iron-gray sea. The house had been built crooked; it seemed to lean over the edge of the cliff, as though contemplating a jump. True to its name, its stones were charcoal-colored, and its collection of peaked roofs looked sharp enough to draw blood.

Alice squinted at the mansion on the cliff. "Is it my imagination, or does the house look more shadowy than everything around it?"

"Father dislikes bright sunlight. He says it gives him headaches. He employed some weather Animism to make sure it's always cloudy." He pointed up at a cluster of fat gray clouds hanging over the house.

"So it's always been like that?"

"For a long time." It had been sunny when he and Olivia were children. After her death, his father started pulling the clouds over their home like a shawl. "There's a pathway up the cliff," Simon said. "Around this way."

The path led them up a sort of natural staircase formed from the rock. The mansion loomed before them, its eaves lined with crouching gargoyles. Blackthorn's narrow windows were dark . . . save for one, on the top floor, which glowed with soft yellow light. The laboratory, of course. Was his father there even now, buried in his research?

"What's that?" Alice asked, distracting him. She was staring at something in the far distance, a small dark lump on the horizon, almost invisible against the steely ocean.

"Oh . . . the island? That's Grunewick Laboratory."

"I know that name. They experimented on people there. During the war."

"Yes. But it's been abandoned for a long time, and the sort of experiments they did there have been prohibited since the Foundation began."

"You mean creating Abominations."

"Yes."

A few heartbeats of silence passed.

"So," Alice said, "we just walk in, then?"

"My father has invisible wards and shields around the house to keep out intruders. They won't stop me . . . assuming he hasn't changed them, since I left home. I don't know if they'll let you through. It's better if I talk to him alone at first."

A tentacle flicked restlessly back and forth on the ground. "Fine. I'll wait."

He looked down at the spot near his boots where sun became shade. Bracing himself, he stepped into the bubble of gloom that encompassed the house. A faint tingling passed over his skin. Instantly, the scenery turned darker; he could still see the sunlit world behind him, but it was muted, as if he were looking out at it through a layer of darkened glass.

He took a deep breath and strode forward, down the narrow, overgrown cobblestone path, through a garden filled with silent fountains, bare trees, and neglected flower beds. He kept walking, past an ivy-strangled statue of an angel, its features almost worn off by the elements.

The gardens had gone wild since Olivia's death.

As he neared the steps leading up to the front door, Simon stopped. Every instinct was screaming at him to turn around. There was nothing but pain in this house. But turning around wasn't an option. Maybe it was inevitable, that fate would draw him back here. This house exerted its own gravity.

He glanced over his shoulder. From outside the garden, Alice waved. The sight gave him a bit of strength.

He grabbed the heavy bronze knocker and knocked twice. "Hello?" he called out. His voice cracked. "It's—it's Simon. Is anyone home?"

No response. He tried the door. Unlocked.

He stepped into the house, shutting the door behind him. The entrance hall was vast, cool, and mostly dark. Gas lamps in iron sconces lined the room, emitting a dim glow. He breathed in the house's smell, which was somehow both musty and medicinal, like old carpet and herbs. There was a hint of something danker, as well, something that hadn't been there before—a rot. At the end of the hall, a set of wide, red-carpeted stairs led to the upper levels.

Simon made his way up the stairs and down a long corridor adorned with red carpets. One of his father's spiders—the mechanical golems that roamed the mansion—scuttled along the wall, gobbling up dust bunnies. It looked the same as all the others; round-bodied, bronze, with green glass eyes and clacking mandibles that resembled a mustache. The spider took no notice of Simon.

As a child, he'd never been afraid of them. They were an ordinary part of life, like books or furniture. Now the sight of them made him tense.

At the end of the corridor was a simple wooden door. Simon drew in a slow breath and raised one fist. His hand trembled.

Before he could even gather the nerve to knock, an irritated voice called from beyond the door: "I can hear you breathing out there. If you're going to come in, come in."

He did.

His father's laboratory was a cavernous, stone-walled room, lit by dim yellow meta-lamps. Mismatched tables and chairs stood here and there, every surface covered with precariously stacked books, loose papers, and specimen jars.

A stone table—more of a raised platform—dominated the room's center. His father stood over the table, a white cloth mask covering the lower half of his face, a scalpel in one white-gloved, bloodstained hand. He was in the process of dissecting a purple, horned imp resembling a cross between a monkey and a lizard. Its limbs were splayed out, manacled to the table, its long tongue lolling out of its slack mouth. Bulbous eyes stared at nothing as Dr. Hawking rooted around in its innards.

Simon tried to speak. It took him a few tries before any words emerged. "Do, uh. Do you want me to come back later?"

"No need. It's already dead. The transplant was unsuccessful. Another failure." He wrenched a knot of copper tubes and cogs from the imp's chest and chucked it into a metal tray. It struck with a clank, leaving a smear of dark blood.

Dr. Hawking stripped off his mask and gloves. The corpse had begun to crumble like a sculpture of ash, bits of it flaking away, streams of green smoke rising into the air as it disintegrated.

Simon shuddered. Poor creature. Had it been summoned here just to die for the sake of some experiment?

He forced himself to look away from its death-frozen face and focused on his father.

Dr. Hawking's appearance hadn't changed. He wore the

same shabby, dark green Animist robes and round wire-frame spectacles, and his rumpled hair was gray. It had been gray as long as Simon could remember. His eyes—as always—never seemed to quite focus on Simon, but to stare at a point just beyond him. "I believe it's customary to give some warning before a visit."

Already, Simon could feel himself shrinking down to the size of a beetle. "Sorry. I realize this is short notice, but—"

Simon's father waved the apology away, grabbed his stout wooden cane from where it leaned against the table, and eased himself into a chair. "I presume you have some reason for being here."

"Yes. As a matter of fact. I needed to talk to you."

"About the creature outside?" At Simon's startled expression, he sniffed. "My wards aren't just for show, you know."

"She's not a creature. She's a girl. A person."

"Not human, though. And not an Eldritch creature either. That means it's an Abomination—an entity created or transformed through forbidden Animism."

Simon's heart lurched. "We don't *know* that."

"But that's what you suspect, isn't it?" His gaze drilled into Simon's. "How much *do* you know about this . . . girl?"

"Not much. She doesn't remember her own past. That's part of the problem."

"And what, precisely, do you expect me to do about it?"

"I—I wonder if she could stay here? Just for a little while.

Until we figure out what happened to her. It's not safe for her, wandering around in the outside world."

Dr. Hawking regarded Simon in silence. His eyes were a cool gray, and despite the bloodshot whites, there was a disconcerting sharpness in them—as if he could pluck Simon's soul from his body and weigh it on some invisible scale. "When you were seven years old," he said, "you brought home a kitten. A filthy, half-starved stray crawling with parasites. You begged me to let you keep it. My answer is the same as it was then." He grabbed his cane and pushed himself to his feet with a grunt. "Now, if you'll excuse me . . ."

Frustration squeezed his throat. "Just *talk* to her. Five minutes of your time. That's all it would cost you."

"It could cost me considerably more than that. Right now, the Foundation and I are not on good terms. I've already been expelled as a formal member and stripped of my title as Master. If they were to discover me harboring an Abomination, they could revoke my registration as well. Do you know what that would mean? I couldn't continue my research. Not legally."

His research. Of course. That was all that mattered to him.

"I'll take full responsibility for her," Simon said. "If anything happens, I'll shoulder the blame."

His father's face remained expressionless, but there was a slight tightening around his eyes and mouth. "Are you that desperate for companionship, that you would give up everything to help a girl you barely know?"

"She's my *friend*."

"Whatever the case, my answer hasn't changed. I won't risk—" He froze. The blood drained from his face as he stared at something behind Simon.

Simon turned. Alice stood inside the doorway to the laboratory, hood down, her disheveled dark hair hanging down around her face. She hadn't bothered to cover her tentacles. They writhed around her like the animated petals of some alien flower. "I got tired of waiting," she said. Her eyes glowed purple in the shadows.

A muscle at the corner of Dr. Hawking's eye twitched. "How did you get past my wards?"

"You mean that place where the air got a little thick and tingly?"

For a long moment, they just stared at each other. Dr. Hawking's face was ashen, his lips clamped together. For the first time in Simon's recollection, he looked . . . shaken. Then his expression went blank. "Well, you're here. You might as well stay for dinner."

Father was nothing if not unpredictable.

"This way." He limped toward the door, his footsteps heavy and uneven. His left leg was mechanical, and had been that way as long as Simon could remember. His father had never spoken of how he'd lost it.

They followed him out of the lab; he locked the door behind them.

One of the spiders clattered down the hallway, moving close to the wall, and Alice tensed, stepping away. The spider held a small feather duster clamped in the end of one metal limb. "Is that—?"

"Golem," Simon said. "Like the creepy clown in the marketplace. There are a lot of them around, but they'll leave you alone. They just do the cleaning."

The spider clattered up a wall and began dusting off an iron sconce.

His father limped ahead, ignoring their conversation. He led them to a spacious but sparsely furnished bathing chamber with stone walls and a claw-foot tub large enough to drown in. He glanced at Alice. "You'll want to get changed out of those filthy rags first. I'll have the golems bring you some clean clothes while you wash. Veera left some of her old things here. They should fit you well enough. Simon, you come with me."

Simon hesitated.

"Go on," Alice said.

Simon nodded, uncertain, and followed Dr. Hawking down the hall. He wasn't sure what to make of his father's sudden hospitality.

His attitude had completely changed the moment he laid eyes on Alice. Why?

Chapter Fifteen

The dining hall was long and high-ceilinged. An elegantly carved table ran down the center. Simon took a seat at one end, his father at the other.

Simon's eyes wandered to a spot on the floor. Olivia's blood had long since been scrubbed off, but a faint stain had lingered through the years, a slightly darker patch on the stone.

Dr. Hawking poured himself a glass of wine and took a long swig. "You say she doesn't remember her past."

"No. Only the last few months."

"And where did you find her?"

"Near Splithead Creek. She was hiding in an abandoned cabin. I went there because we'd received a request for aid from the villagers. They claimed a monster was living in the nearby mountains. Turned out she was the monster. She can transform into a sort of . . . dragon. Or something like a dragon. With tentacles. Though she has those all the time. You probably noticed."

His father shook his head and muttered something under his breath.

"You know something. Don't you?"

"I know that she shouldn't exist," he snapped. "How she came into being, I have no idea. But I can tell you this—you shouldn't be walking around the city with that creature. If you were spotted together . . ."

"Stop calling her a *creature.* Her name is Alice." Simon's hands were clenched into fists in his lap, white-knuckled. His father *was* holding something back. He was sure of it. But he knew, from long experience, that pushing for answers would only make him clamp up harder. "And no one got a clear look at her. We made sure of that."

"Good." Dr. Hawking poured himself more wine. "Have you been taking your medication?"

The question caught Simon off guard. His father had a way of doing that—changing the topic suddenly. He opened his mouth to reply, but the words stuck in his throat. He didn't know how his father would react to the fact that Simon had been weaning himself off the pills. What business was it of his, anyway? "Yes. Of course."

Dr. Hawking nodded.

Soft footsteps broke the silence. Simon looked up.

Alice stood at the foot of the stairs, one hand resting on the banister. Her dark hair was freshly washed and shiny; her gray skin glowed with a clean, healthy sheen. She wore a simple dress—dark gray, tinged with lavender—with long sleeves and pearl buttons running up the front. One of his mother's. It was sober yet elegant, and wide enough to accommodate her tentacles; they trailed behind her, looking almost like a part of the dress, like some elaborate train with a life of its own. He would've thought that feminine clothes would look out of place on her, but no. They complemented—rather than clashed with—her strangeness.

Simon stared.

She fidgeted. "What?"

"Nothing. It's just . . . I've never seen you in a dress."

She glanced down at herself, frowning, and plucked at the fabric. "Is it showing too much?"

"N-no. It's fine. It looks nice."

Snug or not, the dress was, if anything, overly prim. The long sleeves and high neckline resembled something a librarian or a schoolteacher would wear. She looked much more . . . normal. More like a girl, which made him aware that she *was* a girl. And Simon had always been completely hopeless around girls his own age. Alice was so different that he'd forgotten to be nervous around her, but now the old awkwardness came rushing back.

Silly, he thought, that a change of outfit could have such a dramatic effect on him. It was probably evidence of shallowness on his part.

"Have a seat," Dr. Hawking said.

She approached the table and sat next to Simon.

A pair of spiders clack-clacked out of the kitchen, carrying a steaming pot of stew. More came behind with platters of bread and vegetables. Dr. Hawking lifted the pot by the side handles, set it on the table, and scooped the food into his bowl. "Help yourself." He hunched over his plate and began spooning stew into his mouth.

Simon dished out some stew for himself and passed the pot to Alice, who took twice as much. His stomach was a shriveled ball, but he forced himself to take a bite.

Alice polished off her bowl and dished out more stew, then reached up with one of her tentacles, grabbed a bottle of wine, and poured some into her glass. When she realized both Simon and Dr. Hawking were staring at her, she froze. "What? Is this rude?"

"I don't believe there is any established etiquette as to the use of one's tentacles at the dinner table," Dr. Hawking replied. "Though I *do* believe you're too young to be legally drinking."

Alice shrugged. "I overheard you talking to Simon. My whole existence is illegal, isn't it?"

"Fair point."

"Anyway, I've never had wine. I want to taste it." She took a sip, grimaced . . . then took another sip. With another tentacle, she grabbed a hunk of bread from the platter and dunked it in her stew.

A few crumbs fell to the floor. One of the spiders scurried over and swept them up.

Simon stirred his stew around and poked at a potato with his fork.

"Oh for Spirit's sake," she said. "*Eat.*"

He raised his eyebrows.

She flushed, gray cheeks darkening. "Sorry. It's just . . . you never *eat* anything." She pointed her fork at him. "Food is necessary for survival, you know."

"I suppose you're right." He dunked some bread in his stew and took a bite.

Dr. Hawking watched the exchange expressionlessly.

Alice polished off another bowl. "Is there any coffee?"

"No. No coffee." A bit of stew dribbled down his gray-stubbled chin as he ate. He didn't seem to notice.

Once they'd finished, the spiders reappeared and began collecting the dirty plates. Simon had grown up with them, but he'd almost forgotten just how remarkable they were. One reared up on its two sets of hind legs and used its long, many-jointed forelimbs to collect the bowls and stack them atop its back, then clackety-clacked off toward the kitchen.

Dr. Hawking stood, clutching his cane. He fixed his piercing gaze on Alice. "Girl. If you don't mind, I would like to speak to you alone in my laboratory."

Simon tensed. An image of the unfortunate imp, splayed out on his father's dissection table, sprang into his head. "Why alone?"

"Because I have some questions to ask her, and I don't require an audience."

Simon opened his mouth to argue, but Alice placed a hand on his arm. He looked at her in surprise. "It's all right," she said quietly. "This is why I came here. Isn't it? To figure out the truth?"

Alice stood.

He watched, feeling helpless, as she followed his father up the stairs and disappeared.

The minutes ticked by.

Unable to bear the wait, he walked up to the laboratory and pressed his ear to the closed door, but he could hear nothing. The silence was unnerving. With a sigh, he sat down on the floor, his back against the wall.

Father wouldn't actually hurt Alice. Would he?

He was thinking about knocking when, finally, the door creaked open. Simon leaped to his feet. "Alice?" She stepped out and closed the door behind her. "Are you—?"

"I'm fine." Her eyes held a distant, preoccupied look. "He said I can stay here for the night."

Simon waited, but she didn't seem inclined to say anything else.

He cleared his throat. "Well, I'll show you to one of the spare rooms." Simon began to walk, Alice trailing behind him. "So what did the two of you talk about in there?"

"Not much. He asked me some questions about myself,

which I mostly couldn't answer. Then he took a blood sample, along with some hair and nail clippings. He said they would be valuable for his research." She produced three empty glass vials from a pocket of her dress. "He also gave me these, and told me to—and I quote—'fill them with any fluids I can produce and return them to the lab as soon as possible.'"

Simon winced. "Sorry. He can be very forward."

She shrugged and pocketed the vials. "I'm as curious about the answers as he is."

Simon watched her from the corner of his eye. "Did he say anything else to you?"

"He told me to—and again, I quote—'keep your tentacles off my son.'"

A small, choked sound escaped Simon's throat.

"Seems he's rather protective," Alice remarked.

"That's not the word I'd use." Simon's father had never expressed the slightest interest in his personal life before. Why now? Did he just hate the fact that Simon had finally made a friend? Was he already trying to drive a wedge between them, out of sheer spite? "I don't see how it's any of his business," he muttered.

"Well, apparently he has a strict policy against you getting involved with Abominations."

"I hope he didn't call you that to your face."

She shrugged. "It's what I am, isn't it? Anyway, I told him

that I was here to figure out how I could get back to normal, and that was all."

Anger bubbled up in him at his father's outrageous rudeness. He pushed the feeling aside. Dr. Hawking was allowing Alice to stay; for now that was all that mattered.

Most of the spare rooms Simon checked were either being used for storage or were so caked with dust it would take hours to make them habitable. The spiders only cleaned what they were instructed to; evidently, Dr. Hawking didn't consider most of the rooms worth bothering with.

There was one, though, that he knew was kept spotless. The idea of giving Alice Olivia's old room made him uncomfortable, but it would probably be the most hospitable.

Still, when they reached the door, he hesitated, hand on the knob.

"What's wrong?" Alice asked.

"Nothing." He pushed the door open. The hinges squeaked.

Olivia's room was just as it had been when she was alive. The bed was still made, covered with a soft down comforter patterned with flowers. The mirror over the dresser was still polished and bright. A stuffed rabbit with bright button eyes sat on the bed.

Alice surveyed the room. "It's very . . . pink." A brief pause. "Wait, is this—"

"Yes. It was hers." He turned away. "We, um. We should get some sleep."

"I guess so."

He lingered, his eyes searching her face. His mind drifted to the mysterious, egg-like pod in the mountains. "Alice . . . what's your very first memory?"

Her teeth caught on her lower lip. "I remember that it was dark. I couldn't breathe. And then . . . suddenly I was in the forest, and it was raining. But it's like remembering a dream. It's all muddled together." She clutched the hem of the dress and curled a tentacle around her legs. "I don't know what he'll find when he analyzes those samples. I don't know if . . ." Her voice caught. "Simon . . . what if I'm wrong? What if I was never human?"

"It doesn't matter. You're Alice. That's all I need to know."

They stood in silence a moment longer, just looking at each other. Her eyes caught the lamplight like a cat's, shining. Her lips parted, quivering slightly, and for a moment, she seemed about to say something else . . . then she turned away. "Good night," she whispered. The door shut softly behind her.

Simon made his way down the hall, toward his own bedroom. He paused in front of a familiar door—his mother's study. Lightly, he touched the knob. He hadn't set foot in this room since her disappearance. Even when she was here, he hadn't been allowed in the study unsupervised.

He pushed open the door, revealing a round space,

crammed floor to ceiling with bookshelves, the books all still there, covered in a fine layer of dust. Dust, too, lay over the moss-colored carpet with its light golden pattern of leaves. An ornately carved, claw-foot table stood in the center. On it sat an empty teacup, untouched—there was still a faint smudge of red lipstick on the rim, faded with time—alongside a silver comb with a few long, golden strands of hair caught in its teeth. If not for the dust, his mother might have been in here just this afternoon. His throat knotted, and he swallowed until it loosened.

He trailed his fingers over the books' spines, pausing on one. The wrinkled leather felt familiar. He pulled it out, studying the blank cover, which had a mummified, foreboding look to it. He flipped to the first page and saw the drawing of the tentacle curled around the sphere: the symbol of the Chaos-worshippers.

He recognized it. It was the book his mother had given him for a present so long ago, the one his father hadn't allowed him to read. As a child, he'd snuck into her study once or twice and peeked inside the book's pages, but he'd always been too frightened to look closely. It felt as though the tome held some dark power—as though a pair of scaly, clawed hands might reach out of the pages and pull him in.

Silly. Of course.

He flipped through the pages now. Each one contained a detailed ink drawing of a god, followed by a chapter of description. There was Yig, the man-eating serpent—Crom Cruach, a vast, spiny worm with a round mouth full of teeth—Ghatanothoa, which was little more than a mass of writhing tentacles and bulging eyes.

Such beings couldn't truly exist. Could they? They all looked as though they'd crawled out of the feverish hallucinations of a madman.

He turned a page to the chapter marked *Azathoth*. Unlike the others, it contained no illustration, just a blank spot on the page, and a few brief paragraphs beneath that: *There are only a few scattered references to Azathoth in ancient texts. It is referred to as the blind idiot god and the Demon Sultan, as well as a source of unfathomable power. It is unclear, however, whether Azathoth is an actual entity, a symbolic representation of these concepts, or something else altogether. Some scholars have put forth the idea that Azathoth is, in fact, another name for the Outer Realm—a dimension of pure, chaotic energy, which exists between worlds.*

There are those who worship Azathoth, but they are mad.

Simon shivered, closed the book, and slid it back onto the shelf. The amulet lay heavy around his neck. He stood, breathing in the all-too-familiar scent of the study. He ran his fingers over the table, leaving trails in the dust.

"Mother," he whispered into the silence, "where are you? Why did you leave us?"

There was, of course, no answer.

He retreated to his old room. Like Olivia's, it had been preserved and kept clean. It was more or less the same as he'd left it over two years ago.

He washed up then dug through the dresser until he found his old nightclothes. He was surprised to discover that—though snug and a bit short in the legs—they still fit.

He wondered, sometimes, if the medication had stunted his growth as a side effect. Though he'd always been on the small side.

He crawled into bed.

Despite his exhaustion, sleep wouldn't come. He rolled onto his side, staring at the wall, breathing in the smell of his bedding. So many familiar smells in this house. And each one awakened a flurry of memory.

When he and Olivia were very small, they had shared this room. They'd stayed up late, whispering stories to each other by the faint light of a meta-flame.

"What do you want to be when you grow up?" he'd asked her.

"I'm going to be a strong Animist," she said. "I'll be a fighter and a Healer and a demon tamer and a famous inventor, and at night I'll be a bandit and wear a red kerchief over my face as a disguise, but I'll only steal from wicked rich people and I'll give all their gold to hungry orphans. And maybe someday I'll be Queen. Only I won't be a stuffy sourpuss like Queen Saphronia. I'll have lots of parties, and I'll invite people from all over the Continent, and there'll be loads of good food and cakes with lemon icing."

"You can't do *all* those things," Simon said.

"Why not?"

"Well . . . if you're a bandit at night and a queen during the day, when will you sleep? You'll get tired."

"No I won't. I never get tired. What about you? What will you do when you get older?"

"Oh . . . I don't know. I guess . . ." He stopped, frowning thoughtfully. "I guess if you're going to do all that, you'll need someone to help you."

She giggled. "Don't worry about me. What do *you* want?"

"I want . . ." He stared at the ceiling. He thought and thought. But he couldn't find a good answer, even then. He knew that he wanted to do something important, something that made a difference, but he couldn't envision it. He'd envied Olivia for how certain she seemed about everything. It was never a question of *could* she do it. Just *when*.

When they turned six, she wanted her own room. He'd cried himself to sleep the first few nights after she left; the room had seemed cold and empty, full of shadows, and though she was just down the hall, it felt as though a vast gulf separated them. Vast as the chasm between life and death.

Simon's throat tightened.

He thought longingly of the shiny black pill, still sitting in the bottom of the bottle on his nightstand. His tongue crept out to wet his sandpaper lips. A dull, sickly pain had taken root in his skull, pressing against the backs of his eyeballs with each heartbeat. His body was rebelling, crying out for the drug he'd denied it for so long.

Still, he resisted.

Alice had said the pill smelled funny. For some reason, that remark stuck in his head, wriggling in the back of his brain. It did seem strange now, to him, that he had never asked questions, never wondered *what*, exactly, he was taking. A small, cold seed of dread had taken root deep inside his chest.

He climbed out of bed. Still in his pajamas and slippers, he walked down the hall, back to his mother's study, and summoned a tiny meta-flame. It danced over the tip of his finger as he scanned the shelves, trailing the fingers of his other hand over the familiar spines until he found the title he was looking for—*Botany for Animists*.

He slid it out and flipped through the pages. The plants were arranged in alphabetical order, each with a small ink drawing, the parts labeled.

Bloodweed: a dark red grass with stimulant properties, which can be mixed into a paste and used to amplify the effects of certain summoning spells.

Corpse flower: a small white blossom, faintly tinged with

blue. The odor of corpse flower is repulsive to humans, reminis-
cent of rotting flesh, hence the name, but imps and demons find
it intoxicating. Its petals are sometimes used in the training of
demon familiars.

He turned to the back of the book and found the entry
he'd been searching for:

Vinculum root: a black root which, when ingested, acts as a
powerful sedative. It also has the unique property of suppressing
an Animist's ability to use meta. In liquefied and distilled form,
it is iridescent purple. Its odor is distinct and pungent to demons
and other entities, but undetectable to humans.

Simon's mouth had gone dry. Could it be . . . ?

No. Ridiculous. His medicine came from a reputable
Healer. Why would she secretly give him vinculum root?

Unless it hadn't been her idea.

Dr. Hawking, his father, was the one who'd chosen the
Healer, who'd arranged for Simon to be sent there, and
who'd ensured that his medication kept arriving each month,
even after Simon left home. Dr. Hawking had never wanted
him to be an Animist. From the beginning, he'd discour-
aged Simon with probing questions designed to plant seeds
of doubt.

Are you sure your nerves can handle the strain?

Animists must sometimes do unpalatable things for the greater
good. Do you have the stomach for that?

But *why*? Why would his father sabotage him? It didn't

make any sense. He slid the book back onto the shelf and rubbed his damp forehead.

He started to walk back to his bedroom . . . then stopped. Turned.

Breathing quietly, he crept down the hall toward his father's laboratory.

The door was closed. His father, he knew, sometimes slept in his lab. Simon knocked on the door. "Hello?"

No response.

He tried the knob. Unlocked.

Holding his breath, he slowly turned the knob, opened the door a crack, and peeked through. The room appeared empty. His gaze traced the hulking shapes of furniture, outlined by the faint, pulsating glow of the meta-flame dancing over his finger. Dr. Hawking must have already retired to his bedroom. Ordinarily, he locked the laboratory's door when he wasn't inside. Years of living alone had made him careless.

Simon slipped inside, heart hammering his ribs.

What was he *doing*? He didn't even know what he was looking for. And if he was caught . . .

Best not to think about that.

He walked straight to his father's desk and studied the messy papers sprawled across it. They were covered with incomprehensible notes, rows of equations, figures, and graphs that meant nothing to Simon. He shuffled the papers around then opened a drawer. Inside, atop a stack of more papers, sat a tiny bronze key.

He removed it, turning it over in his fingers, and glanced at the row of locked cabinets lining the wall.

He tried a few of the locks before the key clicked into place and turned. He opened the cabinet, revealing rows of jars filled with yellowish fluid. Several contained nondescript bits of tissue, and one held a yellow reptilian eyeball. In the largest jar floated a mouse with dull, moss-green fur. Instead of chisel-shaped rodent teeth, it had tiny saber-like fangs. Its belly was plated like an iguana's. A dozen misshapen eyes protruded from its back. Its mouth was open, its little limbs contorted, as though the poor thing had died squealing in agony.

Attached to the jar was a yellowing label: *Species: Common mouse. Injected with shoggoth cells immediately after death. Revived and lived approx. five minutes before expiring.*

Simon wasn't clear on the legality of attempting to bring animals back from the dead. The prohibition was only against reviving humans. But he *was* fairly sure that the Foundation wouldn't condone these experiments.

On the bottom shelf were a number of thick leather-bound notebooks. He flipped through one—more figures and incomprehensible notes—and picked up another. Several photographs slipped out and fluttered to the floor. Hastily, he picked them up . . . and froze.

The photographs were all of dead bodies, discolored and

bloated, on autopsy tables. One was a girl, thin and pale, her eyes closed, a line of stitches running down the center of her chest and stomach.

Alice.

Dry-mouthed, he turned the photo over, revealing a date scrawled on the back, a date from almost three years ago, and a series of notes printed in black ink: *Alice Tanner. Age of death, approx. fourteen. Homeless. No known family.*

And another note at the bottom, scrawled in his father's spidery cursive: *Corpse acquired approx. ten hours after death.*

Simon's hands were shaking.

From downstairs, he heard approaching footsteps—the distinctive, uneven clomp and shuffle of his father's artificial leg. Hastily, he shoved the notebook back into the cabinet, locked it, and returned the key to the drawer. Still clutching the photograph of Alice, he darted out of the laboratory and down the hall, back to his own bedroom, and slammed the door.

He sat on the edge of the bed, his breaths coming hard and fast. The story from the *Underground* floated through his head. Grave-robbing. Bodies disappearing mysteriously from the city morgue. Experiments.

He looked again at the photograph. It *was* Alice. There was no mistaking that face.

A black hole was opening up inside him, and he was falling. The picture slipped from his hand.

A rippling shimmer distorted the air. The space around him stretched like rubber, the walls elongating and then receding. The warble of distant flutes filled his ears.

And then the world vanished.

⁓

He stood in a desert, looking up at a sky whorled with jewel-like stars. A pair of doors loomed before him. He couldn't remember where he'd been a moment ago, or how he had gotten here.

"Hello, Simon," said a mild little voice, and he turned to see the shadow-thing standing behind him, its eyes blank circles.

"What is this? Did you bring me here?"

The shadow tilted its head. "*You* came here."

"I don't even know where 'here' is." And yet he had the sense that he had seen this place before. He looked around, trying to collect his thoughts. "This isn't the Eldritch Realm."

"No. You might say we are somewhere far beyond that. But you might also say that we are inside you, and that this place exists inside everyone."

Riddles. How he hated riddles. "I'd ask you who you are, but I have a feeling I've asked that before, and you didn't answer me. As a matter of fact, this entire conversation feels very familiar."

"You've retained a bit of memory. Very good. As to who I

am, well. I am you. That's one answer, anyway."

"Pretty sure we're not the same person."

"Well, I'm not the fussy little 'you' that sits at the front desk of your mind, if that's what you mean. I dwell in the dark spaces between your thoughts. I am more 'you' than you."

This line of questioning was going nowhere. "You said I came here on my own."

"It's true. It's the simplest thing in the world, to come here—you merely look between the cracks of the pieces that make up yourself, and you slip through. Like water through a broken vase."

Simon *had* been here before. He knew it. Why couldn't he remember? "Those doors . . ." He stared at them. They loomed, a freestanding, one-sided impossibility. "That's the cathedral," he whispered. "The cathedral of bones."

"So, that's what it looks like to you? Interesting. Would you like to go in again?"

Holding his breath, Simon stretched out an arm. The doors opened, just a hairsbreadth, and green light bled through. He could hear voices on the other side, he realized. They were laughing. Or maybe screaming. Or both. They were, he realized, the voices of everyone who had ever existed, the living and the dead—humans, demons, animals, creatures he couldn't begin to comprehend. The light pulled at him, trying to draw him in.

This place—it was connected to everything. To the entire universe.

His mother's face filled his mind. Was she here, too?

He felt himself pulled toward the doors, toward the light. *Yes.*

"She's waiting for me," he whispered. "Somewhere in there. I feel it."

"Call out to her, if you wish. She may hear you. Though, I should warn you, there are other things listening."

"Like what?"

The shadow shrugged its insubstantial shoulders. "Things."

Simon pushed the doors. They didn't budge.

"There is the matter of the toll," said the shadow.

He remembered this part. "You want some of my essence. So how much can you take before it starts to affect me?"

"That's the question, isn't it?"

He sighed and raked a hand through his hair. "Fine. Just do it."

Its arm stretched toward him, thinning into a tendril, which touched his heart. A chill settled into his bones.

For a moment, he couldn't remember his own name. Or anything else. There was only a frightening blank. *Who am I?* There was someone . . . a girl . . .

Then the shadow withdrew its tendril, and memory rushed back, leaving him shaken.

"Go ahead," the shadow said.

Simon flung the doors open and strode through, into the cathedral. It was just as he remembered: the bone chandeliers, the skeletal birds, the scythe-carrying, winged creature looming over the well of light. Its head tilted, creaking; its jaws parted. One arm stretched out, offering the chalice.

Slowly, like a sleepwalker, Simon approached the well, but this time, he ignored the proffered cup. Instead, he leaned down and submerged his entire head. Cool, misty green filled his eyes. And then there was only blackness. He had the impression of enormous space stretching into infinity. "Mother?" he called. His voice collapsed into echoes then was swallowed whole by the immense silence of the abyss.

A voice called out, tiny and faraway. *Simon.*

His heart leaped. "Mother! Where are you?"

She didn't answer. Instead, a vision unfolded itself in his head: a massive, dark, sprawling shape, like a tree stretching its branches into a pale green sky. The vision winked out an instant later, and there was only the all-swallowing void. He was alone in silence. *"Mother!"* No response.

Then a single filmy yellow eye opened in the blackness.

It was looking straight at him. He heard a voice—a growl like the shifting of tectonic plates. His skull vibrated with the force of it.

"Mnahn . . . grah'n . . . shugg-oth . . ."

The words twisted themselves into his head like vines,

wriggling deeper, trying to anchor themselves into him. They were *pulling*, drawing him deeper, and he felt himself stretched like taffy, the edges of his consciousness softening and blurring . . .

❧

He was back in his bedroom. The world swam around him, soft and hazy and transparent. He could still see the cathedral behind it, like a shape at the bottom of a rushing stream, as though the real world were only a thin layer of paint, a mere shadow cast by a deeper reality.

The memory of that terrible voice filled his mind—the overwhelming sense of darkness and power. That *thing*, whatever it was . . . it could have crushed him. If he'd lingered another moment, it would have. He felt that with a cold, soul-deep certainty.

He grabbed the pill bottle from the nightstand. It slipped from his trembling hands and shattered on the floor. Reality faded in and out around him as he fumbled through the shards, cutting his finger on a jagged edge of glass. Blood dripped to the stone tiles as he grabbed the capsule.

Despite his newfound suspicions, he wanted it. It would calm the terror. He raised it toward his mouth . . . then, at the last minute, he forced himself to lower his hand. *No more.* He dropped the pill to the floor and crushed it beneath his foot. It burst open and sank into the stones, forming a dark stain.

Breathing raggedly, he shut his eyes and pressed the heels of his hands against them. When he finally cracked his eyelids open again, the cathedral's shadow had vanished. His bedroom snapped back into place, real and solid. Exhausted, shivering, he sank into bed and pressed his hands to his face. A low moan escaped him. The memories were a chaotic, nightmarish blur.

He didn't know what he had seen or heard. Didn't even know if it was real, or if the last thread of his sanity had finally snapped.

His gaze fell on the photograph of Alice, lying on the floor amidst the glass shards. A drop of his blood marred her pale form. He reached out slowly, as though his arm were moving through water, and picked up the glossy square of paper.

The door cracked open. Simon stuffed the photograph beneath his pillow.

His father stood in the doorway, silhouetted in the faint light of the hall. "Simon, what's going on? I heard you cry out."

"Nothing," Simon mumbled. "Just a bad dream."

"Your hand is bleeding."

"I cut my finger on a piece of glass. It's not serious."

His father hesitated. Shadow drowned his face; Simon couldn't read his expression. "I'll be in my laboratory. If you need anything . . ."

"I'm fine."

Slowly, the door creaked shut. Simon held his breath and listened to the scrape of receding footsteps.

Once he was sure his father was gone, he sprang out of bed and raced to Alice's room. She was sleeping soundly. He shook her awake. She stirred and groaned, blinking luminous purple eyes at him. "Simon, what . . ."

"We have to go. Now."

She rubbed her eyes. "Leave Blackthorn? Why? We just got here."

Simon raked his hands through his hair. "I snuck into my father's laboratory, and I saw . . ." His eyes lost focus, and he shuddered. "I think he may have done something terrible."

She hesitated. "Maybe it's not what you think. Have you asked him about it?"

Simon's teeth caught his lower lip, and for a few seconds he considered the idea—then he shook his head. "Too risky."

"You think he would hurt you? Your own father?"

"It's not myself I'm afraid for."

A pause. "Just what did you see?" she whispered.

"His experiments. He's been . . . reanimating corpses." Even speaking the words aloud made him nervous.

"So? Maybe it's against the Foundation's laws, but how does that concern us?"

"There's more to it."

Alice pushed the covers aside and sat up. She was wearing

a knee-length cotton nightgown, loose enough to accommodate her tentacles. Not ideal traveling clothes, but nothing in Veera's wardrobe was. "It *must* be bad. You look like you've seen a ghost."

He laughed; the sound emerged a little too high-pitched. A lunatic sound. He clapped a hand over his mouth and muttered, "Excuse me," as though he'd hiccupped or burped.

She stared. "Simon . . . your eyes . . ."

"What?"

"They're green again."

He shivered, shut his eyes tight, and forced himself to breathe slowly. His eyes opened. "Now?"

"Hazel," she said.

He didn't have time to try to puzzle out what was going on with his eyes, or how it was connected to any of this. But he had a feeling it had something to do with the cathedral. With that shadow. "Never mind that," he said. "I'll tell you everything once we're out of Blackthorn. Just . . . trust me. Please?"

She gave him a strange, sad smile. "What else can I do? You're the only friend I have in this world."

A lump rose into his throat. "Alice . . . I'm sorry. I brought you here, and now—"

She sighed. "Well, the food was good, anyway." She stretched out a tentacle and grabbed her patched, ragged cloak from the nightstand, where she had draped it. "Where are we going? Any ideas?"

"The train station. There's a train that leaves Eidendel at midnight—the last one. If we're quick we can catch it."

"Where to, then?"

"I don't know."

She stood and slipped into her cloak. "Well, we'll figure it out on the way."

Part II

In Realms Apart

Chapter Sixteen

Fog lay over Eidendel like a damp woolen blanket. The moon hung overhead, a pale sickle shrouded in clouds. Simon wore his Animist's robe and a pack with a few essentials— biscuits and dried fruit hastily snatched from the kitchen, a change of clothes, and a knife, wrapped in cloth. He took the photograph of Alice, too.

He still wore the amulet, the gift from the newspaper seller. Now he clutched it tight, feeling its smooth warmth against his palm as he and Alice hurried through the moon-lit streets. His thoughts spun in dizzying circles. He knew that something had happened to him after he fled his father's laboratory. He'd seen and heard things that seemed both less and more real than reality—a vision? A dream—but he couldn't bring the memories into focus. Had he really felt his mother's presence, or had it all been an illusion?

He wished desperately that she were here now. She would know what to do.

He pushed the thoughts away. *Just get out of the city. Away from Blackthorn.* He'd worry about the rest later. If he stopped moving now, panic would set in. So he kept running, clutching Alice's hand tight in his, as though he could outrun his thoughts.

The city was silent and still. Unusually still. The glow of streetlamps burned dim yellow circles through the haze. Pale buildings loomed like sculptures carved of bone. The comparison touched faint memories in Simon's head. *A cathedral of bones . . .*

Where had he seen such a thing?

He and Alice walked past a gas lamp, and their shadows flowed across the wall. Overhead, air whooshed, and a breeze stirred the hairs on the back of Simon's neck. He looked up just in time to see a grayish-white, hairless form soaring on leathery bat wings. It circled, looked down with burning red eyes, and screeched, then swooped away into the darkness.

"What was that?" Alice asked.

"A wraith," Simon whispered. "An Eldritch creature."

"So it was summoned by an Animist?"

"Yes." And it had just spotted them, which wasn't good.

Easy, he told himself. As far as that thing knew, they were just two pedestrians out for a stroll at night. But often, Eldritch creatures could see and sense things that humans couldn't. If it sensed what Alice was—

He quickened his pace. There was nothing to do but keep moving.

They hurried through the streets in breathless silence, making their way toward the train station.

"Someone is coming," Alice murmured.

Simon froze, listening. The clip-clop of hooves on cobbles reached his ears. His back stiffened. A patrol.

A line of horses stamped through puddles, splashing water. They were headed straight toward him. "Hide," he whispered to Alice, gripping her arm. They ducked into a nearby alley and waited, holding their breath. The hoofbeats stopped.

"Come out, Swoony. I know it's you. My wraith can smell you."

He recognized the voice. *Oh, Spirit. Not* him.

"Come out, or I'm coming in."

Simon stepped out of the alley, heart hammering. Alice remained where she was, concealed in fog.

Brenner sat astride his horse at the head of the patrol, a pale, winged form crouched on his shoulder, its creepily human-looking mouth open in a toothy grin. The wraith let out another shriek, then vanished in a puff of smoke.

"Handy little creatures, aren't they?" Brenner asked coolly. "They were my suggestion. Every night, the patrols summon a few dozen of them. Much easier to keep an eye on things from the air. Any suspicious activity is instantly reported."

"I'm just out for a walk," Simon said, keeping his tone neutral. "There's nothing suspicious about that, is there?"

"Well, that remains to be seen."

Brenner's minions remained motionless on their mounts. Brenner urged his horse forward until it was standing directly in front of Simon, who stood rigid, fighting the urge to bolt.

Brenner stretched out one arm, holding his whip. Simon tensed as Brenner placed the whip handle under his chin, tilting it upward. Simon didn't move, didn't react. "That cut has healed up nicely, I see." The whip handle pressed harder against his jaw, forcing his head back at an uncomfortable angle. "You remember that incident with the newspaper seller? Apparently, *someone* reported me, and Neeta—*your* old Master—had me disciplined for 'excessive cruelty.' Seven cracks with my own whip."

Simon's eyes widened. He hadn't actually expected Neeta to punish Brenner.

Brenner gave him a hard smile. "She did it herself, the sadistic cow. Told me that if I could take it without crying out, I could keep my position. 'A man who wields the whip must know what it feels like.' Those were her words. At the moment, I'm not feeling very charitable toward whoever reported me. Any ideas on who it was? Well, Swoony?"

He said nothing. It seemed like the safest course.

Brenner kept the whip handle under Simon's chin,

pressing painfully into the soft flesh there. "So. Do you often walk around the city alone at night? Rather a dangerous habit for a weakling like you, isn't it? You never know what you might run into."

"It's touching that you're so concerned for my well-being," Simon muttered.

Brenner's eyes narrowed. "You will address me as 'sir.'"

Simon knew he couldn't afford to antagonize Brenner. Not now. Maybe if he said the right things, Brenner would leave. But at that moment, the pressure of every humiliation and defeat, every cruel taunt he'd ever endured at Brenner's hands, came bubbling up inside him. He met Brenner's gaze, his jaw tense, and replied, "Sod off."

The whip handle cracked across his face, hard. Simon lost his balance, slipped, and landed on his back. The impact knocked the wind from his lungs.

Simon started to push himself to his feet. Brenner leaped off his horse and planted a boot on Simon's chest, shoving down. "Let me go," Simon gasped.

"Or what?" Brenner pressed down harder.

He gritted his teeth. He grabbed Brenner's ankle with his right hand, pressed his left palm to the ground, and drew meta up through the stones. Smoke curled from beneath the fingers of his right hand, and Brenner's pant leg blackened and crackled. Brenner yelped and stumbled backward. "You little . . ." He sounded more stunned than angry. "You *burned* me!"

Brenner's minions let out a collective *ooooh* from atop their mounts, breaking their silence. "You gonna take that, Bren?" one girl asked.

Brenner's eyes narrowed. "Shut up, Haru." He leaned down, grabbed a fistful of Simon's curls, and hissed into his ear: "I warned you not to cross me."

Panic leaped in Simon's chest. He struggled, kicking, fingernails scrabbling against the cobblestones. His ragged breathing echoed through his ears. Brenner shoved him down, pressed a boot into his stomach, and raised his whip.

Simon covered his face with his arms. He heard the whistle as the whip started to come down . . . and then it stopped. Slowly, he lowered his arms.

Alice stood over him, one arm raised, the whip wrapped around her forearm as she glared at Brenner. Brenner's upper lip curled back from his teeth. "Damn it! Get away from—" He stopped, mouth open. The blood drained from his face, and the whip retracted with a *snick*.

Alice's face had changed. Simon could see a long snout, full of fangs, poking out from under her hood. Simon scrambled to his feet, still gasping for breath.

Brenner stood rigidly, face pale. "What are you?" His voice wavered.

She glared at him.

He tugged his whip free and raised it again. "Stay back!"

The whip flicked out, snapping across Alice's face.

She grabbed the whipcord and yanked the weapon out of his hand, tossing it aside like a toy.

The other patrol members edged away. Their mounts pranced and reared, whinnying. "What *is* that thing?" Haru asked, shaky-voiced.

Alice crouched protectively over Simon, a low growl rumbling from her throat. Brenner backed away, white as cottage cheese. "Monster," he whispered.

"Alice!" Simon cried.

Her head turned slowly toward him, and a chill seeped into his veins. Her face was reptilian, covered with dark gray scales. Her eyes had gone blank and feral.

Brenner's voice rose to a scream. "What are you doing? Don't just stand there! *Kill it!*"

Haru yanked a pair of slender blades from sheaths at her hips. They glowed furnace-red. Her horse galloped toward Alice as she spun the blades.

Alice reared up, casting off her cloak in one smooth movement as her body swelled and distorted, ripping through her nightgown. Tatters of cloth fell to the street. *"Alice!"* Simon cried. She didn't seem to hear him. Her jaws stretched wide in a roar. One huge arm snapped out, knocking Haru and her horse aside. Haru tumbled out of the saddle; the horse lunged to its hooves and took off in a flash. Haru had dropped one of her blades. She clutched the other as she crawled along the street, dragging one leg.

Alice towered in full reptilian form, her chest heaving. Her tentacles lashed in a writhing storm around her. Her eyes were glowing orbs of rage.

"*Help!*" squealed Haru. "Galen!"

A bearded patrol member scooped her up, onto his mount. He raised a hand straight up into the air and light burst from his palm. A flare shot into the sky, exploding in a shower of golden sparks. A distress signal.

Alice stalked toward them on all fours.

Galen and the other patrol members turned their mounts sharply and fled with a clatter of hooves on stone. "Cowards!" Brenner shouted. "Come back!" They ignored him. He lunged for his own horse, but Alice was faster. She wheeled around and pounced, pinning him to the street with one clawed hand. The horse—which had been standing motion-less, fear-frozen, until that point—finally turned and bolted.

Brenner thrashed, panting. Alice placed a talon-tipped finger over his windpipe and pressed down. He gurgled, spit-tle bubbling from his lips. She pressed harder, and his eyes bulged.

"Alice, *stop!*" Simon cried out.

She froze. A shudder rippled through her powerful bulk. Her wedge-shaped head turned slowly toward him.

"Please," he whispered.

She blinked, her eyes slowly focusing. She looked down at

Brenner, then back at Simon. Her jaw fell open, and a pained groan escaped her throat. She reared up on her hind legs, bowed her head, and gripped it between massive, clawed hands.

"Alice, it's all right," Simon said. "Let's just get out of here."

Still clutching her head, she backed away from Brenner, and he lurched to his feet. He stumbled, slipped, and landed on his bottom with a thump. He was trembling visibly, his lower lip wet with drool. A dark patch spread across the crotch of his pants. "Help," he whispered. His voice rose to a shout. *"Help me!"*

Alice dropped to all fours. Her amethyst gaze fixed on Simon, and he knew what he had to do.

He grabbed her cloak from the street, scrambled onto her back, and held on. Muscles bunched and flexed beneath him as she broke into a run.

Simon wrapped his arms around her neck, clinging tightly. Buildings rushed past in a blur. It took all his strength just to hold on.

They ran past a scruffy old man sprawled on a staircase, a bottle in one hand. He let out a shriek.

This was no good. The more people saw them like this, the slimmer their chance of escape. "Alice!" He had to shout to be heard above the rush of air. "Change back! You've got to change back!"

She lurched to a halt. Simon spilled off in a tumble, and

the ground rushed up to meet him with a bone-jarring smack. Simon picked himself up, shaking, and gingerly patted himself down. Miraculously, he wasn't hurt. Just a few scrapes.

Alice was dwindling, shrinking back down to human form, small and naked. He handed her the ragged cloak. Fumbling, she grabbed it and wrapped herself in it. She stood, clutching the cloak shut, head bowed. "Simon . . ." Her voice cracked.

They were on a narrow, quiet side street, no one in sight. Simon sagged against a nearby wall to catch his breath. "We lost them, anyway."

Alice's face was fully human again. She raised trembling fingers to her mouth. "I'm sorry," she whispered. "I never meant to change shape. I . . . I slipped."

Simon shook his head. "It was my fault. I made him angry. You might have saved my life."

She looked away. "I probably just put us both in more danger. But I saw you on the ground, and I . . ." She gulped. "What should we do?"

"Get out of the city. Like we planned. I think I recognize this area—the train station isn't far."

Galen had set off a flare, which meant more patrol members would soon flood the streets. They had to reach their destination quickly. Simon clutched Alice's hand, and they ran.

Rain began to fall, slicking the cobblestones. The fog thickened, until Simon felt as though he were pushing it aside with every step. The dull burn of exhaustion crept into his muscles. He was running on pure fear; every time he started to slow, another burst of terror sizzled through his nerves, giving him fresh strength.

"Just ahead," he panted. "Almost there."

They turned a corner, and Simon heard hoofbeats. He froze. Ahead, more horses—at least a dozen of them—paced around the train station. Winged wraiths swooped through the air, pale shapes in the night, their eyes glowing bloodred, like crimson search lamps. Simon ducked into a nearby alley, pulling Alice with him.

"What now?" she whispered.

He bit the inside of his cheek, mind racing in every direction. "This way." He gripped Alice's hand tighter and quickened his pace.

The rain came down harder and faster, soaking their clothes.

They turned another corner, and the dull thunder of hooves reached his ears. More patrols. He veered down another street, aware that they were being driven farther and farther from their destination, toward the heart of the city.

Ahead, a familiar structure loomed through the sheets of water: the Gregor Temple, a soaring construction of gray stone, elegant in its simplicity. He'd been there numerous times as a child. In the front was a single arched doorway with no door.

"Here," he said, breathless. "We can hide in here."

And then what? Simon had no answer, so he ignored the thought.

They slipped into the building.

The space inside was cavernous and empty. A large, round hole in the middle of the ceiling allowed the rain to drip through. The floor of the temple was of white sand, raked smooth . . . all but the center, where a massive Gaokerena, almost as tall as the temple itself, rose up from a circle of earth.

Rain drummed on the rooftop, a hollow sound, and pattered on the leaves. The temple was empty.

Simon sank to the ground and sat on the damp sand, staring at the tree.

There was no one coming to help them. They were alone. He wondered how long they had before the patrols closed in. Twenty minutes? Ten? Not much time to come up with a plan. He felt despair closing in on him. This had been a terrible mistake.

"Maybe we should go back to Blackthorn," Alice said.

"We can't." Even if that were an option, he doubted they'd make it without running into another patrol. The entire city, it seemed, was crawling with them. "I'm sorry, Alice. I've led us into a corner. I—I don't know what to do."

For a minute or two, the only sound was their breathing and the drone of rain.

"What exactly did you see in your father's laboratory?" Alice asked.

He covered his face with his hands.

"Simon."

He wondered if she'd be better off not seeing the photograph. Maybe the truth would just frighten and confuse her . . . but that wasn't his decision to make. He owed her this much. Slowly, he removed the photograph from his pocket and handed it to her. Her breath fluttered . . . then she fell silent.

"There were others, too," he said at last. "Other bodies, I mean." *Bodies.* The word felt so cold, like clay on his tongue.

Alice clutched the photograph, her expression unreadable, blank. "So. This is me."

"It would seem so."

The photograph slipped from her fingers and fell to the white, glittering sand of the temple floor. She didn't move to pick it up.

Rain fell in a shimmering curtain through the hole in the roof, dripping from the branches and leaves of the Gaokerena.

"There was a tree like this in the mountains, too," Alice said.

"You remember?"

"I do now. Maybe I was hiding it from myself." She hugged her knees. "You knew, didn't you?"

"I saw something in the mountains. A sort of . . . pod. It seemed to be growing out of the tree. I didn't know what it was. That's where you came from? Where you . . . ?"

"Hatched. Yes." A tiny, bitter smile touched her lips. "I was a human girl. Then I died. Then I was reborn from a pod growing out of a tree . . . except now I'm this. And I still can't remember a damn thing about who I was. What sense does that make? Am I even alive?"

He thought about Alice's love of coffee. Her wry, subtle sense of humor. The way she'd thrown her arms around him and squeezed him tight. "If you aren't alive, then I don't know what being alive *is*."

She uttered a tiny laugh, though it sounded more like a sob. For a few minutes, neither one of them spoke.

"They're getting closer," Alice said. "I can smell them. They must know we're here."

The weary hopelessness in her voice was more terrifying than anything. "We just have to think. If we give up, it's all over. Remember that situation in the mountain cabin? We got out of that alive. We can do it again."

"You bluffed your way through that. Somehow, I don't think that will work this time."

"Then we'll fight them."

"If we do, we'll both die."

She was right. Try as he might, he couldn't see another outcome. "Then what?"

She uncurled herself, straightening her shoulders. "I'm going to turn myself in."

Panic leaped in his chest. "Alice. No."

"I have to."

"There's got to be a better way. If we can just find a place to hide until morning, maybe the patrols will give up, and then we'll have a chance to escape—"

"And then what would I do? Go back to hiding in the wilderness like an animal? We barely had a plan to begin with, Simon." She smiled wanly. "You've done enough. I won't have you dying for my sake. I have to face this."

Simon opened his mouth to protest . . . then closed it. There was no way he would stand back and allow them to take Alice, but arguing about it was a waste of energy. Instead, he closed his eyes, pressed his hands to the stones beneath him, and began to draw in meta. There was a great deal of it, here—the tree burned with it, glowed with it. Its sprawling network of roots feathered the ground beneath the Temple and spread outward under the street. Simon pulled meta from deep within the tree's heart, filling up his internal stores. He felt the energy pooling inside him like warm wine. His fingertips prickled.

When they came, he would be ready.

"Simon . . ." Alice's voice shook.

His eyes snapped open, and he scrambled to his feet. Alice rose beside him, her tentacles massing beneath her and pushing her upward in one smooth movement.

A row of four cloaked and hooded Animists stood just inside the doorway, blocking their exit. He hadn't heard their approach; they were on foot, having abandoned their mounts so they could move in quietly, like oiled shadows. A woman stepped forward from the group and faced Simon. With one hand, she reached up and pulled down her hood and shook out her dark hair. Her face was grim, with the faintest trace of sadness.

"Neeta," he said. He wasn't surprised to see her. On some level, maybe, he'd been expecting it.

Neeta's cool gaze flicked to Alice. "You will come with us," she said.

Alice rose to her feet. Simon stepped in front of her.

Neeta's hand rested on the hilt of her weapon—a bladed staff, its blades currently sheathed and hidden within the staff itself. During their years together, he had never actually seen her use it. She'd told him that it was only for emergencies. "Stand aside, Simon."

"What are you planning to do with her?"

"That's none of your concern."

"It's very much my concern."

There was a rustle of movement as the three other Animists reached for their own weapons. Neeta held up a hand, and they froze. She regarded Simon coolly. "Don't do anything rash. We're not here for *you*. Just the Abomination."

Simon's fingers twitched, curling into fists.

His best chance would be to create some sort of diversion. He didn't have the power to defeat Neeta and several other top-tier Animists, but he could distract them, at least long enough to let Alice escape.

Of course, then *he* would be arrested. But he didn't care. It was his fault she was in this mess to begin with.

His breathing quickened as he reached for the warm pulse of meta in the center of his being. He felt full, brimming with power; his fingertips glowed with it.

"You should know," Neeta said, looking at Simon, "I spoke to your father tonight, and he told us about the Abomination. In exchange for the information he gave us, he made me promise that you would not suffer any consequences for your part in this. If you do something stupid, however, I can't guarantee that immunity."

It took a moment for the words to sink in. His father had willingly handed Alice over to the Foundation.

A sickening mixture of heat and cold swept through Simon. A red haze crept across his vision. The blood roared in his head. His palms grew hot as meta collected in his skin, crackling.

Alice gripped his wrist suddenly, and Simon gave a start. He met her gaze, and she gave a small, almost imperceptible shake of her head. She turned to Neeta. "I'll cooperate."

"Alice! Don't do this!"

Her fingers tightened on his wrist. "I told you. I won't let you throw away your life for me. Do you understand?" Her voice was a harsh whisper. "I *won't*."

He looked into her eyes. They were calm, steady—but beneath the calm was a terrible deadness. "Please."

"This is my choice." She released his wrist and stepped forward. "My life is already over."

"Restrain her," Neeta said.

A muscular Animist stepped forward and withdrew a pair of iron manacles from his robes. He slapped the manacles around Alice's wrists. Alice stood, head raised, back rigid. Two Animists gripped her arms and led her toward the door. Neeta followed. *"Alice!"* Simon cried out.

He couldn't just stand here and watch them take away his only friend—the girl he had promised to protect.

He ran after them, into the rainy night. A beetle-black coach waited in the street, drawn by a team of stocky horses. The patrol members shoved Alice into the back then climbed into the front seat.

Simon raised both hands, chest heaving. Meta swirled in his chest, sparked through his veins. His palms sizzled lightning-yellow. "Let her go."

Neeta sighed and pinched the bridge of her nose. "Simon . . ."

"I said let. Her. Go."

Alice's eyes widened. Her mouth shaped a word—he

thought it was *no*. Then the coach door slammed shut, sealing her inside.

All sound had fallen away. Simon was alone in the center of a still bubble, pressure building inside him, around him, spinning through the depths of his body and mind. He was an inferno, a beacon. He could feel himself blazing, drawing in power from the ground, the sea, from the very air. The blood sang in his veins.

Neeta took a step back. A flicker of surprise broke through her mask, and he saw something in her eyes he'd never seen there before: fear. His heartbeat raced. He was more powerful than she'd thought.

Neeta went into a defensive crouch and, with a smooth *shhhk*, drew her carved wooden staff. She pressed a lever on the side, and two double-edged blades sprang from the ends. "This is your last warning," she said. "Stand back."

Simon took a step forward.

"So be it," Neeta muttered. Then, in a shout: "Get the Abomination out of here. I'll take care of him myself."

The burly Animist poked his head out the window. "We can summon reinforcements."

"That won't be necessary."

The driver cracked a whip; the horses broke into a trot, and the coach rattled away. Simon started to run after it, but Neeta blocked him. "You aren't going anywhere."

He'd have to go through her, then. So be it. For once,

there was no fear; his uncertainty had vanished, leaving only a sense of calm purpose. He felt as though he could move a mountain with his bare hands.

Neeta gripped her staff, knuckles white, and launched herself at him. Simon thrust his hands out, releasing his power. It rushed at her in a golden torrent, pouring and sparking from his palms. Neeta spun her staff. It glowed brilliant blue, forming a bubble of cool sapphire light around her that deflected the streams of meta.

Neeta stood unharmed, her staff held out in one hand. She beckoned him with the other—*try again.*

He raised one hand, and a golden sphere blossomed in his palm like a tiny sun. Its heat scorched his skin, but he barely felt the pain. He hurled the sphere. It shot toward her, growing as it did until it was larger than her head. She batted it away, like a softball.

"Is that all you've got?" Her voice rose. "Come, Simon. I taught you better than that!" But she was sweating. Her face gleamed with it.

He just had to get through her, and then he could rescue Alice.

Grains of dirt and grit rose from the street, glowing golden. They flowed and arched in the air, a luminous cloud, like hundreds of fireflies moving with a single mind. Simon had no idea how he was doing it; he had never done anything like it. The power flowed out of him and took the shape of his rage.

This was his true potential, then. The last of the vinculum root had burned out of his system, and he'd emerged new and clean. A swirl of exhilaration filled his chest.

He stretched out a hand, and the cloud of glowing dust took the shape of a roaring dragon's head. He drew on the image of Alice in her demon form—the gaping jaws, the brilliant, fierce eyes. The dust-dragon rushed at Neeta.

She flinched as several of the grains hit her, ripping thin cuts through her cheek and arm. The dragon's head shot past her, stopped, looped around in midair, and raced back toward her.

She raised her staff in both hands. Her eyes closed, her staff glowed blue, and the air seemed to thicken around her like an orb of some translucent, viscous liquid. The golden particles struck the edge of the orb and slowed. She had done something to the atmosphere—or to time itself—within the force field. The particles spread out over its surface, transforming the jellylike orb into a glistening golden bubble. Then the grains of sand shot out, lost their glow, and rained to the ground, harmless.

More, he thought. He needed more power.

Teeth gritted, Simon thrust his arms out again, but only a few weak spurts of light shot from his palms. "No." His voice emerged rough and raw. *"No!"* Panting, he shook his arms, as if to jolt loose some bit of strength stuck inside him.

That couldn't be all there was. There had to be more inside

him, more meta, more hidden reserves, more *something*.

Neeta lunged at him, raised the staff high over her head, and brought it down. He tried to bring his arms up, to shield himself, but he wasn't fast enough; the staff smacked into his temple. Stars burst behind his eyes.

He went down, head spinning, and landed on his back with a bone-jarring thud.

Neeta loomed over him. "I won't arrest you, Simon. I made a promise to your father that you wouldn't end up in prison. But you can't attack a senior officer and expect to get away with it. You will be stripped of your registration. As of now, you are no longer an Animist. You will never again set foot in Foundation Headquarters. You are no longer permitted to channel meta. And if you try, you will suffer the consequences." Her expression softened, sagging. "Maybe this is for the best."

She turned and strode away, leaving Simon lying on his back on the cold, wet cobblestones.

Chapter Seventeen

Cold pinpricks of rain struck Simon's face. He tried to stand, but dizziness rolled over him and flattened him against the street. The back of his head pulsed with a dull heat.

Alice was gone. He'd brought her here, to Eidendel, despite her fears. He'd promised her she would be safe. She had put her trust in him, and he had failed that trust.

His vision went hazy and gray. A familiar clack-clacking reached his ears, growing closer. Dozens of thin mechanical limbs lifted him off the street. He was too weak to resist, too weak to do anything as a procession of spiders carried him away.

He faded out.

⌐⌐

When he came back to himself, he was lying on a hard surface. He blinked a few times. A jolt of panic shot through him as his surroundings settled into place: he was on the stone table in his father's laboratory. Dr. Hawking leaned over him, a frown of concentration on his face, his fingers resting against Simon's temples. Golden light wreathed his hands, flickering in Simon's peripheral vision.

Simon scrambled off the table and lurched to his feet, panting.

"Easy," Dr. Hawking said. He stood, leaning on his cane. "Take it easy."

"What were you doing?"

"Healing you. You had a concussion. Sit down."

Simon gripped the edge of the table. Memories were trickling back, settling into place. "You . . ." A hot, black flame of anger licked the inside of his chest. "You betrayed Alice."

His father's expression tightened. "They came to me asking questions. I did the only thing I could. There is no defying the Foundation—not for long. If I hadn't bargained on your behalf, you would be in chains right now."

No—how *dare*—how *could* he—

His mind stuttered, and his thoughts went blank in a flash of rage. He charged straight at Dr. Hawking, one hand clenched into a fist, and drew it back.

His father didn't even try to avoid the swing. His head snapped to one side as Simon's knuckles cracked into his jaw. Dr. Hawking looked at him steadily. A trickle of blood ran from one corner of his mouth, and he wiped it away. "Do you feel any better now?"

Simon glared at him, then turned and walked toward the door.

"Where are you going?"

"To save Alice."

"No, you're not."

He tried the knob. It didn't budge. Jaws clenched, he shoved his palms against the door and pushed with muscles and meta alike. His hands glowed gold, throwing off sparks. *Break!* He visualized the door flying off its hinges. Still, nothing happened. He grabbed the knob and rattled it, pushing against the door with his shoulder.

"Simon. Sit down. We need to talk."

Simon spun to face him. "I have nothing to talk to you about. Let me out!"

"What do you think you can do on your own?" he snapped. "You don't even know where they've taken her."

"I don't care. I have to *try*." His voice cracked. But he could feel the hope shriveling inside him, even as he spoke. He slumped against the door.

"Sit down," Dr. Hawking said.

Simon didn't move. His chest felt empty and numb. "The thing I could never figure out about you," he said quietly, "do you *try* to be cruel? Or do you just not care? The second is somehow worse. Because if you wanted to hurt me, it would at least mean that you felt something, even if it was anger.

Maybe you want to punish me because you wished I had died in Olivia's place. But I don't think that's it. My feelings aren't part of the equation. They never were. I'm only an inconvenience."

"Is that truly what you believe?"

"What am I *supposed* to think?"

Dr. Hawking's lips tightened. He averted his gaze. "I suppose we're long past due for this conversation." He sank into one of the overstuffed chairs and glanced at a pair of spiders standing nearby. "Some whiskey, if you please. And two glasses."

They skittered away, toward the cabinet at the far end of the lab.

Dr. Hawking nodded to the chair across from him. "Sit."

Still, Simon remained standing. "You can explain yourself to me from there."

"Suit yourself."

The spiders returned carrying a silver tray, which Dr. Hawking set on the low wooden table beside him. On the tray was a clear bottle filled with fiery amber liquid and two short glasses.

"If you think I'm going to drink anything you put in front of me, after what you did—"

"Who said anything about you? This isn't a conversation I care to have sober." Dr. Hawking filled both glasses and drained them quickly, one after the other. He slumped in his chair, face turned toward the ceiling. "You saw the photograph, I take it. I suppose you've figured things out by now. You've heard about the bodies stolen from the city morgue?"

Simon's mind flashed back to the conversation he'd overheard between Neeta and the mysterious official in her office, just before he'd left the city. He thought about the copy of the *Underground* he'd seen, the lurid rumors of stolen corpses. "So that was you, after all?" he whispered. "You took those bodies? For your experiments?"

"Your opinion of me is awfully low. No. I had nothing to do with that."

"But . . . why would you have those pictures, if you weren't responsible?"

"They're from the Foundation. When they sent an official here to question me about the grave-robbing, they brought those photographs and left them here afterward with instructions to report back if I uncovered any clues. I was merely cooperating with their investigation. Mind you, I have my suspicions about who's behind all this. Your mother never could resist pushing the boundaries of science and morality. She never met a taboo she didn't want to break." He let out a flat, bitter laugh.

A thin chill slid down Simon's spine. He found himself thinking, suddenly, of Olivia's funeral, his mother's rage, the whispered argument between his parents. "Mother? You're saying *she* took those bodies?"

Dr. Hawking rubbed his forehead with his fingertips. "Veera had been researching cell regeneration for some time. Creatures from the Eldritch Realm have strong regenerative properties. She believed that by injecting the cells of demons into the corpse of a dead animal, she could stimulate the animal's organs to begin functioning again. Some of the subjects *did* appear to return to life. But only for a short while, and they shrieked in pain the entire time."

Simon's mouth had gone dry. "The mouse," he murmured.

"You saw that, too, did you? Yes, that's hers. Foolish of me, I suppose, keeping the results of her experiments here. If they were discovered, the blame would naturally fall on me. But I couldn't bring myself to destroy them."

"That means . . . Alice . . ." The pieces were falling together. "Mother is the one who brought Alice back."

"I don't know that for sure. But it seems highly likely."

In Simon's head, another piece clicked into place. "Olivia." His heartbeat sped. "She tried to revive Olivia. Didn't she?"

"Olivia is dead," he whispered. "The dead do not come back."

"But Mother did it, didn't she? Just like with Alice. She brought her back!"

Dr. Hawking ran his hand over his face. "This is why I didn't want to tell you. Because I knew that once you learned about Veera's research, you wouldn't be able to stop thinking about the possibility."

"How can you not *care*? Your *daughter* might be alive, walking around out there right now!"

"Simon, what she created was not life. It was not Olivia. It was a grotesque parody of her."

"But Alice—"

"Alice is not a reincarnated human; she is a reanimated corpse. A golem made of meat."

"That's not true. You've *talked* to her. You ought to know. She has memories, emotions—"

"Simon, *listen.*" He leaned forward and spoke with a quiet, feverish intensity. "When an animal dies, parasites invade its body. You can see them moving beneath its skin, inside its eye sockets. They eat out its insides and fill it up, so that it looks almost alive. But the animal itself—its mind, its spirit, if there is such a thing—is gone. Now, imagine if it worked a bit differently—if, when a creature died, it was eaten up not by a thousand maggots, but by a single organism that slid into its skin and wore it like a costume. To an observer, it would certainly look like the animal had come back to life. But it would be a lie."

"So then . . . what? What are you saying?"

"I am saying that whoever or whatever 'Alice' is, she is not a human girl." A muscle at the corner of his eye twitched. "Reanimating a body is not the same as bringing back a dead person. Even if your mother succeeded, what she created would not be *our* Olivia. Can't you understand that?"

He dragged in a shuddering breath. "I supported your mother's research, when she first began dabbling in reanimation. Even before we lost Olivia, Veera was always curious about the subject. But the more I saw, the more I learned about the depths of her obsession with curing death, the more horrified I became. The mouse, she viewed as a success, but her failures . . . I saw things that should never have existed, that would haunt your dreams. And then, after what happened . . ." His head bowed. "I couldn't bear the thought of my little girl's remains being transformed into one of those . . . things. I didn't want some half-alive doll stitched together from her pieces. That would have been even worse than putting her in the ground. And you don't know how hard it was to let them put her in the ground, Simon. To accept, in my heart, that she no longer existed. Your mother . . . she couldn't accept it. We both chose our paths. And neither one of us can return."

Simon shook his head numbly. "I don't know how much of this to believe. I don't even know who you are anymore. If this is true, it means you've been hiding it from me for all these years. You lied to me. Not only that, you drugged me!"

"It was *medicine*. You needed it."

"You told me it was just a sedative. But you put vinculum root in the pills. Or are you going to deny that?"

"That was supposed to be temporary," he muttered. "I was planning to tell you. I waited too long."

A chill feathered down Simon's spine. "Tell me what? What are you talking about?"

Dr. Hawking stared blankly ahead, his fingers clenched tight on the glass. "Come closer. I don't have the energy to shout across the room at you."

Simon hesitated . . . then approached, slowly, and sat down in the chair across from his father's. With his anger fading, he felt suddenly small and uncertain and very, very scared.

"You aren't a normal Animist, Simon," he said. "Ordinarily, when a child like you is born, the Foundation eliminates them. Quickly."

"No." His own voice sounded tiny and flat in the stillness. This was another lie. It had to be. "The Foundation might be corrupt, but they don't kill children."

"It's all very humane, I'm told. A strong sleeping draught, a needle full of quick-acting poison. Quiet little deaths behind closed doors." He poured himself more whiskey. "The Queen's eyes are everywhere. But your mother . . . she has the most formidable intellect of anyone I've ever known. She devised a way to deflect the Queen's gaze from you—to hide your power. A metaphysical cloak, she called it."

"*What* power?"

"A power the Foundation fears more than anything. And they're right to fear it." He tilted his glass, watching the amber liquid slosh around inside. "You are a Chaos Animist, Simon. You can tap directly into the energy of the Outer Realm— the space between worlds. But humans can't control that energy. It slowly eats away at their minds, drives them mad, transforms them into something unspeakable. Your mother told you the story, didn't she? How one man destroyed a city, reducing it to a scorched crater, and how Eidendel was rebuilt on the ruins? Do you know what Eidendel means? It means 'out of the ashes.' And that's all that was left—ashes—when he was done. Since then, there have been no Chaos Animists left alive. Until you."

Simon sat, frozen. The floor had dropped out from under him, and he floated, suspended, like a pebble about to fall into an abyss.

Dr. Hawking took another swig of whiskey and coughed. "Your mother wanted to tell you. She believed it was possible to train you." He shook his head. "*Train* you—a six-year-old child. Can you imagine? I said it was far too dangerous, that I wouldn't put you through that. So I placed a block in your mind. A sort of . . . locked door, to prevent you from using that particular pathway. If you tried to access that power, even inadvertently, you would lose consciousness. For a while, it seemed to work."

He thought back to that moment during the mission with Neeta, when he'd fainted. That flash of light.

"The block weakened over time, as I knew it would," his father said. "The drugs were a secondary measure. Vinculum root dampens certain receptors in the brain, inhibits the ability to channel any form of nonmaterial power. Of course, a side effect is that you were unable to use meta effectively. I tried everything to discourage you from becoming an Animist, but—"

"You only started giving me the drugs later. After Olivia died."

Dr. Hawking set the glass down and rubbed his trembling hands over his face.

Simon's heart pounded. A cold line of sweat trickled down his spine. "Father?"

Dr. Hawking pointed at the bottle and gave him a sickly smile. "Sure you don't want some?"

Simon wanted to knock the bottle off the table. "Why don't I remember what happened to Olivia?"

He wouldn't look Simon in the eye. "I had no choice but to lock away your memories of that night. If you'd remembered what you had done, it would have destroyed you."

What *he* had done . . .

The room seemed to be rotating slowly around him. More puzzle pieces were tumbling into place: the gap in his own memories, the vague stories of an unidentified man who had attacked and then fled. The faint, lingering image of a dark figure. A shadow-thing.

"I know that some people believed *I* killed her," Dr. Hawking said. "I allowed those rumors to circulate. It was better than letting anyone suspect the truth." He took his glasses off, set them on the table, and rubbed his watery eyes. The gesture made him look suddenly, strangely childlike. "On that day . . . the day she died . . . your mother and I were arguing about some stupid thing, and you were upset. Olivia started crying. Veera stormed out of the house. Olivia started shouting at me, and I shouted back. You pressed your hands over your ears, shut your eyes, and screamed at us to stop. And then . . ."

A strange numbness crept over Simon; a high, tinny ringing filled his ears.

A knife of memory cut through his brain—an image of his father cowering in the corner of the dining hall, looking small, pale, and terrified. His leg had been ripped off, and blood pooled beneath the stump.

I did that.

"No," Simon whispered.

"The younger the child, the purer and stronger the power," Dr. Hawking said. "And the more easily it escapes."

More flashes. Whirling shadows. Wind howling, bursting forth, as darkness bubbled out of his skin—as if some terrible, inhuman thing were clawing away at him from the inside, straining to escape. Furniture flying through the air. The table falling, pinning Olivia's small body beneath it.

I killed her.

Somewhere through the icy horror, he found himself thinking about the tiny, useless imp he'd summoned back in Splithead Creek, hoping to impress Mayor Umburt. All his life, he'd thought his problem was lack of power. *If I were only stronger,* he had thought so many times, *I could have protected her from the monster that killed her.* He pressed his hands to his temples, as if he could squeeze the newfound knowledge out of his head.

The monster . . . was him.

The room began to shake. The whiskey bottle toppled off the table and shattered on the floor.

"Simon!" His father leaned forward and gripped Simon's face between both hands. His palms were rough, and his skin smelled of whiskey. "Breathe."

"I—I can't—" A dull rumbling filled the air. The floor trembled beneath his feet. A low, inhuman wail escaped his mouth.

Dr. Hawking reached into his robes, withdrawing something. There was a sharp sting in Simon's neck, and a fuzzy blanket of calm settled over him. His vision blurred, and he slumped forward, against his father. Dr. Hawking withdrew the needle from his neck. Simon glimpsed the glass hypodermic tube, filled with iridescent purple-black liquid.

Dr. Hawking slipped the needle into his pocket and leaned down so they were at eye level. "Listen to me." His voice was faintly echoed and distorted. "What happened was not your fault. But you must never use this power again. Not for anything. The risk is too great."

He wanted to shut out his father's voice, to escape into sleep. He was so *tired* . . .

"Do you understand, Simon?"

He nodded numbly.

He drifted in and out of a black fog as Dr. Hawking carried him in his arms, like a small child, up the stairs. He was dimly aware of being lowered into his bed. Dr. Hawking pulled the covers up to his chest. He lingered a moment, staring down at him. Simon tried to focus on his expression, but his vision kept blurring. He heard retreating footsteps, then the click of the door shutting. A tear slipped from the corner of his eye, down his temple. His limbs were too heavy to wipe it away.

Moonlight filtered through the window, spreading softly across the stone floor. The drugs tingled through Simon's veins, dulling the agony.

He hated it—wanted to deny it—but the familiar numbness felt good. After so long without those little black capsules, the injection had catapulted him out of his own body, and he floated on a little cloud somewhere above his pain. He knew the pain would be there for him, waiting, when he crashed back down. But for now, he just wanted to float.

Alice is still in danger, whispered a voice in his mind. She was locked away somewhere, a prisoner of the Foundation. Alone. She needed him. He tried to sit up, but his body wouldn't listen.

He stared at the ceiling through hazy eyes, his thoughts spinning in every direction. He struggled to focus.

Mother hadn't left him to track down Olivia's killer—she'd left so she could continue her research, away from the prying eyes of the Foundation. So she could bring Olivia back. His sister might be alive and well, walking the Earth right now. And his father had hidden that possibility from him, all this time.

The drugs pressed down on his thoughts in a heavy, smothering blanket of nothing. He slipped into darkness.

When he woke, Simon's body felt like rubber. His mouth and head were stuffed with cotton. But he was awake. Judging by the light outside the window, it was dusk or dawn; whether he had been asleep a few hours or a few days, he had no idea.

When he pushed himself to his feet, his legs wobbled but held. Leaning against the wall, he made his way slowly over to the door and tried the knob. Locked. He tried to channel, but when he reached for the warm, ever-present glow of meta, he ran into a cold wall inside himself. The drugs had left him helpless . . . or maybe his father had placed another block in his mind while he was unconscious.

He thought of Dr. Hawking's face, his whiskey-reddened eyes, the way his voice had trembled.

His own father was terrified of him. And why not? Simon had ripped off his leg.

He forced his mind back to the present. *Think.* There had to be another way out. His gaze strayed briefly to the window, but no—it was too small to climb through, and even if he could, the drop would kill him.

A heavy, paralyzing despair crept through his body. He sank to the edge of the bed and bowed his head, burying his fingers in his hair.

No. It was too soon to give up. *Think, think, think.* The fog of the drugs still clung to his mind; he pinched the back of his hand and twisted, focusing on the pain. Slowly, his head cleared. There must be something here that could help him. He patted himself down, checking his pockets—empty, save for a stray coin and a bit of lint. Then his fingers found the amulet, still resting against his chest.

He pulled it off his neck and cradled it in one palm, studying the smooth green stone. At a glance, there was nothing special about it, but the old woman had seemed so strangely insistent about giving it to him.

What were the chances that a scruffy, half-crazed seller of gossip rags possessed an object of real power?

His fingers wandered over the gem's surface. He breathed in. *Focus.* There. He could feel . . . something. A resistance in his mind, similar to the simple spell that held his compass shut. It required meta to open. He focused, gritting his teeth, trying to think past the wall in his mind, to think *around* it. *Just a little.* All he needed was the tiniest thread of meta, the barest flicker . . .

Come on, he thought. *Come on, come on.*

There!

The amulet snapped open. He let out a gasp, fumbling as the amulet slipped from his grip and bounced off the floor. A tiny glass bottle rolled out. Simon picked it up and examined the contents. It was filled with powdery gray ash.

Summoning ash.

He uncorked the bottle and spread the ash in a circle on the floor. He didn't have a knife, so he bit down on his thumb. He had to bite very hard—human teeth weren't that sharp—and tears of pain stung his eyes. At last, he tasted the copper tang of blood. Panting, he squeezed his thumb, and three fat red droplets fell into the circle. "I call upon you, servant of the Eldritch Realm," he whispered. "Claim my toll and lend me your strength."

A puff of greenish smoke filled the air and stung his eyes and nose, making him cough. When the smoke cleared, a tiny creature sat on the floor. It was no larger than a squirrel, and resembled—more than anything—a furry orange newt with six short, plump limbs. A pair of sluglike antennae protruded from its head. It sat back on its haunches and blinked large black eyes up at him. "*Huzzuh*," said a tiny, gruff voice.

Simon stared blankly.

"*Huzzuh?*" the imp said again. He thought he detected a trace of impatience in its tone.

"Uh . . . hello. My name is Simon Frost."

The imp raised its paw—one of the middle set of limbs—and scratched behind its tufted ear.

His hopes were sinking rapidly, but he plunged ahead: "I'm trapped here, in this room. I need to get out. My friend is in serious danger."

The imp peered up at him for a moment, then yawned,

showing a curled purple tongue. A pair of iridescent drag-onfly wings unfurled from the creature's back with a snap. Simon gave a start. The wings were twice the length of its own body, damp and shimmering. They fluttered, then whirred, and the demon lifted off the floor like a fat, furry bumblebee. It drifted toward the window and bumped against the glass.

Simon opened the window.

"*Huzzuh*," it said, with the same inflection as *thank you*, and flew out, vanishing into the darkness.

He paced the room for a while, then stopped, leaning his forehead against the wall. So much for that.

Tap. Tap-tap-tap. Something was knocking at the door. There was a scrape, then a click, and the door opened. The imp hovered outside.

Simon stared, openmouthed.

The imp turned, whirred down the hallway, then paused and glanced over its shoulder at Simon. "*Huzzuh!*" it said, and it sounded almost like *hurry up*.

There was no time for doubt. Simon followed.

They passed the half-open door to the laboratory. If the wet, raspy snores from inside were any indication, Dr. Hawking was passed out drunk at his desk. A sharp twinge of pain lanced through Simon's chest. He ignored it and kept walk-ing, down the stairs and out through the front door. Cool air washed over him as the tiny imp led him through the overgrown garden.

Near the edge of the cliff, illuminated by moonlight, stood a slender figure in a patched, shabby cloak. The fuzzy orange imp flitted over, perched on the figure's shoulder, and folded its wings.

A slim hand reached up and pulled down the hood, revealing a gaunt face and masses of dirty, feather-decorated braids—the newspaper seller. Simon's jaw dropped. "You."

The imp on her shoulder nuzzled her cheek. She scratched under its chin with one finger, and its eyes slitted with pleasure. *"Huzzuh."*

"Thank you, Garzi. You may return now."

The imp vanished in a puff of smoke.

"Who *are* you?" Simon asked.

She smiled. Her face rippled, warped, and shimmered. Her wild hair tamed itself into straight, jaw-length, graying blond locks. Her rheumy, gray-yellow eyes turned clear and green. Her gaunt cheeks filled out, growing smooth and firm. "Much better," said a familiar voice.

It was his mother.

Chapter Eighteen

Simon's mouth opened, but no sound emerged.

"It's been a while, hasn't it?" She stepped forward and embraced him. "I've missed you."

She smelled the way she always had—like arcane powders and herbs. Floral and faintly bitter.

He wanted to hug her back, but he was frozen, arms limp at his sides. A part of him was afraid to accept the reality in front of him, afraid that it was some trick, some illusion or drug-addled hallucination. Still, her scent triggered a rush of memory so powerful, it was like being struck by lightning, and all at once he was a child again. A lump rose into his throat. "You came back," he whispered.

"I never really left you. I just had to . . . go undercover for a while. To take care of some business."

"Mother . . ." His voice cracked. "Where *were* you?"

"That's a rather long story." She stepped back and gave him a small, strange smile—half wry humor, half pain. "I think we have a great deal to talk about."

This was real. After four years, his mother was *here*, in front of him. Questions swarmed his brain. "Why didn't you ever contact me?"

Her smile faded. "I'm sorry, Simon. I *wanted* to. But I had to wait for the right moment."

"You could have at least let me know you were alive."

She shook her head. "If I'd contacted you in any way, you would have tried to find me. And that might have led the Foundation to me. They watched you carefully, you know. I couldn't take that chance. You'll understand everything once I explain, but for now, you must come with me. Quickly, before your father discovers my presence. Believe me, he won't be happy to see me."

Simon hesitated. "Father . . ." His voice shook. "I . . . he told me . . ."

"Olivia is alive, Simon."

He drew in his breath sharply.

It was what he had always hoped for, in his secret heart, yet never dared to believe. His mother had erased his mistake. She had brought Olivia back. "Is she . . ." His voice caught. "Is she . . . the same?"

A brief pause. "Some of her memories haven't returned yet. She may not recognize you at first. But she is Olivia.

Come with me, and I'll show you." Veera pulled a slender silver dagger from beneath her cloak and stuck it into the air. The tip of the dagger disappeared, and she drew it downward, leaving a luminous green line. She sheathed her dagger, then pushed her fingers into the green slit and pulled it open like a curtain. Beyond, he glimpsed another place. Jade sky, black rocks.

She stretched out a hand. *"Hurry."*

He took her hand, and she pulled him through.

The portal sealed itself shut behind them. They stood on dark stone under an alien sky swirled with purple clouds. A sickle-shaped moon hung low in the sky . . . except it wasn't a moon. A bulging yellow eye stared down from its cratered surface. It blinked once. Simon stared. "Mother . . . why does the moon have an eye?"

"Why shouldn't it?"

"Is it . . . alive?"

"Probably. In the Eldritch, the line between animate and inanimate is a little more blurry."

Rock formations towered here and there, forming grotesque, treelike shapes; contorted protrusions, somewhere between branches and tentacles, reached for the sky, and formations resembling half-melted faces peered out from the rock. Simon wasn't sure, but he thought he saw them *moving*, very slowly, from the corner of his eye; when he looked at them straight on, however, they remained frozen. A huge, black, eyeless bird with a serpent's tail flew down from the sky and landed on one of the rock formations. It let out a rusty shriek, then lifted one scaly yellow leg and deposited a dropping on the branch.

Simon didn't need to ask where they were. He'd seen the ink drawings in books. *The Eldritch Realm*, home to demons, imps, and other unearthly beings. Few humans ever had a chance to see it. He'd always assumed the illustrations were exaggerated or stylized in some way, but no—it looked more or less exactly like those black-and-white drawings, everything spiky and warped. It was a world scrawled by the hand of a drunken madman.

Roses grew in clusters near his feet, splotches of brilliant bloodred against the black ground. They swayed lightly back and forth, their leaves twisting in the still, windless air. When he leaned down closer, he saw that their leaves were not leaves, but wriggling green tentacles.

"Hurry." His mother turned and strode forward. "This way."

Simon jogged to keep up. New, bizarre sights tugged at his attention with every step: there was a stream filled with bubbling, steaming purple liquid, and there was a carriage-sized nest perched atop a rock formation, filled with iridescent rainbow eggs. More tentacle-roses grew here and there, some of them sprouting from the sides of outcrops. In the hazy distance, a herd of unfathomably huge, stilt-legged creatures grazed. It was difficult to tell, from so many miles away, but he thought they must be taller than the tallest buildings in

Eidendel. Watching them was like watching a living city.

He struggled to pull his gaze away, to the back of Veera's head. Her graying blond hair shone like platinum in the otherworldly light. "How is it that I never recognized you?" he asked, breathless. "Even if your appearance was different, I should have felt your meta."

"This." She tugged at her cloak. "It's specially crafted to mask my energy's signature, which is how I've been able to go undetected for so long. Disguising myself as a worshipper of Azathoth seemed only natural. They're a fringe cult, so the Foundation doesn't take them very seriously. Most of the time."

Far away, one of the building-sized creatures lowed. The sound echoed, clear and bell-like.

It was all so much; he couldn't take it in. But one thought swam to the top of his mind. *Alice.* How could he have forgotten about her, even for a moment? "Alice needs help," he blurted out.

Veera stopped, so suddenly that he nearly ran into her. "Alice," she repeated.

"She's my friend," Simon said. "She was taken by the Foundation. She may be in danger—"

"Shh." Veera tilted her head, then dragged him to the side, behind one of the massive rock formations. "Something is coming."

"A demon?"

"Shh."

Simon pressed his back against the cold rock. A low rumble emanated from nearby, and the ground vibrated beneath his feet. He peeked around the rock. A huge shape lumbered past—smaller than the stilt-legged beasts, but still larger than a house, covered with wrinkled, leathery gray skin and possessing more than a dozen stumpy legs, its face covered with a multitude of eyes, all colors and sizes. A flat, forked tongue flicked out from a hole in the center of its face, tasting the air, but it didn't seem to notice them. It kept going. An eyeless black bird swooped down from the sky, and the gray beast's tongue darted out and snatched it from the air, retracting into its mouth before its prey had so much as a chance to squawk. Bones crunched between boulder-sized molars. *Gulp.*

Simon squeezed his eyes shut. He listened, holding his breath, as the heavy footsteps receded into silence.

"Mother?"

"It's safe now." She released his arm and kept walking.

"Listen. Alice is—"

"We'll talk once we get home. We need to remain alert."

He followed, his eyes darting back and forth. "Those things . . . do they eat people?"

"Only the unwary ones. Ah, here we are." She approached one of the larger rock formations; it was vaguely treelike, and almost as large as Blackthorn.

In a flash, Simon remembered the tree he'd glimpsed

during his vision, when he was calling out to his mother. This was it. Except it wasn't a tree—it was a sort of natural stone castle. Countless tiny, irregularly shaped windows dotted its surface. They glowed with soft greenish light. When he looked closer, he saw a door set into the stone of the base. His mother opened the door and stepped through it. "My home."

"Did you *make* this place?"

"I discovered it, abandoned, and modified it to my own purposes. I don't know who made it. A demon, probably. They do build things, as it turns out. There are no cities in the Eldritch—demons don't like to cram themselves together, as humans do—but there are structures, here and there."

He followed her inside, looking around at the vast, cave-like entrance hall, the walls lined by rows of lamps. Their glow bathed everything in an eerie greenish tinge.

Veera strode forward. Simon had to nearly jog to keep up. "You've been here the entire time? Ever since you left?"

"It's an ideal place for me to conduct my research in peace."

He caught her arm. "If we're safe here, then please . . . listen. Alice is in trouble."

"As you mentioned." Veera's calm, inscrutable smile flickered briefly, then returned. "We'll talk about that, I promise you. But there is so *much* to talk about. I'll make some tea."

"There's no time—"

"Simon." She took his hands in hers. "Relax. Everything will be fine."

His chest tightened with frustration.

Ahead, Simon heard claws clicking on the stone floor. A small, furry form with pointed ears appeared out of the shadows and strode toward them. It was catlike, with silvery-lavender fur, small, curved horns, and two pairs of crimson eyes. A long, scaly tail swayed behind it.

The creature rubbed up against Veera's legs and let out a rumbling purr. She scooped it into her arms, and it curled up, eyes slitted with contentment. Hesitantly, Simon reached out to pet it. The beast pinned back its ears and hissed at him; he yanked his arm back.

"Careful," Veera said. "Penelope doesn't trust strangers."

He studied the horns and bloodred eyes, and remembered the dead mouse floating in the jar. "She's one of your experiments."

"The first successful one." Veera kept walking, cradling the demon cat to her chest. "All I needed was more time. But your father did everything in his power to hold me back." Bitterness tinged her voice.

They came to another doorway, leading into a dining room with a huge, carved stone table in the center. Candles flickered, wax melting down their sides and forming amorphous shapes on the tabletop. At the head of the table was a towering, throne-like chair, and in it sat a girl of about twelve or thirteen.

Simon's breath caught.

Veera placed a hand on his shoulder. "Olivia," she said. "This is Simon, the one I told you about. He's your brother."

Olivia stood slowly. She was barefoot, clad in a simple white slip. Her skin gleamed like moonlight on bone.

He tried to speak, but the words hit a wall in his throat.

She stared back placidly with all-black eyes. No whites, no irises. Her long, silver hair shimmered with its own unearthly light. She reached up to tuck a lock behind her ear, which resembled a fish's fin.

Finally, he managed to force out a faint whisper. "Olivia?"

Olivia hung back, eyeing him warily, like a wild animal watching from the bush.

He took a slow, unsteady breath. "Do you recognize me?"

She blinked a few times—a moist sound. Her eyes flickered, growing momentarily filmy white, and he realized that she had a second set of eyelids—a nictitating membrane, like a bird's. Her pale gray lips parted briefly then pressed together. "I'm sorry. I don't remember anything about my old life. Mother keeps saying it will come back to me, but . . ." She gave a little one-shouldered shrug, an achingly familiar gesture.

It was Olivia's voice. But . . . wrong. Detached, as though she were half asleep or drugged.

"You know me," he said, desperation creeping into his tone. "Maybe you've forgotten. But deep down, you know who I am. We're twins." He spoke the words like a magic spell, as if speaking them could make them true.

She stared back with her inscrutable black orbs. They may as well have been glass. He reached out to her, and she flinched back.

Something inside him died.

Olivia turned away. "I'm sorry."

"Don't force it," Veera said. She stroked Olivia's hair, as though she too were a cat, and Olivia leaned into the caress. Her eyes flicked toward Simon, then away. She pressed a knuckle to her lips.

Simon told himself to be patient. He was a stranger to her; she just needed time to get used to him. That was all. Still, a voice whispered from the marrow of his bones, a voice that sounded like his father's: *This isn't Olivia.*

Olivia had been sharp and bright, like flame. She had laughed and smiled as easily as she breathed, had reached out a welcoming hand to every stranger. This Olivia had shades of her, but she seemed distant, unreachable as the moon. Or was it his own memory that was faulty?

Veera touched Olivia's pale arm. "Will you give me and Simon a moment of privacy? Here. Take Penelope with you." She placed the demon cat in Olivia's arms, and Penelope immediately snuggled into her embrace, purring.

Olivia ran her fingers through the beast's sleek lavender fur and walked toward the door. She cast one last, furtive glance over her shoulder at Simon, then disappeared.

It wasn't his imagination, he thought. She *was* different. Her essence—the thing that made her Olivia—was gone.

No . . . not gone exactly. Changed. Like hot-burning coal crushed into a tiny, cold, glittering diamond. He *felt* it, on a visceral level. He had known Olivia since before he was a person. Their cells had mingled together in the womb; they had been part of the same whole, and when she'd died, Simon had been cut in half. He would recognize her even if she wore a different face and body altogether.

That wasn't his sister.

Yet Veera seemed to accept her completely.

"Sit down," Veera said. She lowered herself into the throne-like chair, picked up a bronze teapot, and poured its dark, fragrant contents into a cup. "Have some. It's brewed from Eldritch plants. My own recipe."

He remained standing. "No, thank you."

She stared at him for a few seconds then sighed. "You're angry. I suppose that's understandable."

Angry wasn't the word. He felt empty and dull inside. So many times, he'd imagined a reunion with Olivia and his mother. And here he was . . . yet it was all wrong. Veera acted as though she'd simply taken a short vacation, a little jaunt to the Eldritch Realm, instead of abandoning Simon *for years* while he drowned in grief. "You left me," he said. "You left *us*."

"I had no choice," she said, a hint of gentle impatience in her tone, as though speaking to a stubborn child. She lifted the teacup to her lips. A silver ring resembling a tiny snake curled around one finger. "I realize you've suffered. And I'm sorry. I truly am. But what I'm doing here is very important."

"More important than our family?"

"Family is why I came here. Your sister—your previously *dead* sister, need I remind you—is alive and well. She might be a little skittish around strangers, but, well . . . we've had to be very careful, and I'm afraid some of my paranoia might have rubbed off on her." Veera steepled her long, pale fingers. "You must have so many questions. Ask."

He knew he ought to be brimming with curiosity, but it was hard to think past the cacophony of competing emotions inside him. Finally, he managed a single word: "How?"

"Ah. How did I bring her back?" Her smile widened. She always lit up when she talked about her research. "Well, I'd learned from my earlier failures. Injecting demon cells wasn't enough. I needed something more potent." She removed an object from her pocket—a tiny glass vial. Inside it was a slimy grayish lump, no larger than a coin. "This."

Simon had no idea what he was looking at. "What is that?"

"It is a mass of cells with infinite regenerative capacity," she said, "obtained at great personal risk. It's unlikely that I'll ever be able to get more." She tilted the vial back and forth. "I stole it from the Queen herself. If I told you exactly what it was, you probably wouldn't believe me."

"I've seen a lot of things that aren't supposed to exist. Try me."

She hesitated . . . then shook her head and tucked the vial away. "It's safer if you don't know."

"Safer for who? You or me?"

"Both of us. Regardless, this substance is the key. But even with it, I knew I needed a catalyst, of sorts. And I began thinking about Gaokerena trees. There are so many myths around them, so many stories about rebirth and healing. I'm sure you've heard the old tale of the sage whose daughter dies of sickness."

"He buries her beneath the tree, and the next morning, she's alive."

"Just so. Of course, in reality it's not so simple, but I thought . . . what if those stories weren't just stories? What if those trees really *do* have some power?"

In a flash, he remembered the egg nestled at the foot of the Gaokerena tree in the mountains. "Alice," he whispered.

She nodded. "I was rather surprised to see that you'd met her. Fate binds us all together in such unpredictable ways, don't you think? Like a tangled ball of string. Alice was one of my first *human* experiments . . . one I had given up on. After I buried her there, in the mountains, I waited for nearly a year. But nothing happened. Eventually, I gave up on her and moved on, but it would seem she simply had a long gestation period."

He wondered—was that why Alice seemed so much more alive than Olivia? Was she more fully formed? Or was there something else, some deeper difference between them?

She sipped her tea. "In any case . . . the important thing is, I succeeded. I saved Olivia."

"Father said that when you bring someone back from the dead, it's not really them."

"Oh, your *father*." Disgust tinged her voice. "His hypocrisy is really stunning. As if *he* never tried to revive her. His methods were simply less effective." At the blank look on his face, she raised an eyebrow. "Did he block your memories as well? I suppose he must have. You were always so very suggestible."

She said it so casually, but the words hit him like a slap. He flinched.

He told himself that she wasn't being deliberately cruel. She just said things like that, without realizing they hurt. It was how she had always been.

She poured herself more tea. "Olivia's heart and lungs were crushed in the accident, so your father took her down to his lab, opened her up, and tried to replace the damaged organs with mechanical replicas. He'd been toying with the idea for some time, but he'd only tested it on animals and imps. Of course, this wasn't strictly legal. Had she lived, she would have been classified as an Abomination. Under the Foundation's law, it's forbidden to replace more than twenty-five percent of a human being's body with artificial parts.

Arbitrary, isn't it? In any case, she died on the table."

Simon could see it all too easily—Dr. Hawking, his eyes wild and tear-reddened, rooting around frantically in Olivia's innards.

"Your father is a confused, guilt-addled creature, always wrestling with his own desires and regrets," she said, resting her chin on her folded fingers. "We've both committed the same sin, if you want to use that word. I just sin more gracefully."

In a sudden flash, Simon remembered the conversation he'd overheard in Neeta's office. "Those corpses that disappeared from the morgue . . . that was you?"

"I needed materials for my research, of course. But never mind all that. You're here now, with me . . . and Olivia. I want you to stay, Simon. We'll be a family again."

This was like some twisted parody of his deepest, most foolish dream. And despite how wrong it was, a part of him wanted it. Desperately. Even knowing that it was an illusion. "And my father?"

She snorted. "He had his chance to join me, and he refused. Let him sit alone in his laboratory."

A hot, unexpected rush of anger filled Simon's chest. He wasn't sure why he should feel rage on his father's behalf. Dr. Hawking had lied to him, manipulated him, and betrayed Alice. Yet what right did Veera have to judge him, when she'd left them behind to pursue her own goals? For all his faults, at least Dr. Hawking was *there*. Veera had simply left them both floundering in the dark pit of their own misery. "Four years with no contact," he said quietly. "When Olivia died, I didn't eat. I didn't sleep. I wished over and over that I had died in her place. I needed you more than ever, and you were gone. And you expect everything to be all right? For me to just smile and accept this?"

She hesitated. "I'm here now," she said softly. There was a note of pleading in her voice—something he'd never heard there before. Something almost like regret. "Isn't that enough?"

He wanted it to be. But it wasn't.

For so long, his deepest desire had been to return to the past—to the time before Olivia's death. To regain what the universe had taken from him. But things had changed. Regaining his lost mother and sister would mean losing everything else. More than that, it would mean running away from the world. The *real* world. To whatever this was.

"I can't stay," Simon whispered.

Her eyes widened. "Simon . . ."

"I'll keep your secret," Simon said. "I won't tell anyone about you, or this place. But in return, I want you to help me save Alice."

Her expression tightened. "It's too late for her, Simon. By now they've probably taken her to Grunewick Laboratory. Best to forget her."

His mouth went dry. "What?" he whispered. "But Grunewick is . . ."

"Abandoned?" She gave him a thin, bitter smile, which faded quickly. "That's the official story, yes. But it's still in use as a secret prison."

"I've been inside it. It's empty."

"Parts of it, yes, to deflect suspicion. The rest is sealed off. Any Abominations discovered by the Foundation are taken there to be . . . studied . . . before the public can learn of their existence. No one has ever escaped."

"Studied," he repeated. "What do you mean?"

She looked away. "Dissected, usually."

He felt sick.

"I'm sorry," Veera said, avoiding his gaze.

Simon was shaking—not with fear, but with anger. He planted his hands on the table. "Alice is your creation. *You* brought her back. Don't you feel any sense of responsibility to her?"

Her shoulders tensed. "There's nothing I can do."

"If you're too much of a coward to help her, then *I* will. Send me there, to Grunewick."

"I already lost a child once," she snapped. "I broke the laws of man and nature to bring her back. And you want me to send you into the jaws of death? No."

Simon's breathing quickened. He felt something bubbling under the surface, churning beneath his skin. The room began to shake.

Veera leaped to her feet. "Simon!"

He faced her, hands balled into fists. "I'm not asking for your permission."

"Simon." Her eyes were wide. Frightened. "Please. Calm down."

He took a deep, unsteady breath and forced the seething energy down, deeper into himself. His limbs shook. He'd felt the power. But this time there had been no door, no shadow-thing, no cathedral of bones. That dark energy was just *there*, within reach. He'd felt it earlier, too, in Blackthorn.

It could only mean one thing: the spell his father had implanted was gone. There were no more barriers to restrain his power. What would that mean for the future?

No time to worry about that now. "Send me to Grunewick," he said quietly.

A flash of pain crossed Veera's face. "You choose her over me, then? Over Olivia? Does she really mean more to you than your own family? Or . . . do you hate me that much?"

He tried to ignore the ache in his chest. "I'll always love you," he said. "But I can't abandon Alice. I won't. I'm the reason she's in this mess in the first place."

"If you die, there's no guarantee that I'll be able to bring you back. There are certain conditions. The body must be intact, it must be well-preserved—"

"I don't want to be brought back. I don't want to forget who I am. If I die, I die."

Silence. She stared at him with a puzzled, slightly uneasy

expression, as though she no longer quite recognized him. "I forget, sometimes, that time passes differently for adults than it does for children. To me, four years does not seem so long. It was gone in the space of a breath. But now look at you. A man." She let out a flat, soft laugh and shook her head. "Somehow, I didn't think it would happen. Not to you."

Tears prickled at the corners of his eyes. "Mother . . . I have to go, no matter what . . . but if you help me, maybe I'll at least have a chance." When she said nothing, he added, "Please."

She rubbed her forehead. Her eyes were wet and shiny; she blinked them a few times, chasing away the dampness. "I can transport you into Grunewick," she whispered, "but that's all. There are hundreds of prison cells. I don't know where this girl is being held."

"I'll find her."

She nodded. Slowly, she approached. "Take this." She removed her faded cloak and handed it to him. "It will mask your meta, help you pass undetected."

He slipped into the cloak, fastened the clasp, and pulled the hood up.

"There's no guarantee that she's even still alive, you know," Veera said.

"I know."

"There will be guards there. You may have to fight. To kill. Do you think you're capable of that?"

He hesitated. He thought about taking a life with his own hands, watching the awareness fade from someone's eyes. The guards at Grunewick were involved in something cruel and wicked, but still, they probably had families, loved ones. Killing a human being meant orphaning children, leaving behind grieving spouses, parents, friends.

But the alternative was to abandon Alice. If he was going to do this, there was no point in doing it halfway. In the past, he would have hesitated, held back, wondered if this was the right choice. But the time for doubt was over. He knew the truth about who he was now. And he had someone to protect.

"Yes," he said.

"Then take this, as well." She drew a knife from a scabbard at her hip, which had until then been hidden under her cloak. The entire thing, blade and hilt, was a mottled brownish white, like old bone—maybe it *was* bone—and curved. The hilt was intricately carved to resemble a coiled serpent, the blade emerging from its open jaws.

"The Dagger of Yig, the serpent god," she said, "carved from one of his fangs, if the legend is true." She ran a finger lightly along its length. "It can cut through anything." She placed the dagger in his hand. "Use it well."

Simon curled his fingers around the hilt. The blade was smooth, like ancient, finely grained wood. His skin tingled where it touched the weapon. This dagger was steeped in ancient strength; he could *feel* it.

Simon had never expected to carry a weapon like this. Such things were only for experienced, skilled Animists. An unexpected lump filled his throat.

Veera unbuckled the belt and scabbard from her waist and handed it to him.

He fastened it around his own waist and slid the dagger into its scabbard. "Thank you," he whispered. He had to swallow a few times before he could speak again. "I . . . I hope I'll see you again."

"I can't promise that." She stood, arms crossed over her chest, gaze downcast. "Simon . . . there are dangers you can't imagine in that place. The dagger may not be enough."

Simon's breath caught. His muscles tensed. "I can't use my power." The words caught in his throat. "Father said—"

"I know what he thinks. But Chaos isn't evil."

"It killed Olivia."

She flinched, but only a little. "Fire can kill, too, when it slips out of its master's hands. But fire also gives warmth, life, when handled with skill and care. Chaos is far stronger and older than any earthly power, but it is like fire—or gravity, or entropy. A natural force, no more good or evil than the stars. Perhaps a bit more . . . mischievous. In a cosmic sense."

"I suppose that's one word for it," he muttered.

"It's risky, of course. But you already understand that. Just . . . try to stay alive."

"Believe me, I don't want to die." He gave her an unsteady smile.

She leaned forward and embraced him, enveloping him in the scent of herbs. "Are you sure I can't change your mind?" she whispered.

He wrapped his arms around her slender form, knowing this might be the last time he ever saw her. He closed his eyes. "My mind is made up."

She pulled back, brushing at her eyes with the back of one hand. "Then you'd best go."

"How do I—?"

"Like this." She closed her fingers over his, around the hilt of the dagger, and drew it slowly downward, leaving a glowing green line in the air. She worked her fingers into the slit in reality and pried it open. Beyond lay a dimly lit corridor, still framed by a flickering, wavering boundary of luminous green. Simon took a breath, facing the portal. Once he stepped through, there was truly no going back.

"Do you want to say goodbye to Olivia?" Veera asked.

Simon hesitated.

There were so many things he wanted to ask his sister. Did she still like hot chocolate, and daffodils, and splashing in puddles after a rainstorm? Did they even *have* daffodils in the Eldritch Realm?

But there was no time. With every second that ticked by, his chances of saving Alice dwindled a little more. And Olivia had her own existence here, now. She didn't need him. Whatever they'd had between them, as siblings, had been wiped away. *The dead do not come back.* In a way, maybe, his father was right. "Just . . . just tell her to live a good life. That I love her and hope she's happy here. Tell her that I'll always think of her, but it's all right if she doesn't think of me. It's enough, just knowing that she's safe."

"I'll tell her."

Fresh tears briefly blurred his vision. He wiped them discreetly away and steeled himself. He couldn't afford to feel anything—not now.

"Go," she said, placing a gentle hand on his back.

Before he could change his mind, he stepped through the portal. The hole in the air sealed itself shut.

He was alone.

Chapter Nineteen

Simon stood in a narrow corridor lit by gas lamps in bronze wall sconces.

He didn't know what he'd expected. A dungeon? Stone walls and iron chains?

Grunewick looked strangely ordinary; it might have been any old house. The walls were a dingy off-white, the paint peeling and flaking away in places. The floors were of gray, weathered wood.

His own breathing echoed harshly in his ears. He gulped in a breath and held it, listening. Faint noises—they might have been voices, but it was difficult to say—echoed from somewhere below. The hairs on his neck prickled and stood on end.

Nothing to do but start walking.

He crept forward, gripping his demon dagger. His cloak

swirled around him. Its colors, he noticed, had shifted to the same dirty white as the walls, blending in with his surroundings. He pulled the hood up. Icy sweat trickled down his sides.

He passed a dark wooden door with a tiny, barred window and paused. On the other side, something glowed with an eerie bluish light. He peered inside.

A glass cylinder ran from floor to ceiling, filled with luminous liquid. Inside floated a silver-scaled form resembling an eel with a woman's head, mouth crammed with needle-sharp teeth. Dark hair floated around her pale face. Her eyes were milky white, opaque as boiled eggs. She pressed her face against the glass, mouth open.

He backed rapidly away and forced himself to keep walking. His heart knocked against his chest.

Alice, he thought. *Find Alice.*

Behind another door, a man laughed, a high-pitched, jagged sound. There was a *thump*, and the door shuddered. Through the bars, he glimpsed a face like melted wax, dull eyes within pockets of drooping flesh. Two mouths snarled and gibbered.

Abominations.

All this time, he thought. All these years, the Foundation had been lying to the public about this place. He'd spent his life believing that, whatever its flaws, the Foundation had the people's best interest at heart. He'd *defended* them.

Simon turned a corner, stopped, and counted his breaths. *Focus.*

He walked past more cells, checking each one briefly. He tried to ignore the inhuman snorts and howls from behind the doors, the pale fingers stretching through the tiny, barred windows. An overpowering sense of despair emanated from all around him, pressing in on him like something tangible. These poor creatures. He could see no glint of awareness in their rolling eyes, yet he could hear the caged-animal misery in their wails. Where had they all come from? How long had they been here? Had they been born in this place, or . . . ?

Vague conspiracies and rumors about abductions and secret government experiments flitted through his head. He pushed the thoughts away. He couldn't afford to get distracted now, but he had a feeling he'd only scratched the surface of everything he didn't know about the Foundation.

The hallway ended in a single door. He approached it and pressed his ear to the rough wood.

Behind the door, something moved; metal scraped. "Who's there?" called a voice . . . hoarse and cracked with pain, but unmistakable.

He closed his eyes briefly as a rush of overpowering relief swept through him. He wasn't too late.

"It's me," he whispered.

"Simon!"

"*Shhh.*" He studied the keyhole. How to open the door? Maybe the dagger . . .

"Simon, listen." Her voice trembled. "You have to get out of here. These people will kill you."

"I'm not leaving you." He forced the tip of the dagger into the keyhole and turned it with a grunt of effort. The lock broke with a snap, and the door sprang open. Alice was curled in the corner, clad in the tattered remains of her cloak, dark circles under her eyes, a heavy iron collar around her neck, matching manacles around her wrists and ankles.

He dropped into a crouch and quickly sliced off the collar and manacles. The blade glowed green, cutting through the iron as though it were cheese. The skin beneath was reddened and chafed, pearled with blood. "Oh, Alice . . ."

"Never mind." Her eyes were wild, white-edged. She was breathing rapidly. "We have to go. Now. Before they . . ." The words melted into a low, pained groan.

Behind him, he heard a rustle of cloth. He froze, stomach dropping, then slowly turned.

A white-robed, hooded form stood in the hallway, the lower half of its face covered by a pale leather mask, eyes lost in shadow. Simon raised the dagger, gripping the hilt tightly with both hands. The figure tilted its head.

Simon's ragged breaths echoed through the silence. "I'm warning you. Come any closer, and I *will* use this."

The figure made no sound. It raised one gloved hand and pointed at them. Two vaguely reptilian shapes emerged from the shadows behind it and stalked toward Simon and Alice. A chill washed over him.

The creatures were roughly man-sized, and they walked on two legs, but there was nothing remotely human about them. They were white and hairless, with muscular haunches and thick, lizard-like tails. Their necks were long and sinuous, their arms tiny, each ending in a single foot-long hooked claw.

Alice stared, her face ashen. "What are those things?"

"Ghasts." He swallowed, throat tight. "Demon familiars." Ghasts were fierce, and smart, and hungry. Not many Animists had the skill to summon them, but for those who could, they were unstoppable weapons.

The larger ghast took a step forward and licked its muzzle. They had no faces, no eyes—just massive jaws crammed with long, needle-like teeth.

Simon thrust the dagger forward. "Stay back!"

The hooded form snapped its fingers.

The ghasts advanced slowly, tails swaying behind them. Acid-green drool bubbled from their mouths; where it struck the stones, it sizzled.

"Alice," Simon said, "can you transform?"

She rose to all fours. Her body swelled and darkened, and the remains of her cloak fell away. Bones and muscles crackled, rearranged themselves. Her neck stretched out, her limbs thickened, and her jaws lengthened and sprouted fangs.

She growled.

The ghasts circled them like wolves. One abruptly charged straight at Simon, jaws gaping.

Alice lunged and seized the ghast's neck in her jaws. It squealed. She shook it once, like a cat with a mouse; its neck snapped, and she dropped it disdainfully. Its body crumbled and vanished in a swirl of green smoke.

The second ghast took a few steps back then turned toward Simon, teeth dripping. He slashed with the dagger, and the ghast fell back, squealing, a deep gash in its shoulder. Black blood gushed out and hit the floor, sizzling. The ghast let out a bone-shredding scream, then lunged at Simon. He thrust the dagger again, but this time the ghast was ready; its long tail lashed out, knocking the weapon from his hand. One hoof cannoned into his chest and sent him sprawling. He scanned the floor frantically for the dagger. *There*; it lay a short distance away. He crawled toward it and stretched out a hand, but the ghast sent it flying away with another flick of its tail. Its head swung toward Simon.

Alice pounced on the ghast, knocking it to the ground. The ghast sprang back up, leaped onto her back, and sank its teeth into her neck. Green drool ate into her flesh, bubbling, and hissing steam rose up from the wound.

"Alice!"

She roared, rearing up, and flung the ghast away. It struck the wall and slid down. Alice stalked toward the cloaked figure, growling . . . then her legs wobbled, and she staggered to one side. Her neck swayed back and forth. The wound on her back—a patch of raw, wet flesh—sizzled. Simon watched in horror as the patch grew. The acid was eating into her, burning her alive. She dwindled, shrinking back to her human form, and crumpled to her knees. Dark hair hung in front of her face like a curtain as she arched her wounded back, groaning. She scrambled for her cloak and grabbed it, clutching it against her bare, shivering body.

At any other point he might've been embarrassed and flustered at her nakedness. Now it was the least of his concerns.

The masked figure raised one hand. Three more ghasts emerged from the shadows and advanced toward them.

Simon stood in front of Alice, shielding her with his body as best he could, his mind racing in frantic circles.

"Run," Alice whispered.

"I'm not leaving you!"

"If you don't, we'll both die." She cried, gasping. "Get out of here."

Simon gritted his teeth. A scream welled up in his throat. *No.* This wasn't how it would end.

"Simon, *go*!"

The ghasts closed in. Then, all at once, they charged. An

impact jarred him to his bones, and then he was on the floor, a forest of yellowed teeth bared inches from his eyes. A string of drool dangled over him. Hot, foul breath gusted against his face.

"Wait," said a voice. The white-robed, masked figure stepped into his field of vision, looming over him. The figure placed one gloved hand on the ghast's neck. "Don't kill him."

The voice was muffled, but he recognized it, all the same. His mouth opened in shock.

"Neeta," he whispered.

The ghast stepped back. She stood over him, stone-still. Behind her, two more robed forms seized Alice and dragged her back into her cell.

"Alice!"

The door slammed shut with a resounding bang. The two robed forms remained motionless outside it, standing guard.

Neeta removed a heavy iron collar and chain from within her robe and snapped it shut around Simon's neck. She yanked the chain, pulling him upright. He stumbled. His hands flew to the collar, trying to pry it off. "Neeta." His voice emerged thick and choked. "You're one of these people?"

She removed her mask and stared at him for a long moment, her expression inscrutable. Then she glanced at the waiting ghasts and raised a hand. "You may return."

They vanished in a puff of greenish smoke.

"Why?" Simon rasped.

She let out a quiet sigh. There was pain in that sound. "You shouldn't have come here."

It hurt, more than he would have expected. He'd already known that Neeta believed in the Foundation through and through. But despite everything, he'd still admired her, still seen her as his teacher. Had he ever truly known her?

She turned and began to walk, pulling Simon along. The collar chafed his neck.

He stumbled after her, wheezing. He could barely find the breath for words. "Where are you taking me?"

"To the Queen. It will be better for you if you don't resist."

He blinked, dazed. "The Queen? She's here?" That made no sense. The Queen lived in a mansion in Eidendel.

Neeta didn't respond. She kept walking at a brisk clip, half leading, half dragging him along. "I don't know how you found this place, or where you got that weapon. But we will know everything soon enough."

"What are you planning to do to Alice?"

"No more questions."

She led him through a door, into a narrow, stone-walled stairwell with a set of rusted iron steps leading down in a spiral. There were no lamps here. Neeta raised one hand, and a golden ball of meta blossomed above her palm. It cast a faint, pulsing glow over the walls as they descended.

The door at the bottom of the stairwell opened into a

large, empty room. At the far end of the room stood a pair of towering black doors.

Neeta led him to the doors. She started to reach out, to touch the dark material—wood or stone, Simon wasn't sure—then stopped. She took a deep breath and let it out through her nose. Simon saw, to his surprise, that she was trembling. "I should warn you . . . the Queen is not who you think. It is said that she is mostly a symbol these days, and that is true enough. The woman who represents her public face is merely a figurehead. A puppet. Our true ruler— the one who has led the Foundation since its inception—is behind this door."

"But . . . the Foundation has existed for five hundred years."

She met his gaze. "Once you're inside, don't speak. Try not to look her directly in the eye. And don't think anything disrespectful, if you can help it. Once we're in her presence, there is nothing I can do to protect you."

The doors creaked open, revealing darkness. He could see almost nothing beyond, but he had the sense that the space was incredibly vast.

"She's in here?" he whispered.

"The Queen doesn't like light."

Neeta pulled him forward, into the blackness, and the doors slammed shut behind them. Simon blinked, his eyes straining against the thick shadows. "Neeta . . . what . . ."

"Shhh."

He shuffled his feet. He couldn't see the floor, but he could feel a puddle of something slimy and viscous. It clung to his boots. He shuddered.

A wet, snuffling sound broke the silence. At the far end of the cavernous emptiness, a faint, yellowish glow pierced the darkness. Two lights, round and filmy. It was hard to judge their size from this distance, but each, it seemed, was larger than a man. They hung suspended high above him . . . then they flickered, once. *Blinked.*

Neeta dropped to one knee. "My Queen. I have brought you the trespasser, as you ordered." Simon didn't move. She yanked on his chain and whispered, *"Kneel."*

Simon fell to his knees.

The thing in front of him shifted its enormous bulk, emitted a low rumble, and leaned forward, lowering its titanic head. A wet, indescribably foul stench rolled over him. Dimly, he could make out the outline of the thing's face. A writhing mass of rubbery protrusions, like catfish whiskers, covered its mouth. A thick, slimy substance dripped from its jaws, congealing in puddles on the floor. Heavy, scaled ridges sat above its murky yellow eyes.

His mind wouldn't accept what was in front of him. It rebelled, froze. Its gears ground to a halt, leaving his body a shuddering, mute shell.

The enormous eyes blinked. With an odd detachment,

Simon noticed a tiny, scarred notch on the ridge above the left eye.

The thing extended one house-sized hand toward him . . . but it was not a hand, exactly, nor a claw. It resembled a mass of fleshy roots, long fingers branching into smaller and still smaller fingers, the thinnest little more than filaments.

Neeta tensed. "My Queen. If I may speak, he is not accustomed to your touch. He may die if you—"

A single finger flicked toward her. It didn't touch her, but Neeta flinched and stiffened. Her expression didn't change, but her eyes glazed and her breathing quickened. A dark line of blood trickled from her right ear.

The tree-thick finger stretched toward Simon, smaller tendrils wiggling at the end. One tendril touched the center of his forehead—the barest brush of moist, clammy flesh. And suddenly, he couldn't move, couldn't even draw breath. Every muscle had locked into place. A flash of blinding pain filled his skull.

For an instant, he felt something vast and cold touching his mind—a labyrinth of thought, ancient as the oceans, remote as the stars. There was a sense of a great, impassive eye peering into him, and his own tiny, simple thoughts laid bare, spread out like the innards of a worm on a dissection table.

There was a flicker of . . . something. Fear?

It's afraid?

Of me?

Then the damp tendrils were pulling back, recoiling. He dropped to the floor, shivering, head pounding.

Silence filled the enormous room.

Neeta remained on one knee, motionless. A few minutes dragged by as Simon's shuddering breaths echoed through the emptiness. The huge eyes blinked again, once. "My Queen?" Neeta said at last, her voice small and uncertain.

A voice filled his head, but it was nothing like a human voice. It was enormous, deep, and rough, like the scrape of tectonic plates grinding together. It vibrated in his sinuses and made his eyes water, filling every corner of his skull: *KILL IT.*

He heard Neeta's intake of breath, saw her shoulders tense, drawing inward . . . then she bowed her head. "Your will is mine." She seized Simon's chain, pulled him to his feet, and walked briskly out of the room. The doors groaned ponderously shut behind them.

Simon stumbled numbly after her, his head ringing. His brain felt like jelly. He was struggling, and failing, to process what had just happened.

The Queen . . .

The Queen is a demon.

No, he thought. Not a demon. Something greater, older, far more terrifying.

It was the voice.

He had heard one like it before. It echoed back to him from those black times—the ones he could barely piece together.

The chalice. The cathedral.

The Queen was something that, according to the Foundation's teachings, did not even exist. A thing spoken of only in legends and dusty, forbidden texts.

The Queen was an Elder God.

Chapter Twenty

Simon moved mechanically as they ascended the staircase and emerged into the upper levels of Grunewick. He heard a low, feverish moaning and realized it was coming from his own throat. "Spirit," he whispered. "Oh, Spirit."

Neeta paused, casting a glance over her shoulder. Her eyes were empty and dull, but beneath the dullness there was a deep black void of despair. Absently, she wiped the blood from her right ear, then kept walking. "I'm sorry, Simon. An order from the Queen is absolute."

So, he was going to be executed. He felt curiously numb. Empty. "So why didn't she just kill me herself?"

"She doesn't kill humans. Not directly. It's part of the treaty."

"Treaty." His lips and tongue felt like clay. "With a monster."

Neeta stopped in her tracks. Her grip tightened on the

chain, and she turned to face him. Her hair, damp with sweat, clung to her face. "You understand nothing."

"Help me understand. Why would you serve something like that?"

Her features sagged. "I have no choice. None of us do." She didn't look angry. She looked tired, defeated. "She is more powerful than all of humanity combined."

He found himself thinking, suddenly, of the tiny vial in his mother's hand, the lump of grayish slime. Her secret ingredient. A substance stronger than demon cells, obtained at great personal risk.

Had she stolen it from the Queen herself?

He thought of the scar above the Queen's eye, and the pieces clicked together.

What had greater regenerative capacity than a demon? An immortal being. Somehow, Veera had gotten her hands on a tiny piece of the Queen's flesh. With his mother's ability to travel between worlds, it might have been possible for her to enter the Queen's chambers and escape instantly afterward.

Did that mean that Alice was, in some strange way, a relative of the Queen? And Olivia too?

He pushed the questions aside; there were bigger things at stake now. His mind spun. If he was right, his mother had done the unthinkable: had injured an Elder God. Even if it was no more than a tiny notch. The Queen wasn't invulnerable.

"Maybe she isn't as strong as you think," he said. "What

if she could be overthrown?"

"Simon . . ." Neeta shook her head slowly. "Even if it were possible, it would be disastrous. Hard as it may be to accept it, the Queen is humanity's savior. There are worse things than her out there. Far worse. Without her aid, her protection, our world would have long since been devoured by creatures from the Outer Realm." She stopped. Took a breath. "In the beginning—after the War of Ashes—the Queen intervened often and directly in human affairs. As time went on, she began using human intermediaries. The monarchy became a stand-in—her public face, as it were—and the Foundation became her hand. With each passing century, she has governed less and less, guiding us only when necessary, and the memory of the Foundation's origin faded. We made sure it faded. There were always those who could not accept the idea of swearing fealty to an Elder God. And here we are, now, in an age of unrivaled prosperity and peace. Our empire stretches across the Continent. And yet, if she withdrew her protection, it would end in a heartbeat. She is all that stands between us and a thousand hells—entities more evil, more *hungry* than you can begin to imagine. Humanity is a frail, flickering candle in the void. She is our only shield."

"Who told you all that? Her?"

Neeta didn't reply.

Simon thought back to that horrifying moment when the Queen had invaded his head. There had been no hint of human sentiment in that mind. "So, what does she get in return for protecting us from the other Elder Gods? Don't tell me she's doing it out of the kindness of her heart."

"You would not understand—"

"I'm going to die. What difference does it make?"

A brief silence. "In another five hundred years, she will devour half of humankind, leaving the other half to repopulate the Earth so the cycle can repeat. That is the bargain."

"So we're cattle being fattened for the slaughter." He wanted to laugh. He wondered if this was what it felt like to go mad. "And you're all right with this?"

"The cattle in the pasture eat better and live longer than their wild cousins. It's a mutually beneficial arrangement. As we do for them, the Queen does for us. You might say that this is part of a natural order—the cycle of death and rebirth. Better than going extinct."

He gave her a long, empty stare.

"This is not for us to decide, Simon. The world is as it is, and it is beyond our power to change. Do you think I would choose this?" Her voice wobbled like a crystal on the verge of shattering. "We are *insects*. Ants on an anthill. All we of the Foundation can do is protect humankind from a truth that would drive them mad."

Beneath the ashes of despair, a small, hot flame of anger kindled. "That's easy for you to say, when the devouring won't happen in your lifetime."

She shot him a glare. Then her expression softened. "I

won't ask your forgiveness. Hate me, if it's any comfort to you." She kept walking, pulling him along. "If you have any last requests, I'll do my best to fulfill them. I can't tell your father or anyone else the truth about what really happened to you, of course. But if you have any message for him, any last words, I will deliver them."

Simon swallowed, throat tight. "Tell him I'm sorry."

She nodded. "I'll take you to the girl's cell, and you can say your goodbyes."

A terrible hollowness filled his chest. Was this how it ended? "Neeta. Don't do this. Please."

She didn't respond.

"You know this is wrong. You *have* to know."

"It doesn't matter if it's right or wrong, Simon." Her voice was curiously gentle. "It's what must be."

They reached a door with a small, barred window—Alice's cell. He glimpsed her inside, curled up in the corner. He couldn't tell if she was even conscious.

Neeta unlocked the door and shoved Simon into the small, dark room. The door slammed shut. He faced the door, gripping the bars. "Neeta! *Please!*"

She stared at him. Pain lanced across her face, and she looked away. "You should have taken my advice and given up on being an Animist. You would have made a fine tailor. You could have died an old man, safe and comfortable in your favorite chair, a cat purring in your lap."

"I'm allergic to cats."

She laughed, a choked sound. "Simon . . ." She put a hand over her face. Then she lowered her hand, stared at him for a long moment, leaned in, and whispered, "I can buy you an hour, perhaps. No more."

Before he could respond, she turned and walked away, footsteps echoing sharply through the hall. *One hour.* What could he do in that time?

Simon's head still ached and pounded. A wave of dizziness passed over him. He paused to lean against the wall then made his way toward the back of the room. Toward Alice. He fumbled in the darkness until his hand touched her shoulder.

"I'm sorry, Simon," she rasped. He could hear the pain in each breath. "This is my fault. If you'd never gotten mixed up with me . . ."

"I don't regret anything," he whispered. Gently—carefully—he touched her hair, felt the warm dampness of blood. It was everywhere.

"I wish you hadn't come here." Her voice was thick and choked; the words trembled. "I wanted so badly for you to survive. I told myself that I could face this, if I just knew you were alive and safe. And now you're going to die because of me."

"Neither one of us is going to die." He groped through the near blackness, found her hand, and squeezed it. His other hand stroked her hair, fingers trembling. "I'm going to get us out of this. I swear."

Half-lidded, dim purple eyes stared at him through the shadows. She drew a slow, rattling breath. "It's all right," she whispered. "You don't have to pretend for my sake." Arms and tentacles wrapped around him, pulling him closer.

He rested his cheek atop her head and hugged her back— carefully at first, afraid of hurting her, then tighter. He didn't want to let go, but he knew they didn't have much time. "There might be something I can do," he whispered into her ear.

She twitched. "What?"

"Let me at least heal you, first—"

Her fingers dug into his arms. "Don't waste time," she hissed. "My wounds aren't fatal. If you've got a plan, then *hurry.*"

Simon hesitated. Was he really going to do this? *My power killed Olivia.*

His mother's voice echoed in his head: *Fire can kill, too, when it slips out of its master's hands.*

Now the power was his only chance. He *had* to escape . . . not just for himself, not just for Alice, but for the truth. Thousands of lives depended on it. Of course, they would call him a madman. But he'd worry about that later.

He reached, fumbling, for the power that had shaken the floor of Veera's castle. But of course now that he truly needed it, he could feel nothing; Chaos only seemed to flow into him spontaneously, during moments of intense fury or blind panic. It wasn't a pet dog, to come when he called on it. More like an unruly horse—a bucking, half-wild thing.

But he had to harness it.

"I'm going to meditate," he said. "Give me a few minutes."

He couldn't see Alice's expression, but he could sense her confusion. Still, she nodded.

He released her hand and sat, legs folded, arms hanging loose at his sides. He took a slow, deep breath and closed his eyes, centering himself, falling into the rhythm of his own breathing. He could feel the dim glow of meta in the center of his chest, strangely muted and distant; the collar Neeta had clamped around his neck seemed to be interfering, in some way.

But it didn't matter. He was drawing water from a different well.

He allowed himself to sink deeper into the darkness of his own mind.

Breathe. Be. Breathe.

It was hard to be still, knowing that his life—that *Alice's* life—was in danger. They were in the heart of an inescapable prison, surrounded by enemies, and they had less than an hour before those enemies came to kill them. How was he supposed to remain calm under these circumstances?

His mind flashed to his training with Neeta, the increasingly strict and demanding exercises she'd put him through, her voice snapping, "Focus!" as cold water poured down on his head. He had done it then. He could do it now.

The world faded, and he sat alone in the center of everything.

He was stillness and silence, a mere vessel. He was empty.

Chapter Twenty-One

"**Y**ou keep coming back." The shadow-thing stared at Simon with its round, unblinking eyes. Its form wavered and flickered, a person-shaped hole in the air.

The desert wasteland remained unchanged, a sprawling, flat nothingness under a jeweled sky.

"I need power," Simon said.

"Oh. How much?"

"Enough to save Alice."

The shadow leaned toward him, head tilted, its body lengthening and twisting like a snake's. "Alice belongs to the Queen now. If you want to save her, you will have to kill the Queen."

He thought about what Neeta had said—about how the Queen guarded humanity from worse things. What if she was right? What if, in destroying one evil, he unleashed a thousand others? What if *this* thing was one of them?

But what if Neeta was wrong?

If things continued as they were, then the Queen would destroy half of humanity, and the cycle would repeat itself again and again over thousands of years. Countless innocent lives lost, devoured by those monstrous jaws. Was he prepared to let that happen, because of some unknown, uncertain danger that might not even exist?

So much hung in the balance. A decision like this shouldn't be made by one person, he thought. But the choice was his whether he wanted it or not.

"I'll kill the Queen," Simon said.

The shadow chuckled softly. "I was hoping that would be your answer. Are you willing to pay?"

Simon took a breath. Here in this space between worlds, his head felt clearer. The fear and confusion and aching had vanished, wiped away like chalk from a board. He thought about Alice—her fierce will to live, burning hot and bright. More than anything, he wanted to protect her. He knew that the life of one person shouldn't matter in a choice this big, but how could it not? She had given him the courage to question everything he'd been raised to believe, to seek out the truth. She made him want to believe that a better world was possible, that humanity could shape its own future. That no one was an Abomination.

Still, there was one question he had to ask. "Who are you?

Are you a demon? Something from the Eldritch?"

"I belong to no realm."

"Give me your name."

"Names." It let out a little sigh. "Humans are so very obsessed with *words*. You believe that naming things gives you power over reality, allows you to comprehend the universe. But that's not how it works. Words are only labels stuck to the surface of things, don't you see? The boundaries you draw are no more than lines in the sand, to be washed away by the next wave. Everything is everything. Which means, of course, that nothing is anything."

"There must be something people call you."

"Very well. If you must name me, call me Azathoth."

A needle of cold slid through him. "*That* Azathoth? The same one the Chaos-worshippers talk about? The strongest of the Elder Gods?"

"I am no god. I am the darkness between worlds, and between elementary particles, and inside your own mind. I am the emptiness before birth and after death, the ancient indifference of the stars, and of what lies beyond the stars—"

"I get it. You're nothing, but you're very important."

"It's rude to interrupt someone, you know." The blank circles of the shadow's eyes remained fixed on him.

An unexpected, hot rush of anger filled Simon. "You killed Olivia."

"Well, *you* killed her, technically. But I can see why you

might blame me." Azathoth gave a little shrug. "Power, the power you ask for, killed her. Do you still want it?"

Too late to go back. He pushed his anger aside. "Yes."

The shadow reached out and touched a long black finger to the center of his chest. It stroked him once, lightly—then the finger plunged into his heart like any icy knife. Simon gasped. The shadow's eyes narrowed, and a jagged grin appeared like a sickle in its face. Simon stood rigid, mouth open as the finger pushed deeper. He couldn't even scream. The shadow was reaching into him, casually peeling back the layers of his mind like the leaves of a cabbage, seeking some bright center.

Simon felt something being pulled out of him from deep within. The shadow yanked its finger out of his chest, taking with it a string of delicate, luminous white. The string snapped, coiled itself into a ball, and floated above the shadow's palm.

Dazed, Simon stared into the sparkling white sphere. The light was warm and clear and pure. He felt as if he could gaze at it forever. "That was inside me?"

"Yes. Pretty little bauble, isn't it? Everyone has one. The grain of sand in the center of the pearl. You might call it your soul." The shadow's jagged black fingers curled around it. "And now it's mine." The huge jaws stretched open, revealing a glowing red interior. The ball of white light disappeared inside, and the jaws closed.

The ground rumbled. The shadow's body swelled. The massive head tipped back, and a triumphant roar split the air. A spiderweb of cracks spread across the desert beneath Simon's feet.

The doors split open, and green light poured out. Simon walked into the cathedral of bones. The floor trembled. Bone-dust rained from the ceiling. Everything was falling apart. But he kept walking. He felt strange—heavy and light at the same time. He had given up his soul. Was he just an empty shell now? Was he still human?

He'd worry about that later.

The well of green light was still there. The winged skeleton above it crumbled and fell. The chalice rolled toward his feet. Simon ignored it. He climbed over the edge of the well and plunged in.

When Simon's vision cleared, he was looking down at his own body, lying unconscious on the floor of the cell. Alice was shaking his shoulder, calling his name, but her voice sounded small and distant.

He zoomed out, through the door—his consciousness passed through the thick, knotty wood as though it were smoke—and down the corridor.

He could see two white-robed forms walking toward his cell. Guards. One carried a hypodermic filled with black liquid. A quick glance at the liquid's cellular structure told him it was deadly poison. So, here were the executioners, coming to end him and Alice.

He should be afraid. Shouldn't he? Yet there was no fear, no emotion at all, save the faintest echo of amusement. The guards were like beetles coming to slay a dragon.

With a thought, he unmade them.

In reality, it took only an instant, but his perception of time had shifted, and he watched it all happen in exquisite detail. He unraveled their skin and muscles and dissolved their bones, breaking them apart into their atoms. He watched them crumble into dust, then into smoke, which dissipated into the atmosphere.

He felt nothing. He *was* nothing.

And yet he was aware of everything around him—the texture of the walls, the shape of the wooden boards support-ing them, the cool, dusty smell of the air. He could break it all into nothingness with a thought, if he wished.

So. This was what absolute power was like. This was pure existence.

It felt like being awake for the first time.

It felt cold.

And then the burning started. He snapped back into his physical form with a jolt as invisible fire swept down from the crown of his head, engulfing his entire body. He gasped, his back arching off the floor. His father's words rushed back to him: *Humans can't control that energy. It slowly eats away at their minds, drives them mad, transforms them into something unspeakable.*

"Simon!" Alice was reaching out to him, eyes wide.

"Alice," he whispered. "Get away from me."

"What—"

"Get away!"

He thrust out a hand, and the door to the cell crumpled and flew off its hinges. Then he picked up Alice with his mind and flung her out into the hallway, away from him. He shouted into her mind: *RUN.*

A high ringing filled Simon's head. Power flowed through him. It wasn't meta—meta was warm. This tingled through his veins like ice. Simon looked at his own outstretched hand and saw something writhing around it. Shadow bubbled from his pores. The world began to shake. Cracks ran through the walls and floor, splitting them open. Broken bits of tile floated into the air, buoyed up by some unseen force.

The shadow poured out of his body, wrapped around him, cradled him. He breathed it in, swallowed it, felt it pool in his belly and spread through his veins. He had no choice.

The dissonant warble of flutes filled his head. He was breaking open, turning inside out.

There was a moment of mad joy, purer and stronger than any feeling he'd ever experienced. Then all feeling vanished.

Alice ran and ran. Her wounded back seemed to be splitting open with each step, but she kept going. The world was tearing itself apart around her; there were flashes of light, dull rumbles, deafening cracks. Dust and debris flew through the air. Screams echoed down the tunnels.

The ceiling ruptured, and light poured in. A gust of wind seized her and flung her into the air. She plummeted, sea and sky flashing past her vision, and struck icy water with enough force to jar her bones. She sank beneath the surface and floated there in darkness, stunned.

A dull roar filled her ears. She didn't know if it was wind or water or her own blood roaring in her skull. Light glimmered above her, and she felt herself drifting upward.

Her head broke through the waves. Wind screamed, and she felt herself pulled by a powerful current; she paddled frantically, fighting in vain against the ocean, until it swept her past a jutting black rock. She seized the rock and hauled herself out of the water, panting and trembling, clinging with hands and tentacles.

Grunewick loomed against the night sky, a castle-like shadow blotting out the stars. Dark clouds massed over its peaks. The entire building was crumbling, breaking into smaller and smaller fragments.

A dull chime sounded, coming from nowhere and everywhere, vibrating through the sea and Earth—the sound of some unfathomably great bell ringing. Another dissonant blast of sound, like a thousand trumpets, split the air.

Jade-tinted lightning flickered in the sky. Then the clouds split open and a shaft of green light shot through, bathing the entire island. Ripples spread outward from its shores, trembling through the ocean.

Darkness spilled out of the ruins, forming a mass of shadow that expanded, solidifying into an unthinkably vast shape in the sky. It was hard to say what it resembled, because it was impossible to look at directly. One could focus on details—a lashing tendril of darkness, an open mouth, a bulging, unseeing eye. It was a storm with teeth; it seemed to be made, at once, of clouds, of shadow and flesh. But the mind was not designed to take it all in at once. To do so would be to go mad.

Something floated up out of the whirling maelstrom of debris. It was a dull grayish-green, with flailing limbs and bulging yellow eyes, its mouth a mass of writhing tentacles. The thing was larger than a mansion, yet tiny compared to the vast, chaotic darkness surrounding it—a bloated toad, impossibly ugly. It squealed, a harsh, grating sound. Batlike wings—tiny, useless, absurd—protruded from its shoulders.

A pair of amorphous, foggy hands formed themselves in the air, lifting the hideous creature, and squashed it like a grape. A spurt of black and green innards flew through the air, then vanished, whisked away by the storm.

A wild, earth-splitting roar filled the air. Within that

sound were thousands, millions of voices laughing and screaming and howling and babbling. The voice of Chaos.

"Dear Spirit," Alice whispered. "What's happening?"

"The fabric of reality has ruptured."

She turned her head to see a slender, middle-aged woman hovering a few feet above the ocean's surface. Her cloak billowed in the wind; her shoulder-length, graying blond hair streamed behind her.

"Who are you?"

The woman met her gaze calmly. "His mother. I came to see my son one last time."

A rock the size of a house hurtled toward her. The woman raised both hands, and the air shimmered. The rock smashed against an invisible barrier, disintegrating into tiny pieces that rained into the ocean. The shadowy maelstrom in the sky screamed.

"You—you're saying that thing is *Simon*?" Alice asked.

"It's him. But it's also Azathoth . . . or rather, a tiny fraction of his energy." She turned her attention back to the churning mass of darkness. The muscles in her face tightened. "I feared this would happen. We're fortunate that it happened here, far from the mainland. The damage will be contained. But everyone who was inside Grunewick will die. In the case of the prisoners, that's probably a mercy."

Alice's fingers tightened, her nails—now claws—scratching lines into the rock. Simon had done this to save *her*. Guilt hit her like a punch to the chest. She shoved it away. No time for that. "How do we save him?"

"We can't." A spasm of pain crossed her face. "This was his choice."

She forced back panic. "No. He's still in there somewhere. Inside that . . . thing."

"He sacrificed himself to save you. If you throw yourself into that maelstrom, you'll have wasted his efforts."

"Then help me! Help me rescue him!"

Her jaw tightened. "Don't you think I would if I could?" A tremor crept into her voice. Her shoulders crumpled. "I should never have let him do this. I—I should have stopped him. Now it's too late."

Alice gritted her teeth. "You're wrong." She didn't have the strength to transform, but she had no choice. Burning pain ignited her muscles as her skin stretched and her body rearranged itself.

"You will die," Veera said. "For good this time."

Alice ignored her, dove into the water, and swam in a straight line for the writhing mass of darkness. The air was full of choking dust. Her eyes prickled and burned. She dove under the water and kept swimming. Currents rushed around her, yanked her deeper . . .

And then she was spiraling upward, born on a rush of air. Huge chunks of stone flew all around her. One swept past, and she clung to it tightly.

Simon was in here. If she could just find him . . .

A tendril of darkness lashed out at her, and she tumbled down, a gnat swatted from the sky.

She dragged herself out of the water and hauled herself back up again, climbing over chunks of stone. Flying grit stung her eyes and burned her skin. The air around her darkened. She could no longer see Veera, or the sky, or the sea—it had all blurred together. The storm howled.

Ahead, a deeper darkness loomed: a wall of nothing.

She watched, dazed, as the maelstrom stripped away ribbons of flesh from her forelegs. She was disintegrating. If she went any deeper, she would be ripped limb from limb.

Veera was probably right. This was suicide.

With a roar, she hurled herself into the darkness.

Chapter Twenty-Two

There was a jolt . . . and then the world blurred and shifted. The howling faded into silence. The pain vanished.

She was standing on a cracked, hardpan desert, under a sky whorled with stars. The sudden stillness, after the whirling maelstrom a moment ago, left her disoriented. She looked down at her hands.

She hadn't even *had* hands a moment ago. Apparently, she had changed back without even feeling it . . . and she was wearing the lavender dress that Simon had given her. But that wasn't the greatest shock. Her skin was no longer gray, but the soft, warm hue of wheat in sunlight. She examined the nails—small, pale ovals—then patted her lower back. No tentacles.

When she raised her head, she saw a form standing a few yards away, facing the horizon. A breeze stirred his curls.

"Simon?"

He didn't respond.

She walked toward him. "Simon . . . can you hear me?"

Slowly, he turned toward her, hazel eyes unfocused, as though he were staring into a faraway place. "Alice . . . you look different."

"I guess this is my true form." She touched her own face, exploring her features with careful fingertips.

"You're beautiful." His voice sounded oddly faint and echoed. "You were always beautiful." He blinked a few times. "What are you doing here?"

"I came for you. Where *is* this place?"

"I don't know. I think it's somewhere inside my mind. Or maybe a kind of gateway between me and the other realm. It doesn't matter now." He gave his head a shake. "You . . . You shouldn't be here. You should go."

"I'm not leaving you." She gripped his hand. "Come with me."

He smiled sadly. "I can't."

And then, suddenly, his hand wasn't there. She looked down and saw that it had vanished . . . and that his wrist was already disintegrating into tiny, glowing particles, like motes of dust in sunlight. The particles floated away, dissipating into the atmosphere. A chill touched her heart. "What's happening to you?"

"I gave up my soul for this power. Now there's nothing

holding me together."

"I don't understand." She could hear the panic edging into her voice.

"It's all right," he said gently. "I knew what would happen. I'm ready."

"No!" She grabbed his shoulders. His left arm had vanished almost entirely, and more glowing bits were already breaking away from his side. He was disintegrating, unraveling in front of her. She tried to clutch at the luminous golden bits of him as they floated away, but there were too many. They slipped through her fingers and drifted up into the sky, like fireflies.

"It's better this way." Even his voice seemed to be fading. "I killed Olivia. It was me. I have this power. I was never even supposed to exist."

She didn't know what he was talking about. She didn't care. "I've killed too. Or did you forget?"

"Alice . . ." His voice broke. "Please. It might still be possible for you to save yourself. But you have to get out of here. Now."

She held him tighter, breathing hard. More particles of him escaped into the air, glowing and then winking out, like dying embers. "I'm not going anywhere." She pulled back to anchor his face between her hands. Golden flecks glowed in his eyes and hair, then spiraled away. He had grown translucent, insubstantial. It was like trying to hold smoke. Unshed tears shone in his eyes. "Simon," she said. "Do you remember when you first found me? I had already given up on my own humanity. But you were too stubborn to let me go. I'm not letting you run away now."

His lips framed words, but she could no longer hear his voice.

Desperate, she leaned forward and pressed her lips to his—but it was like kissing a ghost. There was a faint chill, a lingering scent, like a half-remembered dream. She tried to hold on to the taste of him, to cling to his shape, even as he broke apart into a thousand fragments of light.

"*No!*"

Panting, she fumbled at the air, grabbing bits of light. But there were too many. Far too many.

Her two hands weren't enough. But she was supposed to have more than two. This small, soft, useless human form wasn't *her*. She was strong and fast and gray-skinned, and she had many arms. Enough, maybe, to hold him here.

As soon as the thought crossed her head, there they were—her tentacles, sprawling around her, familiar as old friends. She reached out, stretching them upward, and *pulled*. She pulled with her muscles and her mind. She imagined her will as a net, and she cast it outward and upward, into the sky, gathering up the scattered bits of Simon and drawing them inward, toward her. She held the memory of him in her head—his wide hazel eyes, his messy curls, his voice, his touch. She called to him.

I know who you are. You are good, and you are kind, and you have to come back.

Come back. Please.

I need you.

The golden specks floated toward her, clinging to her skin. She let out a sob of relief as she pulled them together, and the specks coalesced into a shining ball of light, like a miniature sun, small enough to cup in her palms.

Even now, she could see it starting to break apart again.

Oh no you don't.

She clutched it between her hands and *squeezed.* She reached into herself and drew upon a power she barely understood, a power that slept in the core of her being. It felt vast, that power. Vast and deep and ancient and *hungry* in a way that frightened her. Here, in this strange place, she could somehow sense it more clearly than she could on Earth. *What am I, exactly?*

Then she pushed the thought aside. Focus. She had to save Simon. Everything else was secondary.

Threads of green light crept through the gold, knitting the sphere together. She wove the strands of her essence through his and anchored the fragments of his being together, holding him there with her will, panting and trembling with effort, until at last she couldn't hold on anymore. She released her grip, and the sphere floated before her. The luminous green threads formed a pattern like cracked glass over its surface—a vase that had been shattered and then glued back together. It held.

She clutched it to her chest and curled in around it protectively. It pulsed against her heart, warm.

A thin, flutelike whine filled the air. She tensed as the desert shivered beneath her feet.

Overhead, the stars began winking out, one by one.

Chapter Twenty-Three

There was no gap in her consciousness. One moment she was in the desert, the next she was splashing in the ocean, floundering with limbs and tentacles to stay afloat. Waves lapped at the hard, metallic scales covering her body.

She was back in her own world.

The howling wind had quieted; the ocean had stopped spinning, and the air was still. The last bit of flickering green light faded from the sky, leaving it black and empty. A faint, reddish light edged the horizon. Dawn or the last glow of sunset, she wasn't sure.

Grunewick had been utterly obliterated. There was only a low, naked mound of rock where it had been. The sea had swallowed the rest.

Weakly, she paddled toward the island and hauled herself up onto the rock. She'd swallowed quite a bit of salt water;

her throat and eyes burned. She sneezed and sprayed a stream of red-tinged liquid from her nostrils. Bloody gashes marred her sides and legs, burning and stinging, even as the wounds shrank and healed. She lay, shivering. She was alone.

Then she spotted a small, pale, limp human form lying on the rock.

Gasping, she crawled over to him. *Simon.*

She rested her head against his chest and listened. A heartbeat reached her, faint and small. She exhaled a breath of relief . . . but when she looked down at him, her relief turned to dread.

His eyes were closed, his face pale and still. Large, dark patches marred his naked body. There was one on his right arm, another on his side. Several more covered his legs up to the knees. They weren't burns—not ordinary ones, anyway. They were pitch-black. Looking at them was like staring into the void. The edges squirmed, very slightly. She realized, horrified, that the dark patches were *growing*, bit by bit, thin, lacy black lines creeping over his exposed skin, claiming more and more of him.

No, she thought. *I saved him.* I saved him.

She glimpsed a flash of blond hair from the corner of one eye and turned her head as Veera crouched down beside her. If she was at all taken aback by the sight of Alice as a huge, scaly demon, she didn't show it.

"What's happening?" Alice asked, or tried to ask. It came

out more like, "Russ-hah-nig?" The words were rough, distorted by a mouth not meant to pronounce human speech.

Veera approached and crouched next to Simon. She reached out to touch his cheek with the tips of her fingers. "His existence is being unraveled," she said softly.

Alice wanted to scream. She had dragged his soul back from the edge of oblivion. But in this realm, a soul was nothing without a body. He needed both . . . and his body was breaking down.

"He has a few hours, at most." Veera lowered her head, hair falling around her face like a curtain. A drop of water fell, landing on Simon's cheek. "I can't help him."

"What about his father?" Alice tried to ask. She only managed, "Faa . . . zah?"

Veera froze. "His father?" For an agonizingly long moment, she was silent. "Perhaps . . . yes. It's a tiny chance, but still . . ." She turned, drew a dagger, and cut a glowing green slit in the air. Beyond, Blackthorn loomed, a jagged silhouette.

Veera bent over and pressed a kiss to Simon's pale forehead. Then she turned to Alice, her expression grim. "Go."

Alice's tentacles snaked out, wrapped around Simon, and lifted him onto her back. She glanced at Veera. Then she leaped through the opening.

She found Aberdeen Hawking lying in bed. An empty silver flask lay on the floor where it had fallen from his hand. A dribble of amber liquid formed a small puddle on the pillow under his mouth.

She didn't know how he'd react to her demon form; she transformed back, grabbed a sheet to wrap around herself like a cloak, and shook his shoulder. He groaned, batted at her hand, and rolled away.

She slapped his face, hard. He looked up, blinking. "Alice?" he murmured thickly.

"Get out of bed! Your son is dying!"

"What . . . Simon?"

She hooked her tentacles under his arms, hoisting him up. *"Move!"*

With Alice half carrying, half shoving him, he stumbled down the stairs and into the entrance hall. Simon lay on the floor on his back, motionless, wrapped in a blanket. Dr. Hawking crouched and gingerly peeled the blanket back. He drew in his breath sharply when he saw the black patches.

Alice hovered nearby, tense. "Well?"

Dr. Hawking raised wet, red-rimmed eyes to her. "There's nothing I can do." His voice cracked. "His very cells are breaking apart, as we speak."

She grabbed him by the robes with both hands and dragged him toward her. "I swear on my own grave, if you turn weak on me now, I will gut you." She squeezed the words between sharp, gritted teeth. "For Spirit's sake, *try!* Even if there's no hope, even if it's impossible . . . just *try!*" She released him and gave him a shove, breathing hard.

Dr. Hawking drew in a shaky breath and ran his hands over his face. He looked down at Simon. His curls were damp, matted with water and blood, stuck to his face. The spider lines of blackness were creeping up the side of his neck, toward his brain.

"Help me get him to the laboratory," Dr. Hawking said.

Alice lifted Simon with her tentacles. Dr. Hawking wrapped an arm around him, and together, they carried him upstairs. Simon was frighteningly light, like a husk.

Dr. Hawking cleared a spot in the center of the laboratory. "Here," he said. She lifted Simon onto the stone table. Dr. Hawking pulled on a pair of thin rubber gloves and tied a cloth mask over his nose and mouth. He turned to Alice. "Wait downstairs."

"What are you going to do?"

"You asked me to save him. I'm saving him." He shoved her into the hall and shut the door.

Alice paced the hallway.

How long had it been? Four hours? Five?

From within, she heard clanks and scrapes. And other, more disturbing sounds . . . like a blade cutting bone.

When she couldn't bear it anymore, she opened the door a crack and peered in.

In the center of the room, next to the stone table, stood something resembling a huge fish tank filled with green liquid. Simon's head floated inside.

Alice pressed a hand to her mouth to stifle a gasp.

A forest of tubes ran from his neck, through the bottom of the tank, and into a humming machine below. His eyes were closed, as though he were sleeping peacefully. He yawned, and a few bubbles drifted from his open mouth.

Dr. Hawking hunched over a table, gripping a handsaw and a screwdriver. On the stone table lay an array of mechanical body parts—a torso, a leg, a hand reaching upward, as though grasping for something. Dr. Hawking turned to the tank and laid a hand against the side, murmuring something under his breath.

A tiny, strangled sound escaped Alice.

Dr. Hawking spun to face her. His eyes were wide and bloodshot. He put down the screwdriver and marched up to her. "Do not disturb me," he growled.

The door slammed.

Chapter Twenty-Four

Simon rose up slowly through layers of fog. The sound of a thousand ticking clocks filled his dreams, echoing through his head. He felt weightless, buoyant, and then as heavy as stone. There were red flashes of pain and spells of blissful, dark numbness.

He opened his eyes. He was in his bedroom, sunlight spilling in through the window, curtains billowing in the breeze. Outside, he could hear the surge of waves against the shore, steady as a heartbeat.

He'd been in agony a short while ago . . . or had he? He couldn't remember clearly what had happened, only that he'd felt as though his body were on fire. But now the pain was gone. In fact, he felt better—lighter, somehow—than he'd felt in a very long time.

"You're awake."

He turned his head, startled, to see Dr. Hawking standing in the doorway. Simon opened his mouth. At first, his voice didn't want to cooperate. It took him a few tries to speak, and when he did, his voice emerged faint and scratchy. "Alice . . . where . . ."

"She's fine. Sleeping."

A rush of relief filled him. Alice was safe. That was all that mattered. Still . . .

He had done something, hadn't he? Something terrible. He swallowed, throat tight. "What happened?"

Dr. Hawking hesitated. His face, Simon noticed, was paler than usual. "How much do you remember? Anything?"

He started to shake his head—then stopped. There were vague impressions, but they felt like a fading dream now, and he had the sense it would be better for his sanity if he didn't think about them too carefully. "I remember a bit," he murmured.

I killed an Elder God, he thought, stunned. He hadn't dreamed *that*, had he? He had plucked the ancient, immortal Queen—the secret ruler of humanity—out of her lair and squashed her like a fat spider.

It had been satisfying. He recalled that much. But he remembered, too, what Neeta had said about the Queen protecting humanity from worse evils. It was hard to imagine anything more threatening than the creature he'd seen in that dark room. If Neeta had been telling the truth, then how long would it take for those other evils to realize that the Queen was gone?

Everything *looked* fine, from what he could see through the window. The sky was blue, dotted with puffy clouds; the sun was shining. But appearances meant little.

"How do you feel?" Dr. Hawking asked. "Are you in any pain?"

"Pain? No. I'm fine." That seemed strange, now that he thought about it. Hadn't he . . . died?

He lifted one arm, curled and flexed his fingers . . . then stopped, staring. His hand was no longer made of flesh, but of delicately jointed bronze. He turned it over and examined the back. Was he dreaming? When he placed his hand against his chest, he felt—not a beat—but a steady ticktock.

Dr. Hawking cleared his throat. "I realize this must be a bit of a shock. But it appears the procedure was successful."

Simon's head fell back to the pillow, and he stared at the ceiling. His mind floated in a fuzzy cloud. Gingerly, he touched his neck, felt the seam where flesh became metal. He remembered, suddenly, his mother telling him that Dr. Hawking had tried to save his sister by replacing her damaged organs with mechanics, and how he had failed. He raised one hand again, slowly, opening and closing his fist. It was . . . a lot to take in. But he was alive, which was more than he had dared to hope for. "How much of my original body is left?"

"Your head, obviously. Your left arm. Part of your lower body, though I couldn't salvage the legs. Your heart is now artificial, as are most of your other organs, though you still have a rudimentary digestive tract, so you should be able to eat . . . though you don't actually *need* to. Overall, I would say around seventy percent of your body is now mechanical."

Seventy, he thought, dazed. Well over the limit set by the Foundation. He was more golem than human.

His father continued: "I installed a device inside your new heart, similar to the one that powers my spiders, which constantly draws in meta. You'll never have to worry about running out of fuel, so to speak. Your mechanical organs should last at least as long as the organic ones . . . probably longer. Though there's no precedent for this, it's conceivable that, with proper maintenance and occasional repair work, you could live up to two hundred and fifty years." A pause. "Although, of course, your existence is no longer strictly legal."

So, he was in the same boat as Alice.

Yet now, he felt only a quiet gratitude for the cool softness of the pillow against his cheek, the blue of the sky outside his window, the distant sound of waves. *I'm alive.* The rest could wait.

He sat up and carefully touched his left leg, now smooth, rigid, and cool. There was still sensation. Muted, strange, like something felt through a layer of cotton, but there.

"I gave up my soul to save her," he said quietly. "At least, I think I did. But . . . I still *feel* like the same person. How can that be?"

Dr. Hawking shrugged. "I have always considered the soul a rather overrated concept. The brain is far more useful."

Simon touched his chest. A vague memory stirred—a sensation of drifting apart, dissolving. Azathoth had ripped out the linchpin holding his mind together. Simon had felt himself unraveling, becoming nothing. And then . . . warmth. A soft, welcoming glow, like a lighthouse guiding him back home.

Alice. Alice had done that. She had saved him—somehow.

Was it love? Was that what had allowed him to stare into the darkness and return with his soul intact? His father would probably scoff at such a sentimental notion. But Simon could think of no other explanation. Maybe, sometimes, the answer really *was* that simple.

"You said you remembered a bit," Dr. Hawking said softly. "What was it like? When you used your power."

A shudder gripped Simon. He had become something more than human . . . but something much, much less, too. In that brief span of time, he'd been a consciousness too vast and all-encompassing to care about the destruction he was causing, because—at the time—it had seemed so meaningless, like stepping on an anthill. Now he felt sick. His mind flinched away from the memory. "I killed people," he said.

And Neeta . . . had he killed her, too? He couldn't even remember. His heart ticked faster.

His father gripped his hand firmly. "Simon."

He blinked a few times, snapping back to the present. His father released his hand. "You were not yourself," Father said. "You bear no responsibility."

He'd said the same thing about Olivia's death. Simon knew it wasn't that simple. But panicking and falling apart wouldn't help anything, either. He closed his eyes for a few seconds, hiding in darkness, then opened them again. "How many dead?"

"I don't know."

Whatever happened, he decided, he would face the future when it came. He had spent most of his life being afraid; it was simply too tiring. It was all he could do, right now, just to lie in bed, feeling the strange lightness of his new body. "I don't feel cold," he murmured. "But I don't feel warm, either." He turned his head toward his father. "I saw my mother, you know. And Olivia."

His shoulders stiffened, but he said nothing.

"Did you know? About them?"

Dr. Hawking looked away. "I won't ask your forgiveness."

Simon said nothing.

"Your mother and I . . . when we first met, we told each other that we would never have children. Because we were both the same sort of people. I never believed myself capable of being a decent father. In that, it seems, I was right. But still, when she announced she was pregnant with twins, I . . . I thought maybe I could *try*." He lowered his head. "I made so many mistakes. And now you will live the rest of your life as an Abomination, because I was too cowardly to let you go. We are the same, your mother and I."

"Thank you," Simon whispered. "For saving me."

A subtle tension eased out of Dr. Hawking's shoulders. He nodded and blinked his eyes dry. "I'll, uh. I'll let Alice know you're awake."

It was the first time, in Simon's memory, that his father had called her by name. "Where is she? I'll go to her."

A pause. "Are you sure? Can you stand?"

Simon sat up and pushed aside the covers, looking at himself for the first time. He was wearing loose drawstring pants, but everything from the waist up was bare.

As a child, he'd had a toy, a small metal man that could be bent and posed; his new body resembled, more than anything, a life-sized version of that toy. The skin was slightly reddened where it joined with the metal plates. It itched, but there was no pain. In the center of his chest was a convex glass circle that glowed with soft golden light. It pulsed like a heartbeat.

Simon swung his legs over the edge of the bed and straightened slowly. His new limbs wobbled, but held. Standing felt different—a strange balancing act. But he would get used to it, he supposed. "Where is Alice?"

Dr. Hawking turned. "Follow me."

Simon took one small, careful step, then another. His bare feet clicked against the stone floor as they walked down the hallway, toward Olivia's old room. "For a full day, she refused to leave your side," Dr. Hawking remarked. "I ordered her to get some sleep, and she agreed, on the condition that I wake her when you regained consciousness." He knocked on the door. "Alice? He's up."

There was a brief pause . . . then the door sprang open. Alice stood there, dark bags under her reddened eyes. At the sight of Simon, they widened.

He gave her a tiny smile and interlaced his hands behind his back, feeling suddenly shy. "Er . . . how are y—"

She flung her arms around him and buried her face in the crook between his neck and shoulder. "Don't ever scare me like that again," she said, voice trembling.

He stiffened in surprise . . . then hugged her back, tightly.

Dr. Hawking retreated, giving them privacy.

Alice clung to him for another few minutes, then pulled back, wiped her eyes with the back of one hand, and looked him up and down. She tugged him into the room by his arm, and they sat side by side on the edge of the bed. "Does it hurt?"

"Not really." He absently touched the luminous circle in the center of his chest. "I know it looks strange, though."

"Strange?" She laughed, a choked sound. "Have you forgotten who you're talking to?"

He looked into her violet eyes. "I suppose we have even more in common, now."

She smiled, a tiny, complicated smile—wry and bittersweet and knowing. "I suppose we do."

Chapter Twenty-Five

A powdery blanket of snow lay over Eidendel. The shops were decked with holly boughs and red bows.

"I still think this is a bad idea," Alice muttered. She hung back in an alley, swallowed up by her cloak. A scarf covered her nose and mouth, leaving only her eyes visible.

"I've been working on my illusion-crafting over the past month," Simon said. "It's just a few small tweaks, but still, no one should recognize our faces."

"Even so . . ."

"You can't stay cooped up in Blackthorn all the time," Simon told her. "You said just the other day you were feeling claustrophobic, that you were going to explode if you didn't get outside. Well, here we are." He stretched out a hand to her. "We won't stay out long, I promise. I just want to show you the Gaokerena tree in the Gregor Temple. They always decorate it for Solstice. It's probably the most beautiful thing in the city right now."

She hesitated . . . then stretched out an arm and placed her hand in his. He led her out into the street, and they resumed walking. No one spared them a glance.

Still, Simon kept his guard up. Despite what he'd said, he knew this was risky. They were Abominations, trespassers in the world of normal people. And everyone in Eidendel was still talking about what had happened several months ago—the hole in the sky, the bizarre phenomenon that had destroyed Grunewick. The island was far enough from the shore that no one in the city had been harmed—though a handful had gone temporarily mad during the incident, raving and screaming. There'd been headlines and endless articles speculating about the incident, but experts had no answers. The *Eidendel Underground* was the only paper to run an accurate story—AZATHOTH APPEARS IN SKY, DESTROYS SECRET GOVERNMENT LABORATORY!—though of course no respectable person believed it.

People were confused and on guard. If Simon were wiser, perhaps, he would lie low. Or leave the city entirely.

Still, hiding away in darkness and shadows didn't feel right, and fleeing seemed even worse. For better or worse, Eidendel was his home, and he was tired of hiding. What was the point of being alive if you weren't going to *live*?

He and Alice made their way down the street, past the

warm, golden, glowing squares of shop windows. The snow covered everything, muffling their footsteps. The world felt soft and silent, wreathed in white.

Simon glimpsed a face in the crowd, and his artificial heart lurched. *Neeta.*

She wore an eyepatch and walked with a limp; she looked as though she'd aged ten years in the span of a few months. But it was unmistakably her.

He stood frozen, gripping Alice's hand tightly. His gaze briefly met Neeta's, but he saw no recognition there.

He kept walking, head down, gripping Alice's hand tightly. They turned a corner, and he glanced over his shoulder. No sign of her. He exhaled.

She's alive. The revelation filled him with a quiet gratitude, mingled with unease. If Neeta had survived, it meant there was still someone who knew what had really happened to Grunewick. But she probably believed that Simon was dead. As long as she thought that, he was safe. Hopefully.

"I guess the illusion spell is working," Alice whispered.

"I suppose so." Maintaining it was exhausting. Their actual faces hadn't been altered, so appearing as someone else meant constantly projecting the illusion into the minds of everyone around him, and with a crowd this size, that was a daunting task. But Simon found that, with his new body, he was able to channel larger amounts of meta than ever before.

He hadn't used Chaos-energy since his transformation.

He hoped he would never need to again. He still *felt* it, like a shadow lurking in the corner of his mind—a dark potential. But now that he understood what it was, he could control it, keep it locked away.

They reached the Gregor Temple, and the tree within. Strings of softly twinkling golden meta-lights, replenished daily by the Animists who tended the Temple, encircled the Gaokerena's trunk and festooned its branches, along with an assortment of silver bows and golden bells. Its leaves had fallen; without the decorations the tree would have appeared gray, skeletal, and faintly foreboding. But now it glowed with warmth and cheer.

Simon's breath plumed in the air as he gazed up at the tree. "My family and I used to come here when I was small, every Solstice. My father was never much interested in tradition, but Olivia always bullied him into coming with us. And even if he never said so, I think he was glad she did." A faint smile touched his lips.

He realized Alice hadn't spoken for a while and glanced over at her. She was staring at the tree with an unreadable expression.

His mind flashed to the Gaokerena in the mountains, the broken fragments of shell.

Then she reached out and took his gloved hand in hers. "You're right," she said. "This was worth the trip."

They stood, holding hands, as the snow fell softly through the open ceiling.

Simon shivered a little. "It's cold," he murmured.

"Can you still feel the cold?"

"I can, sort of. It's just . . . different."

She placed a hand on his arm and squeezed. "Can you feel this?"

A flush rose into his cheeks. "Yes." He could feel her gaze on him, and he wondered what she was thinking. He placed a hand against the meta-core in his chest—the glowing circle, hidden by layers of clothing.

"Simon?"

He swallowed, his hand trembling a little. "I still think about it sometimes. That moment when I let the power consume me. What I saw, what I felt . . ." His eyes drifted out of focus. "It felt awful. But at the same time, it was incredible. And . . . I feel like I still haven't come back entirely. Like maybe I never will. I'm not sure I know who I am anymore, or *what* I am."

"You're Simon," she said. "You're my friend. And more. That's all that matters."

He looked into her eyes. She smiled and squeezed his hand.

He'd never felt more human than he did in that moment.

Epilogue

Night.

A faint creak broke the silence. Simon stirred in bed, rubbing at his eyes. His door was open an inch.

"Hello?"

No response.

He slid his feet into a pair of slippers and padded across the room, through the door. The hallway was quiet and dark. Moonlight slanted in through a nearby open window—had it been open earlier?—and lay in a silvery bar across the floor.

A slender form stepped out of the shadows, into the moonlight.

The sight of her hit him like a splash of ice water. For a long moment, they faced each other in silence. "Olivia?"

He hadn't seen her, or his mother, since his visit to Veera's castle in the Eldritch Realm. He hadn't thought Olivia would *want* to see him.

"What are you doing here?" he whispered.

She pulled a blade from a sheath at her hip and held it out to him: the Dagger of Yig. "Mother found it in the rubble. We thought you might want it back."

"Is she . . ."

"She's fine. She came to check on you a while ago, after Father saved you . . . though you were still unconscious. She believes you're angry at her."

"I'm not. Please tell her that."

Olivia nodded.

He took the dagger, feeling its weight and warmth in his palm. "Thank you."

She pulled a lock of hair behind one delicate, fin-shaped ear. Her dark, inscrutable eyes glinted in the pale moonlight. "You did something extraordinary, you know."

He hesitated. "The Queen . . . is she really dead?"

Olivia gave him a mildly reproachful look. "It will take her a hundred years or more to knit her body back together. To her, that's only the blink of an eye. But for us, well . . . it will give us time to figure something out. Mother is already working on it."

"Neeta, my teacher . . . she said there were other, worse things out there. Things that might attack humanity once the Queen was gone."

Olivia gave a small shrug. "To trade a known horror for the unknown is always a risk."

He asked the question that had been hovering in the back of his mind ever since his reawakening: "Do you think I did the right thing?"

"We can never know what's right, in the moment we make a choice," she replied. "Only later, when we know the results, can we figure right and wrong." For a moment, she seemed inscrutably old and somehow very young at the same time. And he wondered, again, why she was so different from the Olivia he remembered—and so different from Alice. Cold, where Alice was warm. Withdrawn, where Alice was outspoken.

It was as though Olivia had never fully come back. As though she had been ready to move on, and so only pieces of her returned.

"We never really had a chance to talk," she said.

"I didn't realize you wanted to."

She averted her eyes. "Mother still thinks I'm her," she said. "The old Olivia, I mean. Sometimes . . . when she looks at me, I feel like she's looking at someone else. I'm afraid I'm going to disappoint her."

"No matter who you are, you're still her daughter. I know it's confusing. Sometimes I don't really know who I am to my father, either—or who he is to me. Maybe I'll always be figuring it out. But that's what it is to be human."

"Human." She shook her head, as though the words were a bitter joke.

"A person, I mean." He rubbed his thumb idly over the carved hilt of the dagger. "Listen. I don't want you to feel like you have to fill the old Olivia's shoes. Just be who you are."

Her lips curved—the faintest ghost of a smile, tiny and sad and mysterious. "You seem like a kind person. She was lucky to have you for a brother."

A dull ache filled his chest, and for a few seconds, tears prickled in his sinuses. Then the urge to cry retreated. "Give Mother my love."

She nodded. "Goodbye, Simon. Maybe we'll meet again someday."

Then she crawled out the window, lizard-like, and was gone.

Simon gazed out at the slowly brightening sky, the gray-green ocean. Waves crashed and surged against the shore in an ancient heartbeat.

Things would never return to the way they'd been. For the first time, though, that acknowledgment didn't feel like the end of the world. There was a path forward. It was crooked, and he couldn't see where it led—there were too many twists and turns, too many questions—but he would find out, one step at a time.

Simon Frost laid a hand against the icy windowpane and stared at his own reflection in the glass. His eyes were bright green—brighter, it seemed, than they had ever been. But he felt no fear, only a strange *awakeness*, as though he'd shaken off the last, clinging cobwebs of an old dream. As though both the world and Simon himself had been remade on some deep and invisible level, and every particle of existence had shifted ever so slightly to make room. For what, he couldn't say.

A few stars still glinted, defiant against the coming dawn. The world stood glass-still, poised at the edge of a new day, like a cat about to leap. The horizon shone with a faint, eerie greenish tinge, and the surge of waves held an otherworldly hum, like countless voices blending together in a wordless chorus . . . or the warble of distant flutes.

Or perhaps it was just his imagination.

Acknowledgments

〜⦁〜

Thank you to Claire Anderson-Wheeler, my amazing agent, for her hard work, dedication, and invaluable feedback.

Thank you to Kristen Pettit, my talented editor, and the entire team at HarperCollins for believing in this book and helping me guide it toward its final form.

Thank you to my delightful family for giving me both the security and freedom to flourish and for nurturing my creative spirit when I was a kid.

And thank you to my wonderful partner, Joe, for all his love and support. I'm truly lucky.